PURE DEAD TROUBLE

Debi Gliori

ALFRED A. KNOPF ✦ NEW YORK

THIS IS A BORZOI BOOK PUBLISHED BY ALFRED A. KNOPF
Text and illustrations copyright © 2004 by Debi Gliori
Jacket illustration copyright © 2005 by Glin Dibley

All rights reserved under International and Pan-American Copyright Conventions.
Published in the United States by Alfred A. Knopf, an imprint of Random House
Children's Books, a division of Random House, Inc., New York, and simultaneously
in Canada by Random House of Canada Limited, Toronto. Distributed by
Random House, Inc., New York. Originally published in Great Britain by
Transworld Publishers Ltd. in 2004.

KNOPF, BORZOI BOOKS, and the colophon are registered trademarks of Random House, Inc.

www.randomhouse.com/kids

Library of Congress Cataloging-in-Publication Data
Gliori, Debi.
Pure dead trouble / Debi Gliori. — 1st American ed.
p.   cm.
SUMMARY: Danger continues to find the members of the eccentric Strega-Borgia family
at their Scottish castle, this time in the form of a butler who wants to blow up a nearby
corporation and a demon who seeks the all-powerful Chronostone.
ISBN 0-375-83311-0 (trade) — ISBN 0-375-93311-5 (lib. bdg.)
[1. Magic—Fiction.   2. Witches—Fiction.   3. Demonology—Fiction.   4. Family life—
Scotland—Fiction.   5. Scotland—Fiction.   6. Humorous stories.]   I. Title.
PZ7.G4889Pur 2005
[Fic]—dc22   2004058607

Printed in the United States of America
August 2005
10   9   8   7   6   5   4   3   2   1
First American Edition

This one's for Michael, who saw a forest
while I was moaning about being up to my eyeballs in matchsticks.

Contents

Dramatis Personae

THE FAMILY

TITUS STREGA-BORGIA—thirteen-year-old hero

PANDORA STREGA-BORGIA—nearly eleven-year-old heroine

DAMP STREGA-BORGIA—their two-year-old sister

SIGNOR LUCIANO AND SIGNORA BACI STREGA-BORGIA—parents of the above

STREGA-NONNA—great-great-great-great-great-great-grandmother
(cryogenically preserved) of Titus, Pandora, and Damp

THE GOOD HELP THAT WAS HARD TO FIND

MRS. FLORA MCLACHLAN—nanny to Titus, Pandora, and Damp

LATCH—StregaSchloss butler

MARIE BAIN—possibly the worst cook in the Western Hemisphere

ALEXANDER IMLACH—temporary butler

THE BEASTS

TARANTELLA—spider with attitude

SAB, FFUP, AND KNOT—mythical dungeon beasts

NESTOR—Ffup's infant son

TOCK—crocodile inhabitant of StregaSchloss moat

MULTITUDINA, THE ILLITERAT—rat, mother to multitudes, and Pandora's pet

THE SLEEPER—Scottish unreconstructed-male mythical beast

ORYNX—salamander and unwilling slave

THE INCIDENTALS

JOLENE AND LEX MCHAIL—American tourists on a quest

DR. PENELOPE UMBRA—research scientist for SapienTech UK

THE IMMORTALS

ISAGOTH—Defense Minister of Hades (Wet Affairs)

S'TAN THE BOSS—First Minister of the Hadean Executive

ALPHA—centaur and librarian

THINGS I'M NEVER GOING TO SAY TO MY KIDS

For heaven's <u>sake</u>, this room's a complete pigsty. (19)

What did your last slave die of? (42)

Turn that racket <u>down</u>. (27)

Are you deaf, or what? (1)

Read my lips: No, you can't go out tonight. (3)

What time d'you call this? (12)

No, I haven't washed them yet. (23)

No, it won't be ready for at least an hour. (13)

Stop sighing, Titus. (8)

You asked for seconds, now eat them. (2)

D'you think that stuff grows on trees? (5)

Right, that's <u>it</u>. (279)

This time, you've gone too far. (276)

Nope, you blew it, pal. (145)

Not <u>now</u>, Titus. (103)

Jeez, Titus, when I was your age . . . fade to
blah de dum de dum de blah drone drone yawn zzzzzz.
(3,872)

Phwoarrr, Titus, was that <u>you</u>?
(3, none of them me, actually)

Nothing to Declare

The Strega-Borgias stood out from the crowd clustered around the silent baggage carousel at Glasgow Airport mainly because of the pallor of their skin and the somber black of their clothing. Surrounded by sunburnt holidaymakers scantily clad in shades of lagoon turquoise, screaming orange, and eye-watering pink, the Strega-Borgias looked as if they had recently returned from a funeral; indeed, as if all five of them had narrowly escaped being buried themselves.

Signora Baci Strega-Borgia propped herself against the handle of a baggage trolley and yawned. Her husband, Signor Luciano Strega-Borgia, shifted the sleeping weight of their youngest daughter, Damp, onto his other shoulder and closed

his eyes wearily. It was three hours past midnight and every one of the two hundred and fifty passengers just off the delayed flight from Milan had several desires in common: to collect their luggage, find a bathroom, and head for a horizontal surface upon which to fall into a much-needed sleep.

The baggage carousel lurched to life with a juddering series of hiccups and began to turn, each orbit bringing suitcases tumbling into view, some of which had suffered horribly in transit. A teenage boy lurking on the fringes of the carousel buried his face in his hands and uttered a heartfelt groan of denial at the sight of his backpack wobbling toward him.

"No . . . ," he whispered. "Please, let it not be mine." He peered through his fingers at the eviscerated luggage bearing the Strega-Borgia crest and his name scrawled on a label that drooped from a shredded strap.

"If I were you, Titus, and thank heavens I'm *not*, I'd just turn and walk away." Pandora Strega-Borgia raised her eyebrows and regarded her brother through slitted eyes. "Mind you," she added, "if I were you, I'd never have tried to import five ripe Gorgonzolas in my backpack either. . . ."

Around Titus and Pandora the crowd thinned abruptly, noses wrinkling in disgust, muttering about the catastrophic effect of nasty foreign food on innocent Scottish stomachs. As Titus dragged his backpack off the carousel, the smell of rotting cheeses intensified, causing Pandora to cough and turn swiftly around in search of less-polluted air.

Across the concourse, Baci Strega-Borgia caught sight of

her familiar black hatboxes and flight cases that held her essential travel kit of broomsticks, collapsa-cauldrons, and ceremonial hats, not to mention the little ventilated crate in which her portable frog collection had traveled the long hours between Italy and Scotland. It's hard to imagine a white face turning even paler, but somehow Baci managed it.

"The frogs . . . ," she whimpered. "Oh heck. . . ." She reached out with black-gloved hands and plucked the battered remains of the ventilated crate from the carousel.

"If that's what I think it is," Luciano muttered, "we'd better grab the rest of our stuff and get out of here, pront—"

Climbing past the rubber flaps through which suitcases trundled from the hold of the plane into the airport was a naked young man, loudly complaining about the flight, the weather, the lamentable lack of footmen, and his current state of undress. Behind him came another vociferous complaiant, also regrettably unclad. Around them the crowd parted, some covering their eyes in embarrassment, others round-eyed and open-mouthed in amazement, their attention focused on the growing number of naked young men clambering off the carousel to join their kin, who stood shivering in a huddle on the concourse floor.

In the confusion, the Strega-Borgias hurled their luggage onto a trolley and stole away, hissing instructions to each other as they headed for Customs and Excise and, hopefully, their waiting car.

"Don't turn back." Luciano propelled his wife ahead of him, her long black cloak billowing behind her.

"But they're my *frogs*," Baci wailed, torn between delight that her amateur dabblings in magic had worked and horror at her part in turning her crated amphibians into escapee royals-in-the-buff.

Luciano quickened his pace, causing Damp to wake up and gaze over her father's shoulder to where Titus and Pandora were following behind, faces no longer pale but brick-red with shame.

"I don't think I've ever been quite so embarrassed in my entire life," Pandora complained as the family drew to a halt at the customs booth. Behind them, Titus saw several armed police officers moving purposefully toward the baggage carousel.

"Keep moving," Luciano said, attempting to look as innocent as possible for the benefit of the customs official, who regarded the family with complete indifference. Holding their breath, the Strega-Borgias rolled past, along the Nothing to Declare channel and out, at last, into the waiting throng of chauffeurs, taxi drivers, and other people's relatives, all waiting for travelers off the delayed flight from Milan.

In vain the Strega-Borgias scanned the faces in front of them, looking for their butler, Latch, who had been instructed to meet them on their return. After three fruitless circuits of the crowd, during which he'd been run into with laden trolleys, had his toes stepped on by women in high heels, and been mistakenly embraced by a drunken Glaswegian, Luciano lost what remained of his temper.

"Oh, for heaven's *sake!*" he exploded, causing Damp to

cover her ears and emit a startled squeak. "Remind me *never* to go on holiday ever again. It's been a *complete* catalog of disasters from start to finish. Not only have we just endured a journey from Hell in an overcrowded sardine can accompanied by decomposing cheeses and rampaging frogs, but now we can't even return to the comforts of home because our feckless employee hasn't bothered to sh—"

"Darling, calm down." Baci tugged at her husband's arm, uncomfortably aware that heads were beginning to turn in their direction. "Look, if Latch has forgotten, we can always take a taxi, or rent a car, or—"

"Perhaps we could just unpack one of your precious broomsticks and *fly* home," Luciano hissed, shaking off Baci's arm and glaring at his family.

Titus wearily removed a cell phone from his pocket, keyed in the number for home, and passed the phone across to his father. Baci slumped over the handle of their luggage trolley while Pandora tried to give the impression that she was in no way whatsoever related to this family of deranged travelers. In her father's arms, Damp listened to the unanswered ringing as Luciano waited for someone at StregaSchloss to pick up the phone.

A long way north, the moonlit silence in the great hall was broken by the insistent shrilling of a telephone. The sound echoed off walls, suits of armor, mirrors, and windows, penetrated through wooden doors, chimed along rows of crystal glasses and china, and at length reached the pantry, where

Multitudina, the free-range Illiterat, lay snoring beside a half-gnawed KitKat. Her whiskers twitched and her pink nose wrinkled peevishly as she surfaced from sleep, blearily aware that something was demanding her attention. Multitudina stretched all four legs, flexed her claws, and sniffed the air for clues. She dragged herself upright and scuttled out of the pantry, across the flagstones of the kitchen floor, and along the corridor leading to the great hall.

"Somebody get that, would you?" she squeaked, outraged that her beauty sleep was being disturbed by thoughtless callers. "I don't do telephones," she explained to the empty hall, adding, "Come on. Pick—up—the—phone."

Just as suddenly as it began, the ringing stopped, but by then Multitudina had stumbled upon the body of Latch, lying like a human draft stop across the front doorstep.

The rat was all too aware that humans didn't voluntarily lie in crumpled heaps unless something was seriously amiss. She also dimly understood that it was up to her to do something about it. That something probably involved calling for medical assistance, so she hauled herself onto the hall table and regarded the telephone with little idea of how to make it work. In some confusion, she peered at the instructions written below the receiver.

"Fire, please, amblans . . ." she translated, her illiteracy normally a source of rodent pride, but on this occasion proving to be a major handicap in her efforts to summon help. "Fire, please, amblans . . . ," she muttered, and then, in a flash of understanding, "Fire, police, ambulance!" Delighted with herself, she peered at the number and began to press the requisite buttons, but no matter how many times or how determinedly she thumped the numbers written next to FIRE POLICE AMBULANCE, all she could hear was a computerized voice demanding that she replace the handset and redial.

The Broken Latch

A sullen gray dawn was beginning to break over Lochnagargoyle as a taxi pulled up at the gate on the northern boundary to the StregaSchloss estate. Barely awake, Titus fumbled with the taxi's door and dragged himself out into the damp air. Ahead of him, faint shapes reared out of the mist: ancient oaks in full leaf, the distant silhouette of the jetty, and the dew-soaked meadow looking like a sheet of beaten silver. Stiff and sandy-eyeballed, Titus drew in a deep lungful of Argyll air and, lifting the latch, pushed the heavy metal gates open and waved the taxi on. With a yawn that made his jaw creak, Titus slumped back into the vehicle's interior, wondering as he did so why it was that at five a.m. he felt so utterly ravenous. He was barely conscious, but his

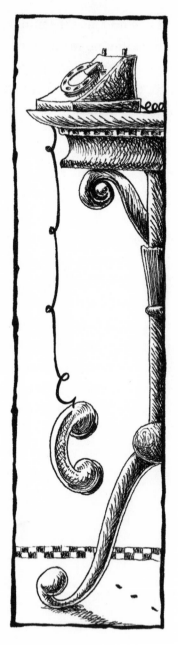

stomach was loudly signaling that it was wide awake and impatient to begin the day's work. Titus laid his head against the glass of the window and groaned. Since Latch had forgotten to pick the family up at the airport, he'd probably also omitted to replenish the contents of the fridge, pantry, and bread box.

In the front passenger seat, Signor Strega-Borgia stared straight ahead, his thoughts running parallel to those of his son. Even the sight of StregaSchloss and the knowledge that cool linen sheets, feather pillows, and deep, dreamless slumber were within reach failed to give Luciano any comfort whatsoever. He closed his eyes, attempting to divert his thoughts onto matters more conducive to sleep than his current desire to slam doors, hurl suitcases, and vent his rage at Latch for letting them all down. Luciano had just managed to talk himself into staying calm, saying nothing, and dealing with his feckless employee after catching up on some much-needed rest when the taxi driver drew to a halt on the rose-quartz drive and demanded a sum of money so outrageous it made Luciano's eyes water.

"You *can't* be serious," he squeaked; then, adopting a more macho tone and forcing his voice to drop two octaves, he added, "That's daylight robbery. Our *flights* cost less than that."

The taxi driver regarded him with utter indifference, his fish eyes betraying no sign that the sum in question was open to negotiation.

"Come on," Luciano attempted. "Be reasonable. I'm not a millionaire. I'll give you half of what you're asking, but that's as far as I'm prepared to go."

Titus caught sight of the taxi driver's expression in the rearview mirror and immediately averted his eyes toward the front door of StregaSchloss, wishing he was on the other side of it instead of being forced to witness his father doing this full-on tightwad number.

"Listen, pal," the taxi driver growled, "this here's anti-social hours, you live in the back of beyond, I've ripped the bum aff my motor driving up yon track. I'm never gonnae get a return fare back to Glescae, your wain needs a diaper change, and there's something that's *stinkin'* in your luggage. . . ." He paused, narrowed his eyes, and poked Luciano in the chest with an extended finger. "And youse're telling porkies about no being millionaires. Lookit yon"—he indicated the honeysuckle-draped walls of StregaSchloss—"only someone wi' wads of dosh would own a hoose like yon. So get a move on, pal. Ma meter's still running."

"Dad. . . ." Titus leant forward and grabbed Luciano's arm.

"Don't interfere, Titus," Luciano hissed. "Highwaymen are, as a rule, exceedingly dangerous and don't take kindly to being interrupted while robbing innocent travelers." He removed his wallet from an inside pocket and peered at the lamentable lack of cash within.

"Dad, it's *urgent,* look—"

"Titus, will you quit trying to interrupt?" Luciano snapped, turning back to the taxi driver. "Um. I'm frightfully sorry, but I don't appear to have any cash. D'you take credit cards? A check?"

"DAD!" Titus yelled. "There's a *body* on the doorstep. . . ."

In the confusion that followed, all thoughts of taxi fares and running meters evaporated. Running across the drive and up the stone steps, Luciano discovered why Latch hadn't arrived at the airport. Lying sprawled across the brass doorstep, Latch showed no flicker of consciousness whatsoever in his open eyes. Only the slow rise and fall of his chest beneath his shirt indicated that he was still alive.

"Dinnae try to move him," the taxi driver advised as he bent over the butler, his face gray with concern. "You find something warm to cover him with, and I'll phone for an ambulance."

From her hiding place in the hall cupboard, Multitudina silently wished him good luck. God knows, she'd tried her best, but the telephone had refused to cooperate.... She decided to offer assistance and scuttled across the hall, skidding to a halt beside the taxi driver's sneaker-clad feet, where she paused for a few moments to catch her breath. Overhead, the taxi driver was issuing directions to StregaSchloss for the benefit of the ambulance crew; silhouetted against the pale light of dawn coming through the front door, the Strega-Borgias were gathered around their fallen butler, their faces hollow with fright as they tried to comprehend what had happened. Luciano gently laid a picnic blanket over Latch, bending low to whisper in his ear, "Don't worry, help is on its way. Just hang on and we'll get you sorted out...."

Scaling the taxi driver's leg in two seconds flat, Multitudina emerged on the telephone table, where her arrival produced dramatic results. With a scream, the man dropped the receiver and backed away. Multitudina, sensing that yet again she'd failed in her attempt to assist, tried to make amends. Leaping back down onto the hall floor, she hurtled toward the open door, clambered onto Latch's blanketed form, and, to everyone's horror, began to administer the kiss of life to the inert butler.

At this, all Hell broke loose, but throughout the screams, sobs, and general hysteria, Latch lay unmoving, his brown eyes as empty of intelligence as if they were made of glass. Baci knelt beside him, gently stroking his outflung hand, ignoring the histrionics of the taxi driver who, after consigning all inhabitants of StregaSchloss to perdition, fled out of the front door as if pursued by demons. As Luciano pointed out afterward, the one bright spot in what had proved to be one of the worst days of his life was the fact that he'd escaped having to pay two hundred and fifty pounds to a highway robber. But this saving brought scant comfort when set against the sight of Latch being wheeled into a waiting ambulance and taken away in the pouring rain.

Signora Strega-Borgia headed upstairs carrying Damp. After discovering that the fridge was indeed empty, Titus had also gone to bed, but with little hope of sleep due to the noises coming from his stomach as it demanded, in turn, breakfast, elevenses, and now lunch. Titus lay in darkness, curtains drawn, the familiarity of his surroundings failing to soothe him into sleep; for no matter what configuration of pillows, duvet, and limbs he adopted, he was unable to shake the image of rain falling into Latch's open eyes. Watching the ambulance driving slowly away from StregaSchloss, Titus had been horrified to find his own eyes growing damp, a situation he couldn't blame on the dismal weather since he'd been inside the shelter of the front door at the time. Beside him, Pandora looked every bit as stricken as Titus felt, and as the ambulance disappeared into the rain, she turned and fled upstairs.

Shortly afterward the police had arrived and the door to the kitchen had been firmly closed, remaining thus for the hours measured out by Titus's bedside clock as it ticked past morning coffee, then lunchtime, and began its approach to the hour when its owner might expect afternoon tea. Showing no respect whatsoever for Latch, Titus's stomach launched into a loud and peevish complaint.

Feet of Clay

Returning to Strega-Schloss after her annual holiday, though by less conventional means than those adopted by the Strega-Borgias, was Mrs. Flora McLachlan, nanny to Titus, Pandora, and Damp, maker of possibly the best chocolate brownies in culinary history, and no mean slouch at advanced witchcraft. The nanny swooped low over the peaks of Mhoire Ochone, dipping in and out of the mist and scattering sheep as they foraged on the lower slopes. Pheasants clattered from the long grass, their frantic wings beating a tattoo of alarm at the soundless arrival of a flying human in their midst.

Meanwhile, up ahead, the vast silhouette of Strega-Schloss dwarfed the shapes of the home-coming beasts, their

backs bent under the weight of their dirty laundry, which after a fortnight's camping was overwhelming both in quantity and offensiveness.

With a deep sigh, Mrs. McLachlan brought her flying rug down in a clump of birch trees, anchored it by touching the earth with her hand, and stepped off onto what had appeared to be a mossy hummock, but was in reality a peat bog of spectacular stickiness.

"My poor *shoes*," the nanny groaned, squelching onto firmer ground and glaring reproachfully at her magical rug. As she rolled up the rug and stuffed it into her handbag, she decided that sometimes it would be far simpler just to take the bus. However, she reminded herself, reaching out to retrieve her muddy shoes from the clutch of the bog, sometimes life was far from simple. She'd had to land her flying rug in the bog rather than on the drive in front of StregaSchloss because she preferred not to advertise the fact that she was a true witch, owning and operating a flying rug being proof positive of her exalted status within the hierarchy of sorceresses. Why, Baci Strega-Borgia would turn a deep shade of green if she discovered that her employee was such an advanced adept, especially since Baci had failed her most recent examination at the Institute of Advanced Witchcraft. Not only failed, but skirted perilously close to being expelled after an incident in the Amphibian Laboratory. . . .

Moreover, Baci hadn't exactly been too forthcoming with this information, pretending to her husband and children that she'd passed her exam with flying colors. . . . Mrs. McLachlan snorted, recalling her discovery of the dismal exam results jammed down the leg of a suit of armor in the great hall, a hiding place that Baci had used for any items of mail that she deemed too sensitive for the family's inspection. From under a cluster of unpaid bills from various dress shops, Mrs. McLachlan had extracted a small crumpled sheet from the institute that bore witness to Baci's lack of magical wisdom. What was it she'd failed again? Mrs. McLachlan dimly recalled her employer only scoring twelve percent for Transformation (Baci's wand control verged on the disastrous) and twenty-seven out of one hundred for Hunch, Prescience, and Sibylline Awareness—although the latter result could be explained by her obsession with the baby that she was currently growing in decidedly non-magical fashion. Mrs. McLachlan's expression softened; she dearly loved Baci, despite her employer's obvious failings, but the nanny's loyalty was tempered by a profound desire for Baci to replace witchcraft with a less dangerous hobby like waterskiing or paragliding. . . .

Aware that she was beginning to sink into the bog, Mrs. McLachlan took several steps backward, squeezed her feet into her ruined shoes, and set off across the moss toward StregaSchloss, each squelching footstep reminding her that, for all her magical powers, she still had feet of clay.

Barging into the kitchen in search of food, the beasts were initially oblivious to the presence of two members of the local constabulary, who sat drinking cups of Luciano's rocket-fueled espresso and wondering if he kept any biscuits in the house.

"We're back," Ffup said, somewhat redundantly, since dragons of her size rarely needed to announce their arrival in anywhere smaller than the Kremlin.

"And you wouldn't believe how *hungry* we all are, aren't we, Nestor, my poppet?" Ffup continued, blithely unaware of the terror that this statement engendered in the hearts of the visitors. Ffup reached behind her wings and unstrapped her backpack, placing it on the kitchen table between the trembling police constables. "Poor Nestor," she murmured, "I'm sure you could just *murder* a bacon sandwich right now. . . . In fact, you're so ravenous you could probably eat an entire piggly-wiggly, couldn't you, poppet?"

One of the constables fell backward off his chair, a keening wail coming from his open mouth, and the other launched himself into Luciano's lap with a loud scream as Ffup dragged her infant out of the backpack.

"Huh—hull—hullp," the policeman gasped, his weight propelling Luciano's chair backward, causing both men to crash onto the kitchen floor, directly beneath the looming bulk of Knot, the yeti, whose matted fur, after two weeks of camping, was teeming with fleas, lice, and slittered ramen noodles in equal measure. To crank up the terror factor by several notches, Tock came ambling into the kitchen, his claws clicking on the flagstones as he made for the fridge, his crocodile grin wide in anticipation. Flinging open the fridge door, he groaned.

"There's nothing to *eat*," he complained, turning his attention to the pantry and ignoring the gibbering policemen, who, judging by the identical stains on their trousers, had lost bladder control at the sight of yet another ravening beast.

Heavy footfalls sounded in the corridor, followed by a series of deafening metallic clatters and crashes. Pushing the damp policeman to one side, Luciano leapt to his feet, yelling, "What on earth was *that*?"

A small figure appeared in the kitchen doorway, clutching a battered handbag in one hand and a pair of mud-caked court shoes in the other. Smoothing a stray wisp of hair out of her eyes, Mrs. Flora Morag Fionn Mhairi ben McLachlan-Morangie-Fiddach scanned the kitchen, her gaze gliding serenely across the stained policemen, the grinning crocodile, and the matted yeti, until it stopped at Ffup and Nestor.

"Och, for heaven's sake, lassie," the nanny scolded. "The poor wee mite. Come to nanny, pet, and let's see if we can do something with that diaper."

Wriggling out of his mother's arms, Nestor flapped across the table and launched himself into Mrs. McLachlan's pillowy chest with an ecstatic squeak. Turning to the ramen-noodle-besmirched Knot, Mrs. McLachlan shook her head and emitted a series of *tuts*, murmuring, "I'll *never* get the tugs out of your fur. . . . Just look at the state of you. Did you forget to pack your comb? And whatever have you been eating? Worms?"

The crashing sounds from outside increased, interspersed with beastly howls and curses, as if some creature were engaging in battle with a massive horde of aggressive dinner gongs. Mrs. McLachlan frowned as Tock sidled out of the pantry, a jar of pickled eggs clasped in each forepaw.

"I don't *think* so, dear. Put those back where you found them and go help your fellow beast with the laundry," the nanny commanded.

"Awww. Please? Can't I have just one egg?" Tock pleaded, the words dying on his lips as he met the glacial chill of the nanny's gaze. "Um, yes. Er, no," the crocodile mumbled, replacing the jars in the pantry and edging into the hall. "Right away. Your wish is my command. Laundry duties, here I come. . . ."

Ignoring the policemen, who were attempting to salvage what little remained of their dignity as they picked themselves off the floor, Mrs. McLachlan addressed the source of the din coming from the hall. "When you've finally disentangled yourself from that suit of armor, Sab, *dear,*" she said patiently, pausing as more clatters and clanks threatened to overwhelm her instructions, "come into the kitchen and wash your claws before afternoon tea."

Only once did Mrs. McLachlan's impervious armor of serenity desert her. The news of Latch's sudden collapse seemed to affect her far more than Luciano had anticipated. Indeed, at one point he thought the nanny was about to pass out, so pale did she become. Then, visibly pulling herself together under the beady-eyed scrutiny of the policemen, Mrs. McLachlan began to do a passable imitation of some obscure ten-armed Aztec deity: simultaneously changing Nestor's diaper; rustling up a trayful of scones; laying the table with blue-and-white china, homemade jam, bone-handled butter knives, and linen napkins; before finally, with Nestor on one hip, swooping into the kitchen garden to pick a bunch of tightly furled pink rosebuds, which she dropped into a vase in the middle of the table with a small flourish.

"Afternoon tea," she announced. "Shall I pour?"

Order, in the shape of Mrs. McLachlan, had returned to StregaSchloss.

Ring Fever

Night fell on Lochnagar-goyle, turning its waters a dark, glassy green. Beneath the surface swam creatures whose names conjured up visions of the deep: brittle stars, moon jellies, and the alien shapes of lobsters, their shadowy blue shells and slow-mo locomotion making them the favored diet of the vast Sleeper, who regarded the loch as larder, living quarters, and laundry rolled into one. Recently groomed, he lay in the shallows, chewing thoughtfully on a wild mint bush to freshen his breath and thus avoid being named "fish-face" by his fiancée when she came to kiss him good night. Overhead, bats flittered across the water, cutting swaths through the clouds of gnats that plagued the lochside every year from May till October.

The presence of the gnats was tolerated by the local population purely for the insects' tourist-dampening qualities; for without gnats, Lochnagargoyle's shores would have become a Mecca of bingo parlors, amusement arcades, and tartan tat tourist shops, its waters crisscrossed by Jet Skis and powerboats, leaving a tidal flotsam of diesel scum, Styrofoam cups, and floating beer cans. Without the aggravation of gnats, Lochnagargoyle would have been ruined—its peace shattered, its wildlife trampled, and its celebrity resident hounded to death by paparazzi.

Watching the bizarre courtship ritual between this celebrity resident and Ffup, one could be forgiven for wondering what could have possibly attracted them to each other in the first place. For a start, the physical differences between Ffup and her beloved Sleeper—the fact that they weren't even of the same species—might have given them both pause for thought. Ffup, a purebred dragon, was only a quarter the size of her monstrous aquatic swain, who, in turn, being a wingless loch-dweller, had little in common with a fire-breathing aeronaut. Furthermore, the Sleeper regarded courtship and its rituals as too soppy for words, but his fiancée had her heart set on a white wedding with bridesmaids, flowers, froth, and a three-tiered cake.

Eavesdropping on this ill-matched pair's prenuptial conversation from the safety of a moored rowboat, Tarantella, tarantula extraordinaire, found it almost impossible to keep her lipsticked mouthparts shut. In her experience of courtship, she had literally devoured all her lovers, finding little use for them other than as a food source after they had fertilized her eggs. Far simpler that way, she mused, regarding her recent clutch of eggs with deep maternal pride. They would never know *their* father, she thought happily, patting her abdomen at the memory. Their father was . . . well, he wasn't much of a conversationalist, but he certainly had been *de*licious.

On the other side of the jetty from Tarantella, Ffup sat dangling her tail in the cool waters of the loch, watching as her infant son, Nestor, said good night to his father.

"Na na na, JAGGY!" Nestor wailed, pushing his father's bristly face out of range. "FISHY—*wahhh* . . ."

"Oh, for heaven's sake, haven't you even bothered to *shave* today?" Ffup groaned.

"Och no. Weel . . . ," the Sleeper admitted reluctantly.

"And you've got bits of lobster jammed between your teeth," Ffup continued, reaching out to pluck her infant away from such dental corruption.

"Wid youse quit that?" the Sleeper demanded. "Aw that nagging. Jis leave me alane, wumman."

Ffup ignored this, settling Nestor across her vast lap and wrapping her wings around him for warmth. "Right. I've brought my list."

"Nnaww. Ochh heck," the Sleeper moaned under his breath.

"Whooo, and let me tell you, this is the mother of all lists. It's, like, *really* long. Going to take me *hours* to read it all to you." Ffup smiled blissfully, producing an irregularly rewound roll of toilet paper on which was written a vast "To

Do" list. "Number one," she began, "the ring. We need an engagement ring. Well, *I* need an engagement ring and *you* need to buy it. Number two . . . number two . . . ah—are you listening?"

"I'm all ears," the Sleeper lied, closing his eyes and letting his vast coiled body slump sideways into the loch.

"Why do I have the distinct impression that this wedding isn't important to you?" Ffup murmured, unrolling another length of toilet paper and peering at what was written on it. A deep bubbling snort came from the Sleeper, followed by a despairing *tchhhh* from the rowboat as Tarantella limped along the mooring rope and hoisted herself onto the jetty within earshot of Ffup.

"Listen up, airhead," the tarantula hissed. "Read my lips. There are more important matters at stake than your forthcoming nuptials. As the world goes to Hell in a handbasket, don't you think it's a tad irresponsible to be idly debating whether toasters make appropriate wedding gifts for dragon brides?"

Ffup spun around, alarmed at being spoken to by a disembodied voice. Unable to see Tarantella, who she assumed wouldn't be seen dead anywhere near water, the dragon peered into the darkness, clutching Nestor close to her body.

"Whoaaa . . . spooky," she whispered, her scaly hide breaking out in the dragon equivalent of gooseflesh, a state of affairs that caused Nestor to wake up and emit a dismayed squeak.

"Did you hear that?" Ffup gasped. Another bubbling snore

came from the aptly named Sleeper, his relaxed body sliding deeper into the loch, oblivious to his fiancée's distress. Utterly unnerved, Ffup leapt to her feet, the roll of toilet paper unspooling from her grip and bouncing into the water.

"Please. No!" she squeaked. "Don't hurt me. I'm just an innocent bystander. Whatever I've done, I didn't mean it. I'm sorry. . . ."

Tarantella groaned. This was all *so* unnecessary. The idiot dragon had launched into full-on hysteric mode and, judging by the little puffs of steam coming from her nostrils, was about to blow any . . . second . . . now.

"*Aughhhhh!* HELP! Save MEEEEEEEEEEE!" Ffup shrieked.

Yup, thought Tarantella. Time to pack up the children and leave town.

With a colossal *whooomph*, Ffup hurled twin bolts of flame from both nostrils, an action that instantly turned an area in the middle of the jetty into a blackened pyre and parboiled an innocent lobster that had the misfortune to be swimming nearby. Clutching Nestor to her chest, the dragon shot inelegantly into the night sky, her wings flapping frantically as she attempted to put as much distance between herself and the Voice as possible. Large cigar-shaped bundles fell from her vent, some pockmarking the surface of the loch, others thudding onto the jetty and releasing the pungent odor of dragon dung.

"Give me strength," Tarantella muttered, slitting her eyes at the retreating silhouette of Ffup as the panic-stricken beast flailed homeward, her flight path marked by the fecal equivalent of Hansel and Gretel's bread crumbs. Disgusted, the tarantula turned away and looked out over the loch. Its tidal lapping sounds were punctuated by an occasional hiss, as little flakes of smoldering jetty fell into the dark waters below. Of the Sleeper there was no sign, save for a few bubbles marking where he'd slid from view to better pursue his bachelor slumbers.

"Thanks for listening," Tarantella grumbled as she began the long journey back to the home comforts of Strega-Schloss. Tarantella now walked with the aid of a stick ever since an attempt on her life had resulted in the amputation of one of her legs. To her disgust, ahead of her lay four hours of effortful limping instead of her hoped-for twenty seconds of air travel courtesy of Ffup.

"Really 'preciate the lift," she added bitterly. "Knew I could count on your assistance in a crisis. *Not.*"

The tarantula's tiny figure limped across the seaweedy pebbles of the foreshore, still muttering to herself and occasionally pausing to rant at the night sky. "If you could have just pinned back your ears for one minute," she bawled, after wallowing through a particularly malodorous puddle of dragon poo, "you might have heard what I've been trying to tell you. Who knows, you might even have taken the time to view the evidence. . . . And believe me, if you thought I was so scary that you had to keech your breeks, when you find out what's *really* happening, we'll all have to run for cover, 'cause you'll bury *Scotland* in keech."

Her voice echoed back at her—*eech, eech, eech*—as she

reached the high-tide mark and paused for breath, aware that she was standing surrounded by evidence of what she'd been trying to tell Ffup. In clots of darkness that speckled the loch shore with pockets of decay were the corpses of hundreds of white mice, mute witness to some vile corruption at work in the darkening waters of Lochnagargoyle.

Toil and Trouble

The following morning, in the absence of Latch, Pandora volunteered to cycle to the nearby town of Auchenlochtermuchty for breakfast essentials. Returning home laden with croissants, coffee beans, and enough breakfast cereals to remodel the south face of Bengormless Mountain in mushy wheat should the need occur, Pandora overtook a taxi negotiating the rutted track that led from the village to Strega-Schloss. To her dismay, the hunched figure sitting in the rear of the taxi was that of the Strega-Borgias' very own Marie Bain, arguably the worst cook in the known universe. As she pedaled faster and faster to reach home first, Pandora realized that this was her last chance to eat a decent breakfast for the foreseeable future. Once Marie Bain took charge of the kitchen, such simple tasks as warming a croissant would become the culinary equivalent of rocket science; breakfast would turn into a tense and stressful state of affairs inevitably resulting in piles of inedible carbon, clouds of black smoke, and monumental tantrums thrown by the thwarted cook.

Leaping off her bike and leaving it to crash onto the rose-quartz drive in front of StregaSchloss, Pandora pounded up the steps and through the front door, arriving in the kitchen breathless and wild-eyed. Sitting at the kitchen table with headphones clamped to his ears, Titus was playing a particularly frenetic drumroll with two wooden spoons on a dishpan, his foot thumping the pedal of the trash can, causing the lid to bang up and down in a manner that he fondly imagined was similar to that of a set of cymbals.

"TITUS!" Pandora bawled, ripping open the packet of croissants and hurling them into the roasting oven of the range. "Like, *hello*? Listen up—Marie Bain's on her way here."

Tssss, sss, CLANGGGG, tacka tacka brrrrt, Titus replied, his eyes screwed up in an expression of extreme pain, his mouth opening to screech, *"I'm drownin' in your venom, I guess I loved too much, your lovin' feels like poison, you've got the killer touch. . . ."*

"Nice . . . ," murmured Pandora, reaching out to replace Titus's cymbals with the compost bucket.

"It's a kitchen confidential, it's a love cooked up in Hell . . . ," Titus continued, bringing his foot down into a rotting swamp of furry zucchini, slimy banana skins, and several past-their-sell-by-date eggs, their shells shattering under his sock-clad toes. His eyes flew open in shock, the wooden spoons falling from

his hands as he leapt back from the table with a roar of disgust.

"Whaaaa? Eurghhh, urk, eurchhhhh!" Hopping on one foot, he headed for the door to the kitchen garden, where he removed the offending sock and hurled it outside into the shrubbery.

Pandora smiled sweetly at her furious brother, deftly avoided his windmilling arms, and declaimed, "Titus Strega-Borgia, drummer with the amazingly talented Alien Brothers, welcome to breakfast television." She stepped out of Titus's path, holding an imaginary video camera to her head and extending a balloon whisk in place of a microphone. "Tell the world, Mr. Borgia, just how *did* you feel when your sister told you the news about Marie Bain's return?"

"WHAT?" Titus paused, a haunted expression crossing his face. "What news of Marie Ba—? Oh NO. She's *not*—?"

The rattle of an approaching taxi caused his face to turn ashy gray. Pandora bent ovenward and retrieved her tray of hot croissants. "Quick. If we eat them all now, she'll never know."

Outside, the taxi door slammed and the familiar voice of the bane of the Strega-Borgia kitchen could be heard greeting Signora Strega-Borgia in pained tones.

"What a pig," Pandora observed as Titus crammed a fourth croissant into his mouth, wincing at the heat but nevertheless determined to consume as many as possible before—

"No, he's not on holiday, Marie. I'm afraid poor Latch is unwell. Shocking news, yes. Terrible. No, we don't know yet. Come and have a coffee while you tell me *all* about your holiday." Signora Strega-Borgia's voice echoed down the corridor, the volume increasing as she approached the kitchen.

Titus reached out for the last croissant and, at a nod from his sister, wedged it into his already overloaded mouth just as the kitchen door swung open to reveal his mother and the unbecomingly suntanned Marie Bain.

Not so much a suntan, Titus thought unkindly, as a major brush with an overheated grill. He stood up politely, just as a stray croissant flake lodged irritatingly in his throat.

"Arrrghhhruff," he growled, hoping to dislodge the offending morsel, but only succeeding in causing the blockage to embed itself still further in his trachea.

"Rrrghurk?" he managed, turning to Pandora and wildly gesticulating at his throat.

"Oh, for heaven's *sake*, Titus." She crossed the room to grab her brother from behind and, with a practiced grip, executed a perfect Heimlich maneuver, which caused the entire contents of Titus's mouth to eject themselves and land with impeccable accuracy on the floor between Marie Bain's feet.

"Oh lord, *no*. I'm so sorry," Titus blurted, horrified for once at his own excesses. "Look, don't move, I'll get a mop—I . . . um, ah . . ."

With a stifled wail, the cook fled upstairs to the comforts of her bedroom, where, if previous tantrums were anything to go by, she would remain for the next week until, wooed downstairs with flowers, apologies, and promises of salary increases, she would once more resume the mantle of bane of the Strega-Borgia digestion: Marie Bain, the enteric entity.

"That's the amnesiac's family on the phone for you again, Sister." The staff nurse's voice had a soft Highland burr

somewhat at odds with her perpetual air of bristling efficiency and her tendency to reduce even the most arrogant of
consultants to meek little lambs after one of her legendary
tongue-lashings in the rinsing room.

"Sister?" she said, with quiet menace. "Shall I tell them
you're chust too busy?"

Halfway through her only cup of coffee in the previous
eight hours, the harassed ward sister leapt to her feet with a
guilty start. "No, Nurse. I'll take it. Thank you. . . ." Stifling an
exhausted yawn, the ward sister picked up the phone.

"Good morning. Ward Two, Sister Fraser speaking. Is that
you, Mrs. McLachlan?"

Across the room, the staff nurse checked her watch, tutted
impatiently, and, grabbing a long rubber hose with a rubber
bulb attached to one end, set off to inflict terror on her
patients.

"No. Not a lot to report, really. He appears to be quite com-
fortable. . . . Well, as far as we can tell, everything appears to
be working normally. No sign of any visible trauma. . . ."

From down the corridor came a quavering voice raised in
supplication. "No, no please, no. Not *that* thing. Get away
from me, woman. I don't need an anemone . . . an enemy . . .
an enema*aaargh*."

"Could you hold on a moment?" Sister Fraser dropped the
phone into an overflowing laundry bin and bolted down the
corridor.

"Mr. Latch?" she gasped.

Latch stood in a corner of the ward, holding a brimming

bedpan at arm's length, his skinny legs quivering beneath a hospital gown of spectacular brevity. Tethered by various tubes and wires to several items of medical impedimenta, he was hampered in his attempts to evade the ministrations of the staff nurse, who was steadily advancing on him, holding an extended enema tube like an offensive weapon.

This drama had engulfed the entire ward, and indeed, appeared to have its own healing effect, for several of Latch's more moribund fellow patients were standing on their beds and joining in the rebellion by waving their bedpans in sympathy.

"Not another step closer," Latch advised, "or I won't be responsible for the consequences. . . ."

"Mr. Latch," the staff nurse said, "would you chust behave yourself. What a carry-on. Such foolish behavior. . . . Chust who do you think you arrre?"

An abrupt change came over Latch's features. His face crumpled, his eyes filled with tears, and his mouth opened to howl, "That's *it*! That's the problem, don't you see? I don't know who I *am*. Help me . . . oh God, help me please. WHO AM I?" He slid down the wall, oblivious to the fact that his hospital gown was failing utterly to preserve his modesty, and, curling himself into a ball, began to sob in a truly abandoned fashion.

In the great hall at StregaSchloss, Mrs. McLachlan stood keeping a watchful eye on Damp while she waited for the ward sister to return to the phone. Damp was deep in conversation with a wood louse she'd spotted crawling across the baseboard below the main stairs. The wood louse, in the way of such creatures, was politely ignoring the hot-breathed attentions of the two-year-old, and was waiting for an opportune moment to make its escape.

"So," Damp said to the wee bug, "wee bug, d'you want to be my friend?"

And the wee bug said, "I don't know, Damp, maybe later. I'm a bit busy right now. Why don't you go ask Mummy?"

But Damp said, "Mummy's busy being sick, wee bug...."

"Oh, that's *marvelous!*" Mrs. McLachlan gasped. "I'm *so* relieved to hear that. Does that mean we could come in and visit him today?"

Damp looked up at her beloved nanny and the wood louse took the opportunity to vanish into the woodwork.

"Of course he's upset," Mrs. McLachlan soothed. "But don't worry, we'll soon remind him who he is. I'm sure that once he sees us, his memory will come flooding back...." She paused, listening very carefully, her smile fading, to be replaced with a frown. "No, he's a *butler,* he doesn't work with chemicals.... What is it you think he's been contaminated with?" There was a pause, then Mrs. McLachlan staggered, as if reeling from some invisible blow. "*Sulfur?*" she gasped. "Are you absolutely sure?"

Sensing from Mrs. McLachlan's voice that something was wrong, Damp staggered across the hall and patted the nanny's knees consolingly. With the phone under her chin, Mrs. McLachlan reached down to scoop Damp up into her arms and hug her tight.

"But it's passing out of his system, you say?" she continued, her voice trembling slightly. "Oh, well, that's a blessing. Who knows what happened? Nothing to worry about. No... Indeed. Give him our love then, and let him know we'll come in to see him this afternoon.... Marvelous... Thank you. Good-bye." Mrs. McLachlan dropped the phone and bit her lip hard enough to draw blood. Her mind launched into a freefall. *Sulfur. The odor of Hades. Sulfur was the indelible mark of the Pit. It was the calling card of a demon. And Latch had been all alone at StregaSchloss... alone and very vulnerable....*

A small hand patted her face, drawing her back to the present. Mrs. McLachlan gazed into Damp's wide-open eyes. "Oh lord, child," she whispered, "I think we're in deep trouble."

Damp's face fell and her bottom lip gave an exploratory wobble. "Hubble bubble?" she said in a small voice.

"A wee bit more than that, pet," Mrs. McLachlan muttered distractedly, as Titus emerged from the kitchen, tunelessly droning another lyric culled from his extensive repertoire.

"By the PRICKING of my THUMBS," he roared, unaware that Mrs. McLachlan also knew the words.

"... something WICKED this way COMES," she intoned, causing Damp to bury her head in the nanny's pillowy chest with a howl of terror.

The Truth About Hell

Luciano Strega-Borgia threw open the library door and yelled down the hallway, "Titus! For Pete's sake. Turn that racket *down*! Are you deaf, or what?" And with parental honor thus satisfied, he retreated to the seclusion of the library and waited for the din to cease.

Three doors along, Titus rolled off his bed and pressed the pause button on his CD player, emitting a martyred sigh as he did so. Then he opened his wardrobe door: stuck to its reverse side was a length of computer paper on which he'd written several phrases in common usage. Producing a gnawed pencil from the interior of the wardrobe, Titus amended his hidden list, adding another tick to "Turn that racket *down*."

Titus smiled. Twenty-*seven* occurrences since May. Pretty good going. However, "Are you deaf, or what?" was a new entry and, in the interests of statistical accuracy, had to be included on the list. Laboriously, he wrote it down, after "For heaven's *sake*, this room's a complete pigsty" (19) and "What did your last slave die of?" (a staggering 42 occurrences).

Smugly determined *never* to use such worn-out wrinkly phrases himself when he had the misfortune to become a parent, Titus plugged his headphones into the CD player, unpaused the current track, and fell back onto his bed, exhausted by the effort.

In the library, Luciano too was feeling exhausted. Unable to stop worrying about Latch, he had lain awake all night. As dawn broke over Lochnagargoyle, he slid quietly out of bed and crept downstairs to the library, seeking comfort in the writings of long-dead Roman philosophers. Later, after breakfast, he returned to the library clutching a vast pot of coffee and spent the remainder of the morning on the telephone to various domestic staffing agencies in the hopes of temporarily employing a butler to stand in for Latch. By lunchtime he was sandy-eyeballed, awash in espresso, and thoroughly fed up. The agencies had furnished Luciano with lists of possibilities, e-mailed and faxed extensive butler résumés and butlering references, and generally buried Luciano under mounds of promotional literature, so much so that he was now close to giving up the search and doing without until Latch had recovered. Perhaps they didn't need a butler right now? Surely they could manage without—

The telephone rang, jolting him back into interview mode.

"Hello. Strega-Borgias. Luciano speaking."

"Er. Aye. It's . . . it's about the job," a stranger's voice said.

"Yes?" Luciano sighed. Frankly, giving interviews by telephone was about as much fun as pulling teeth. "And you are . . . ?"

There was a long pause, followed by a deafening burst of static.

"I'm sorry, you're breaking up. I can't hear you," Luciano muttered as the static was replaced by crackling hisses, through which the mystery voice could barely be heard.

"*Cssssss* agency this morning, *pssst chhh shhwishhhh*, ten years' experien*shhhh pssss*, I'm on the train, CHHHSSSST . . ."

Quietly, Luciano replaced the handset and groaned as it immediately rang again.

"YES?" he barked.

"Hello, ees that Herr Strega-Borgia? I haff a vish to spik pliss viss heem?"

"Then you'd better go back to night school, *hadn't* you?" Luciano hissed, through teeth clenched so tight, his jaw ached.

"I'm sorry? I am telephone about ze yob of butter?" the voice continued. "I am here telling about vy I am ze perfect vun for zis yob? I am Herr Meister Ludwig von Esterhaze. . . . I am being several years in ze yob of butter at VeingartenSchloss een Transylvania, unt I am now vishing to . . . how you say, improve my celery?"

38

Luciano's hand stole across his desk until it reached the wall socket for the telephone. With a desperate snatch, he unplugged the phone and sighed with relief. A Transylvanian butler? He shook his head sadly. With a wife who fondly imagined herself to be a full-on witch, the *last* thing he needed was a butler with vampire potential.

Across the desk, his computer emitted a discreet *ping*, alerting him to an incoming e-mail. Leaning forward, he pressed ENTER and a letter appeared on the screen.

FROM: aimlach@domestic_angelic.co.uk

TO: luciano@stregaschloss.co.uk

SUBJECT: Temporary domestic staff needed in Argyll area

Dear Luciano Strega-Borgia,

The agency Domestic Angelic informed me this morning that you had an unforeseen vacancy for a butler/handyman in the Argyll region. I wonder if you might consider me for this position? My name is Alexander Imlach, I'm 28 years old, recently graduated from the University of Edinburgh with a degree in Ecology; prior to that I assisted my (now, sadly, deceased) parents in running a large country house hotel in Cornwall.

Although I have never been employed as a butler before, I imagine that my experience as front-of-house manager at the Standing Stones in Port Isaac might have, in some way, qualified me to fill your temporary staffing vacancy? By chance, I happen to be visiting a friend who lives near Loch Lomond, and if you were interested in interviewing me today I could be on your doorstep in under an hour.

Under an *hour*? What on earth was the boy driving? Luciano wondered. A rocket? Intrigued, he read on:

Lochnagargoyle and its environs have long been an area dear to my heart. As a child I had the great good fortune to spend a summer camping near the forest of Caledon. The memories I have of that enchanted time are of great comfort to me, all the more so since my parents are no longer in this world.

Luciano retrieved the telephone cable and plugged it back into the wall socket. That *poor* boy, he thought, dabbing at his eyes as he scrolled down to find the telephone number at the end of Alexander Imlach's e-mail. All alone, orphaned, with only fading memories of a trip to *Argyll* for solace. . . . Luciano shuddered. The boy's parents, may they rest in peace, must have been quite insane. Camping on a loch shore in Argyll was the nearest thing to Hell that he could imagine. With rain, mist, freezing-cold water, and gnats in such quantities that they fearlessly invaded your eyeballs and nostrils, only holidaymakers of a masochistic disposition considered driving their tent pegs into Lochnagargoyle's infested foreshores. Suspecting that his search for a temporary Latch-substitute had struck pay dirt, Luciano dialed and sat back to wait.

If Luciano could have seen what Hell was really like, he would have been forced to amend his incorrect comparison of its discomforts with those experienced under a tent in Argyll.

For a start, Hell was *far* hotter. Down in the Hadean Pit burned an eternal furnace that spewed forth sulfurous fumes and gobbets of magma like a subterranean volcano. Sunk in darkness, Hell's passageways and corridors bore evidence of recent modernization in keeping with a brutalist school of architecture. Hell never slept, no dawn bathed it in the light of a new day, and no stars shone in its bloody skies. Resembling a nightmare version of a chemical refinery, Hell's machinery perpetually throbbed, clanked, and shrieked; foul miasmas and odors rolled down its metal walkways, and its residents automatically sprinkled their morning muesli with ground-up headache pills and stirred aspirin into their bedtime cocoa.

One of these unfortunate creatures was slumped across his

obsidian desk, hissing down a cell phone and having a Bad Hades Day.

"How many times do I have to go through this?" he groaned, rolling his red eyes and pulling a hideous face before realizing, too late, that he was on videophone. "No, not you, darling. It was just a muscle spasm. Let me run it past you one more time. I. Have. To. Work. Late. At. The. Office. *Capisce?*" He paused, then closed his eyes in pain. "Whaddya mean, my supper's in the succubus? Who d'you think you're talking to? A minor demon?" Standing up, all the better to pace around his office, Isagoth, Defense Minister of Hades, snapped his fingers to summon a tiny creature poised by the door. Rushing forward, this creature revealed itself to be a salamander, its fiery body unscarred by its tendency to burst into flames on command.

"Whaddya mean, what's a lighter doing in my office? Whaddya *think* it's doing?" Isagoth bent down to light a black cigar against the salamander's igneous scales. "Just *don't*," he advised, exhaling a plume of filthy brown smoke. "Don't give me that I-thought-you'd-given-up stuff. If you had my worries, believe me, you'd smoke too. So cut me some slack, huh? Get off my case. All I'm asking is that you put a few beers in the fridge for when I get home. . . . Uh-huh. And, well, yeah, if you'd pick up my suits from the dry cleaner's, I'd sure 'preciate it. . . . Oops, gotta go. Missing your pointy little head already . . . Byeeee." Isagoth hit the off switch, but not before catching a glimpse of his wife's face on the video screen, incandescent with rage and wearing too much eyeliner, as usual; in the background were the remains of his microwaved dinner dripping down the walls of the dining room.

And now, as if his misery wasn't quite complete . . . He spun on one cloven hoof and punched a button next to a wall-mounted screen, which promptly displayed an alarming image of a demon engaged in some grisly ritual.

"Marsssturrr." The demon's voice hissed out of concealed speakers as it turned to face Isagoth, its features impassive, its hands covered in what could only be blood. "The sssubject has proved to be rather . . . ssstubborn in its rresssistance to quessstioning." The demon shrugged and turned to one side to allow an uninterrupted vista of the chamber beyond.

"Eeeeyewww. Puh*lease*. *Spare* me." Isagoth gagged, his hastily gobbled lunch reappearing in his gullet in a voyage of rediscovery. "I don't need to see what you're doing, moron. The hands-on stuff is *your* job, remember? Me: Master. You: scum. Isn't that how it goes?"

"Yerrsss, Marsssturrrr, but I think—"

"Just do your job, minion. No one requires you to think. Mindless violence, that's your brief. And—"

"Marrsssturr?"

"Get a move on. Break all four of his legs if you have to."

"Done that, Marrsssturr. I'm just removing his appendix with a blunt—"

Bringing his fist crashing down on the off switch, Isagoth closed his eyes and swayed on his cloven hooves. Eurrrgh. Gross. Disgusting. And even worse, he thought, his eyes snapping open and an agonized moan escaping his lips, his own fate would likely be similar if he failed in his mission to retrieve the Boss's bauble on time.

Returning to his desk on legs that suddenly felt too flimsy

to support his weight, Isagoth shuffled through his case notes until he found the relevant file. He hardly needed to look at it, since by now he could almost reel off its contents from memory. Doggedly, he forced himself to scan the pages, searching for clues he might have overlooked in the previous thousand re-readings.

"The Missing Chronostone," he read, his eyes watering in the smoke from his cigar.

1. FINDING THE CHRONOSTONE
(This is an almost impossible mission, or, to look on the bright side, it's almost as easy as emptying the Pacific Ocean armed with one rusty teaspoon.)

2. LIKELIHOOD OF SUCCESS IN FINDING THE CHRONOSTONE
(Zilch, but let's not be too negative, huh? Say 0.000001% chance of success.)

3. PREVIOUS ATTEMPTS AT FINDING THE CHRONOSTONE UNSUCCESSFUL
(No kidding—the last attempt ended up with my predecessor being reincarnated as an insect and coming to a sticky end thanks to a vengeful tarantula armed with nothing more than a lump of pine resin.)

4. IMPORTANCE OF CHRONOSTONE
(Whooh. Pretty important. Like, it's up there with the big ones. Ones like drawing breath, not being dead, etc.)

5. What exactly is the Chronostone?

(On this point, the Boss was distinctly unforthcoming. Quote: "It's a diamond, about the size of an egg, and it's mine, right?" Discussion over. I had a trawl through the Hadean Archives and came up with the following: "Chronostone—a.k.a. Pericola d'Illuminem, Precious, and Ignea Lucifer." Magical? Yes, but not in itself. The Chronostone is an unlimited power source that renders its owner omnipotent. Normal rules don't apply. With the Chronostone on board, you could turn lead into gold, make Time run backward, undo Death's dominion, rip the wings off angels, and become an irresistible babe-magnet.)

(Cancel that last bit. Too frivolous by far, but no *wonder* the Boss wants it back, eh?)

6. Consequence of failing to find the Chronostone

(Oh, puhleeaze. Let's not go there.)

Coughing uncontrollably and wreathed in smoke, Isagoth replaced the case file in a drawer of his obsidian desk and slammed it shut. He wished he'd never heard of the Chronostone. He was way out of his depth.

Part of Isagoth was still in denial, in fact. Every morning he'd wake up with a feeling of creeping dread, a sense that somewhere out there his future was rushing toward him on an unstoppable black tide, and there was nothing he could do to avoid it. This feeling was further compounded by the daily e-mails thudding into Isagoth's in-box from the Boss, e-mails which were becoming more impatient as the weeks rolled past.

"Face it, Isagoth," the demon muttered to himself as yet more messages *pinged* into his in-box, "if you can't find the Chronostone, you're toast. The Boss is *not* interested in excuses; he *doesn't* want to hear that two thousand years of combing the earth for an egg-sized diamond have produced nothing; he just wants his precious stone back, no matter *what* it takes to get it." Inhaling deeply, he read the latest communication from Below.

TO: isagoth
FROM: the pit

progress???

   that drumming sound you hear is not the sound of approaching thunder.

   nor is it the stonking bass riff from the alien brothers' recent hit single "get ur finger out."

   no.

   it's the sound of my claws drumming on my desk, eagerly awaiting your daily update on developments.

   do tell. i'm all agog.

Agog? wondered Isagoth. What sort of word was that? It didn't even come close to describing the kind of state he suspected the Boss would be in. Grinding his half-smoked cigar under one hoof, the demon began to type his reply, which, in common with every e-mail he'd sent, was composed of a groveling mixture of half-truths, overheard gossip, willful rumors, and utter fantasies: in short, lies, lies, and yet more lies.

The Magic Word

Clutching Damp's hot little hand in her own, Mrs. McLachlan tiptoed along the hospital corridor, trailing the scent of lilies from the flowers she'd picked for Latch's bedside, her sensible shoes squeaking on the polished linoleum. The nursing staff were closeted in the duty room writing reports, and Mrs. McLachlan and Damp sailed unchallenged into Ward Two. The majority of this ward's patients were clustered round a vast television, the main function of which appeared to be to induce sleep, for judging by the snores coming from its audience, all Latch's wardmates were out for the count.

In the opposite corner of the ward, Latch lay propped up on pillows, staring at the wall across from his bed. His eyes flickered in Mrs. McLachlan's

direction without giving any hint of recognition. She, in turn, gave no indication of her dismay at witnessing her colleague so hideously transformed. Latch looked as if he'd been marinated in turmeric: the skin of his face and hands was deep yellow in color, and Mrs. McLachlan caught a passing whiff of sulfur, undiminished by the strong smell of hospital disinfectant, exactly as the ward sister had reported.

"Hello, dear," the nanny said softly. "Och, it's such a relief to see you looking so . . . *well*. We've all been so worried about you, but it seems you're now on the road to recovery."

Latch frowned, his hands twisting the bedsheets, his feet stirring slightly under the covers. A look of faint alarm crossed his face as Mrs. McLachlan helped Damp out of her jacket, lifted her onto a nearby chair, and placed an overloaded shopping bag on his bed.

"Now," the nanny said firmly, "we've brought you some wee things to make you feel at home while you're getting better." She reached into the shopping bag and handed Latch a magazine, smiling encouragingly as she did so. "Your *Gentleman's Gentleman* came this morning—it's a new postman on the StregaSchloss run, so naturally he had a hairy fit when Tock waddled out of the moat to say hello. . . . We had a bit of bother trying to persuade the poor man to climb down out of the wisteria and be introduced properly."

Latch stared blankly at the magazine in his hands. Its cover bore a photograph of a man in a black suit, white shirt, and black tie, extending a silver salver on which was a newspaper. "BUTLER OF THE YEAR" was emblazoned below the man's elbow, under which was printed several utterly meaningless phrases: "Hot Tips for Firing Footmen"; "Cellar Duties—A Wine Buff's Guide to Choosing the Perfect Vintage"; and, puzzlingly, "Which Way to Pass the Port? Etiquette for the E-Generation." Now totally at sea, Latch looked up at the bearer of this strange magazine for some hint as to how he should respond. No clues were forthcoming as she hauled a heavy object out of her shopping bag and passed it over to him with an apologetic smile. "Now . . . I know this is silly of me, but I just thought you'd like to keep your hand in while you're here. It's your *iron,* dear—don't look at it like I've handed you an unexploded bomb. . . ."

She's a madwoman, Latch thought, trying to smile reassuringly lest he set her off into some unimaginable display of psychosis. He wondered whether, if he screamed for help, anyone would hear. She was standing up now, towering over him, fussing with a bunch of flowers she'd brought. . . .

"Och, I can't see a vase *any*where," Mrs. McLachlan complained. "And these poor wee flowers are collapsing in the heat." She patted Latch's hand and set off across the ward in search of something to put the lilies in, leaving Damp staring wide-eyed at Latch in his hospital gown.

"Pretty," the child decided, reaching out a small arm to stroke the material.

Latch shrank away, wishing to put as much distance between himself and this unknown child as possible.

"Ahhhh," Damp breathed, her face crumpling with the

rejection. "Lats doesn't like me anymore? Poor Lats. *Poor Damp*. Why you all yellow, Lats? Why you in bed, Lats? Want story?" And without waiting for a reply, Damp helped herself to Latch's magazine and, carefully holding it upside down, opened it and began to interpret the pictures inside. "Look, Lats," Damp said. "Wunsa pona time, there was a beautiful . . . man in a big black car and he had a magic . . . plate with a paper on it and"—she turned the page with some difficulty, since the magazine was nearly as big as she was, and continued, a small frown appearing on her face as she struggled to understand the picture in front of her—"and there was a big . . . poo on a plate and it said, 'Lats. I'm not supposed to be here on this nice plate. . . .' "

Intrigued, despite himself, Latch reached out for the magazine. "Hang on a minute. Can I see that picture?"

Damp looked up at him reprovingly. "But Lats, what's the magic word?"

Crossing the ward carrying a vase brimming with lilies, Mrs. McLachlan stopped, held her breath, and prayed that Latch could remember what Damp meant. Just one word, one tiny word that would give her hope that his memory loss was not irrevocable. Damp flapped the magazine, open to display an ad for hideously expensive cigars, at Latch and repeated, "Lats, what's the magic word? Not seeing poo on plate until you ask proply—"

"*Please*," Latch gasped. "Please . . . please, *please*. That's the magic wor—wuh—*wahhh*."

Scrambling up onto his bed, Damp wrapped her arms

round his neck and clung to him as he burst into tears of relief.

In the dungeons below StregaSchloss, the beasts were taking their accustomed afternoon nap. Curled into a vast hairy ball, Knot slept soundly, a thin trail of drool pooling beneath his matted mouth. In an adjacent stone alcove, Sab was trying to concentrate on the crossword puzzle in the daily paper, despite interruptions from Ffup, who reclined on a pile of straw and was simultaneously feeding Nestor, repainting her talons with nail polish, and keeping up a running commentary on the current state of play with regard to her wedding preparations.

"I mean, it's not as if I'm asking for the *moon*, is it? You only get married *once*, after all—No! Nestor, don't touch; Mummy's talons aren't dry yet. See, I think I'm really being, like . . . quite *reasonable* about the whole wedding, but he says I'm an extravagant airhead—"

"*Lightweight commander; not sea or ground.* Four down, seven letters . . . Oh heck, I *hate* these kind of clues."

"And d'you know he's even trying to wriggle out of buying me an engagement ring? Says he can't possibly afford even the smallest, squittiest diamond? I mean, like, how tight is *that*?"

"*Did moan about tangled gem.* Two across . . . hmmm. That's an anagram, isn't it?" Sab muttered to himself, scratching his head.

"Are you listening to anything I've been saying?" Ffup demanded.

"Urrrgh. Hush, woman. This is difficult. Dido man? Do dam in? Mad doin'? Maid nod ... DIAMOND!"

"Y-e-s," Ffup said with exaggerated slowness. "Well *done*, Sab. What a conversationalist. *What* rapier-like wit, what a stunning contribution to the debate, what—"

Interrupting Ffup's tide of sarcasm came a wavering voice, its whispery tones echoing down the steps that linked the dungeons with the wine cellar upstairs.

"I've lost my mouse ... ," it moaned pitifully. "I could have sworn I left it on top of the fish sticks. ..." A trembling hand came into view, its fingers vibrating in sympathy with their owner's voice as it quavered, "Are you down there, Titus, dear? I'm afraid I've crashed the computer again."

"What are you *doing* out of your freezer?" Sab demanded, leaping up in time to catch the stooped and wrinkly figure of Strega-Nonna as she tottered and fell down the last few steps into the dungeon, her feet entangled in a long gray cord, at one end of which dangled the missing computer mouse. Undismayed by her own terrifying frailty, the ancient woman continued to bemoan her fate, her sticklike arms twitching as Sab tenderly carried her back upstairs.

"I just cannot figure out what's the matter with the infernal thing," she mumbled, waving a dismissive claw in the direction of a large freezer, beside which lay a state-of-the-art laptop surrounded by defrosting bags of assorted leftover soups.

"*I* was surfing, you know," she explained proudly, displaying her newfound grasp of technology, a skill completely lost on Sab, who, incorrectly assuming that the old lady was referring to some form of geriatric water sport, closed his eyes in horror at the sudden vision of Strega-Nonna, clad in a bikini, skimming the waves on Lochnagargoyle.

"Tried to log on to blastfromthepast dot com," she added, patting Sab's snout and gazing around with interest as the giant beast squeezed through the aisles of the wine cellar and into the kitchen, where he deposited Strega-Nonna on a rocking chair beside the range.

"Very kind of you, dear," she yawned, sinking into the warm cushions. "Wonder if you could fetch me my computer manuals and see if young Titus is about? Maybe his agile young brain can help his addled old great-great-great-great-great . . ." Her voice trailed off in midsentence as she fell fast asleep, drained by her tussle with a technology invented hundreds of years *after* she was born.

Sab peered at Strega-Nonna, noticing how frequent cycles of freezing and defrosting were taking their toll on the old lady's skin: her cheeks had fallen inward, giant gray circles ringed her eyes, and her lips had disappeared completely as her mouth shrank into a tightly pleated dimple. It was such a pity, Sab thought, reaching out with a sheathed paw to stroke Strega-Nonna's halo of white hair; such a tragedy that this beloved ancestress couldn't let go of her absurd desire to find a cure for old age—a desire that, bizarrely, had kept her alive for centuries, suspended in ice until medical science addressed the problem of aging. In common with all griffins, Sab had loved and lost many human companions down through the years—some to the battles and wars that humankind appeared powerless to avoid, others to the plagues and famines that had swept across earth at various stages in its evolution. Any humans spared by such calamities lived out their allotted span and succumbed to the ravages of Time, which eventually claimed them all.

In comparison to humans, griffins seemed almost *immortal*. Sab had long ago given up celebrating his birthday, since with hundreds of repetitions such a celebration not only lost meaning but also served as a reminder of all those human friends he'd never see again. . . .

"Hey. Why so glum, chum?" Ffup bounded into the kitchen, her flailing tail crashing against the china cupboard and rattling all the china decorating its shelves. A small moan came from a lidless willow-pattern teapot, long employed by the Strega-Borgias to store small, precious things like marbles and buttons, usually after they'd been rescued from the bowels of the washing machine or vacuum cleaner. The moan grew more pronounced, until finally Tarantella appeared over the rim of the teapot, a tiny pair of tweezers clasped in one hairy leg, her mouthparts gathered in an outraged pout.

"A little hush, please, if you will," she hissed. "I've reached a very delicate stage in my beauty preparations, and any sudden movements might have catastrophic consequences."

"Say again?" Ffup advanced on the tarantula, her hot breath causing Tarantella to recoil toward the safety of the teapot.

"I'm plucking my eyebrows," she said severely. "*Not* that it's any of your business, I might add, but I'd hold you personally responsible if I plucked out one of my eyes by accident."

Ffup winced and immediately became statue-still. "B-b-but, how can you tell?" she whispered.

"Tell *what?*" Tarantella snapped.

"Where your eyebrows begin and your . . . your . . ."

"Are you implying that I'm overendowed in the hairiness department?" Tarantella's voice was chilly in the extreme.

"Um, gosh, *heavens,* no, never, ah . . . er . . ." Ffup began to tiptoe backward, heading for the door to the kitchen garden.

"Because, you understand, I would take a very dim view of such slander," Tarantella continued, raising the tweezers to her eyes and squinting at her reflection in one of the marbles below her body.

"Absolutely. Yes. No, I mean, I never meant . . . AUUK!" There was a colossal crash as Ffup's hind legs became entangled with her tail and she fell backward into a posse of empty milk bottles awaiting collection at the back door.

"Dear me," said Tarantella conversationally. "There goes my favorite eyeball. . . ."

Emitting stereo screams of utter horror, Ffup and Sab fled the kitchen, leaving the tarantula reclining languidly on the rim of the teapot, her tweezers gripping a small marble, a huge grin of victory spreading across her mouth.

Muddy Waters

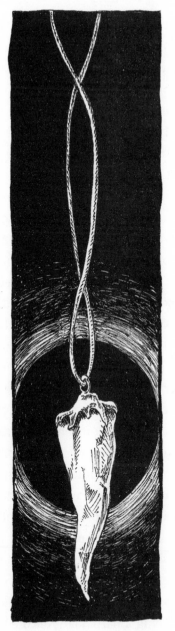

Deep in the murk of the StregaSchloss moat, Tock was in the throes of an interior-decorating crisis. As the temperature rose over the summer, the waters of the moat had slowly evaporated. Now, in the heat of early August, the moat was beginning to smell very peculiar. Strange bubbles rose to its surface and burst, releasing fetid miasmas and swampy gases. The water had turned an opaque shade of bile green and colonies of mosquitoes had moved in. Maddened by their continual whine and revolted by the stench of stagnant water, Tock decided he couldn't put it off any longer. Torn between effecting a moat makeover and simply redecorating and tidying up, the crocodile had finally settled on the radical solution. Groping blindly in the moat's silty depths, Tock's claws at last found purchase on a rusty iron chain, which, when pulled, proved itself to be attached to a vast iron plug. As he tugged and heaved on the chain, Tock wondered if he was making A Big Mistake. Emitting a distant *thwungggggg*, the submerged plug broke free from its moorings and obligingly allowed itself to be dragged several meters across the moat floor, before subsiding once more into the mud from whence it came. Too late, Tock thought, as the moat began to drain, slowly at first and then gaining momentum, faster and faster, the outgoing waters spinning in a slurping spiral into which was sucked the crocodile's entire water-lily collection, nearly followed by the crocodile himself.

"Aukkk!" Tock squawked, clinging to the moat's stone perimeter and watching in dismay as nearly all of his personal belongings were devoured by the gulping maw of the drain.

Half buried in the silt, stranded by the vanished water, was a collection of highly incriminating evidence relating to several unsolved disappearances in Argyll over the previous two decades. Blind skulls, gnawed femurs, embedded ribcages, half a rusting machine gun, and a drowned cell phone all bore mute witness to Tock's ability to guard StregaSchloss with extreme prejudice. As a willing but recent convert to vegetarianism, Tock was finding these all-too-visible reminders of his carnivorous past a little, well . . . close to the bone.

Did I *really* eat all those bodies? he wondered, appalled at such proof of his lack of good taste. And what a *mess*. What a complete pigsty. To think I've been *swimming* in the same water as those bones. But what a *waste* of good protein, he thought, eyeing a particularly bloated specimen of human thigh. Still a lot of good eating on that one. Tock dragged the waxy white thigh out of the mud and considered it thoughtfully.

Moments later, after rinsing the thigh in the kitchen sink, he placed it carefully in the meat drawer of the Strega-Borgias' fridge and waddled back to the moat, feeling faintly virtuous at the prospect of *his* meat-free lunch. This had been thoughtfully laid out for him on the warm stone of the moat-side, wrapped in muslin to protect it from gnats. Settling back with a watercress sandwich in each claw and one clamped between his teeth, Tock was the first resident of StregaSchloss to meet the prospective candidate for the job of temporary butler replacement.

At first there was the sound of a distant insect: an angry buzzing drone that swelled and grew until it sounded like a swarm of hornets, then a chain saw, and finally, ripping the air asunder, the scream of a supersonic fighter jet. The noise hammered at Tock's eardrums and echoed off the south face of StregaSchloss, the aural equivalent of assault and battery. Forgetting that he'd just drained the moat, Tock dived back-ward off its edge, expecting to plunge into the cool liquid silence of his home; instead, he found himself rudely slapping full-length into a patch of moat sludge which bore signs of having once been a reptile restroom.

"Oh, for Pete's sake!" he bawled, annoyed more with him-self than with the source of the deafening din, which, having reached an unbearable pitch, confounded the crocodile by stopping. Dead. Huh? Tock was utterly confused. He listened to a silence now broken only by birdsong. . . . Then the sound of approaching footsteps on the rose-quartz drive reminded him of his guard duties and, shaking his head to remove the last fading echoes of the Mystery Din, he crawled over to the edge of the moat, teeth bared in greeting to whoever this might be visiting StregaSchloss.

"I simply cannot apologize enough." Luciano's expression conveyed how utterly aghast he'd been to find his prospective butler locked in mortal combat with the overzealous Tock.

"A ghastly mistake," he mumbled, his mouth pressed to the keyhole of the first-floor washroom, where Alexander Imlach was attempting to scrub off all traces of mud after rolling around in the moat with a ravening reptile.

"My fault entirely," Luciano whispered, aware that it was hardly Tock's fault for chewing the leather-clad apparition that had climbed off its motorcycle and attempted to gain entry to StregaSchloss. . . .

The bathroom door opened and Alexander Imlach limped out, his face dotted with Band-Aids and deathly pale despite a scalding shower to remove all traces of moat slime from his person.

"Come and have some tea," Luciano said, taking the young man's arm and leading him downstairs to the kitchen.

"I'm fine, really," Alexander said, smiling reassuringly at the gathered Strega-Borgias and taking a huge bite of carrot cake. "I took some herbal remedies, put my aromatherapy gel on the worst cuts, and boosted my immune system by applying rhythmic pressure around my seventh chakra."

The Strega-Borgias stared blankly, aware that no matter

what, they owed it to this young man to at least pretend to be listening as he spouted such incomprehensible nonsense. "Besides," he added indistinctly through a mouthful of mashed cake, "I had a hunch something like this might happen. A sort of . . . crocodile vibe. Plus, my iridologist warned me about crossing the great water—"

"More tea?" Mrs. McLachlan interrupted, adding under her breath, "Or does that count as *drinking* the great water?"

Enthralled, Pandora gazed at Alexander, half hoping he would turn his attention on her, but simultaneously half dreading being the object of his wide blue stare. He appeared to be completely at home, relaxed and friendly, drawing all the Strega-Borgias into the circle of his charm. All, that is, except for Mrs. McLachlan, who was acting as if she suspected young Mr. Imlach of harboring something contagious and was regarding him with an expression composed of equal parts dismay and annoyance. Oblivious to the nanny's chilly stare, Alexander had turned his attention to Baci, who was visibly glowing under his scrutiny.

"Fascinating," he murmured. "I've never had the privilege of meeting a real live witch before. . . ."

Mrs. McLachlan closed her eyes briefly as Baci rose to the bait.

"Oh, not a real live witch *yet*," Baci admitted truthfully, eyes sparkling. "Just a student. Well . . . a second-year student, actually."

Across the table from her mother, Pandora gritted her teeth in annoyance. Her mother's knowledge of witchcraft, even after a year of cramming was . . . well, it was *dangerous*. Even now, somewhere near Glasgow Airport were several innocent frogs, temporarily transformed by Baci's inept magical practices into a group of naked and clueless royals, doomed to be thrown into prison for offenses against public decency, not to mention illegally attempting to enter Britain. . . . Honestly, Pan thought, rolling her eyes, why were parents so *embarrassing*?

Titus, too, was wilting under the heat of Baci's enthusiasm for her craft. Please . . . stop, he begged her silently; no more; enough.

"Of course, Transformation was the main subject we studied last year," Baci continued, producing, to Titus's horror, a Disposawand from the pocket of her linen shirt. "Shall I demonstrate?"

Mrs. McLachlan stood up and began pointedly to clear the table with rather more than necessary force.

"Let's see . . . ," Baci murmured. "What shall I use?"

"Please, take this." Alexander groped beneath the collar of his shirt and produced a silver chain, from which dangled a chunk of quartz in the shape of a large tooth. "It was a twenty-first birthday present from my late parents—it's a dowser's crystal that I use to channel my psychic energy."

Over by the sink, Mrs. McLachlan rolled her eyes and emitted an exasperated *tchhh*.

"It's also a charm," Alexander blithely continued, "ensuring the wearer long life, riches, and fertility."

Baci turned a deep shade of pink, but gamely accepted the offered crystal and placed it on the tablecloth in front of her.

"Mum—" Titus began.

"Not *now*, Titus." Baci narrowed her eyes in concentration.

"One hundred and *three*," Titus muttered under his breath, inwardly vowing to update his cliché chart accordingly, and slumping back into his seat with a loud snort.

Ignoring Titus, Baci began to spin her wand in a slow circle, her eyes squinched shut as she brought the Disposawand down on the crystal with a determined *thwack*.

There was a loud crash from the kitchen sink as the teapot slipped out of Mrs. McLachlan's hands, followed by an answering *chingggg* as the crystal flew out from under Baci's wand, bounced off the table, and rolled across the floor to disappear under the kitchen cupboard.

"Where's it *gone*?" wailed Baci, dropping to her knees and groping blindly in the dust beneath the cupboard.

"Hold on, I'll get a flashlight." Luciano stood up and headed for the wine cellar.

"Wait a minute," said Pandora. "Does anyone actually know *what* we're looking for? I mean . . . what did you change the crystal into, Mum?"

"I . . . er . . . ," Baci groaned. "Um. It was the *Orba Occultis*, I think."

"Huh?" Pandora frowned. "The *what*?"

"The Hidden Globe," Mrs. McLachlan muttered, drying her hands on a dishtowel. "A device that predicts the future life and eventual death of its owner and assorted dabblers too eaten up with curiosity to realize that a little knowledge is a dangerous thing. Commonly known as a crystal ball. Although," she added in an undertone, "why *he'd* want a crystal ball is quite beyond me. He's got the psychic skills of a lemming. . . ."

Mortified, Baci apologized profusely as Luciano, flashlight in hand, attempted to locate the missing object. He hauled out into the unforgiving daylight an assortment of long-lost items, all of which had vanished ages ago in the dust and hair balls beneath the cupboard. Deep in its shadows, Multitudina watched nervously as her favorite hiding place was invaded by a human hand.

"There goes the neighborhood," observed Tarantella, scuttling up the back of the cupboard, only marginally hampered by the gleaming new marble she clasped under one leg. Reaching the safety of her willow-pattern teapot, she was just about to add the new marble to her fake-eyeball collection when she spotted herself reflected in its glassy depths. Peering into the marble, a small smile crossed her pink mouthparts.

"I see a tall, dark stranger . . . ," she intoned, adding somewhat prosaically, "Oh *dear,* it's the coal man. Oh well, never mind. You will cross the great water and . . . be wrapped in a fluffy bath towel. Great fortune will be yours—you will win at Monopoly. Heed the advice of the wise woma—" A shadow fell over the tarantula and she looked up into Mrs. McLachlan's eyes.

"The wise woman advises you to hand that over immediately," the nanny whispered, extending a hand. Tarantella clambered aboard, catching a passing glimpse of Mrs. McLachlan's palm magnified in the glass of the marble.

"Wow. I've never seen a life-line like *that* before."

"Indeed," Mrs. McLachlan sighed. "That's probably why I never have my palm read. It's illegible."

"Written in hieroglyphics, more like," Tarantella breathed. "Are you quite sure you're *human?*"

Mrs. McLachlan didn't dignify this with a reply. Instead, raising her voice, she announced, "Found it."

"My goodness," Baci gasped, astonished that, for once, one of her spells had actually *worked.*

"Bravo!" cried Luciano, relieved that his wife hadn't turned the young man's crystal into a frog—or worse.

"It's not very big, though," Pandora said critically, peering at the tiny object.

"Maybe it's just a baby." Baci patted her tummy. "After all, I *am* quite good at babies. . . ."

"Well, I think it's quite marvelous," gushed Alexander, reaching out to retrieve his transformed crystal. "In fact," he added, "don't change it back. I think I prefer it this way."

Eeughhh, thought Titus. *What* a crawler. He tried to catch his sister's eye to share a moment of teenage disgust at the mysteries of adult behavior, but Pandora's attention was elsewhere; to Titus's annoyance, she was gazing at Alexander with what could only be described as spaniel-eyed devotion. Revolted, Titus crammed the last slice of carrot cake into his mouth and headed for the wine cellar to reboot Strega-Nonna's computer.

Despite an alarming tendency to hurl china around and launch into full-on hysterics at the slightest provocation, Luciano Strega-Borgia had a heart of solid marshmallow, and thus found himself unable to resist the orphaned charms of

Alexander Imlach. A scant two hours after his arrival at StregaSchloss, the young man found himself hired as Latch's temporary replacement.

"Please, call me Zander," he said, shaking Luciano's hand so vigorously that the older man felt his teeth rattle.

Pandora, watching from an upstairs window as Alexander's motorcycle sped back along the track toward Auchenlochtermuchty, realized he'd got the job when the young man took both hands off the handlebars and punched the air victoriously before vanishing behind a dusty copse of ancient oaks.

Neither Fish, nor Fowl, nor Good Red Herring

The following day, in celebration of the arrival of Alexander into the StregaSchloss household, Pandora decided to cook dinner. However, what had seemed like a marvelous idea at ten o'clock in the morning was, by teatime, beginning to assume the proportions of a culinary nightmare. Evidence of Pandora's efforts lay all around the kitchen: teetering stacks of burnt pans, two sinks full of greasy baking dishes, and, mercifully hidden in the roasting oven, a leg of lamb that obstinately remained raw, wet, and utterly unappetizing. Moreover, some thoughtless person had lost the balloon whisk, leaving Pandora hot, cross, and close to tears as she attempted to whip egg whites with a bent fork. Through an open window she could hear a distant splashing as Tock continued his ambitious home renovations, which appeared at this stage to involve removing endless quantities of accumulated mud from the bottom of the moat.

Stopping to offer encouragement, Ffup peered over the edge of the moat down to where Tock stood, his back legs submerged in ooze, his front legs clutching the battered shovel with which he was attempting to implement his transformations.

"Wouldn't a soup ladle do the job more quickly?" the dragon suggested as another shovelful of slime slapped onto the rose-quartz at her feet.

Tock paused and squinted up to where Ffup stood silhouetted against the evening sun. "I think I've accidentally strayed into a hippopotamus heaven," he said, straightening up with a groan. "I mean, have you ever seen this much mud before?" He propped himself wearily against his shovel and waved a slime-encrusted claw about for emphasis. "What a dumb idea. . . . I wish I'd never started this."

Pandora agreed wholeheartedly. The egg whites had steadfastly refused to turn into pillowy meringue peaks, preferring to remain in a liquid pool on a baking tray in the oven, dripping onto the floor and spot-welding themselves for all eternity in little blackened balls of burnt sugar. Meanwhile, the potatoes had boiled themselves to mush while she anxiously waited for the lamb to turn into something more akin to the glossy picture in the cookbook, and not like a chunk of raw roadkill. . . .

Mrs. McLachlan entered from the kitchen garden and laid down a handful of fresh herbs on the table. Tactfully avoiding mentioning Pandora's tear-stained face, the nanny opened the oven door a crack, wondering if she dare assess the damage.

"It's just *awful*," Pandora wailed. "I just know it's the worst meal anyone will *ever* have eaten. I'm a rubbish cook—even Marie Bain's never made food *this* disgusting. It's totally—"

"Hush, child." Mrs. McLachlan pulled on a pair of oven mitts and handed Pandora a knife.

"What's *that* for?" Pandora demanded. "Should I use it on myself? HORROR IN ARGYLL AS LOUSY COOK STABS SELF AFTER RAW LAMB INCIDENT?"

"Being rude isn't going to put food on the table, dear," Mrs. McLachlan advised. "Why don't you chop some herbs while I see if we can do something about your wee lamb?"

"Toss it in the bin, I think," the thwarted cook muttered, turning her back on Mrs. McLachlan and applying herself to the herbs. It was the nanny's gasp of horror that alerted Pandora to the possibility that her cooking was even worse than she'd expected. Mrs. McLachlan stood back from the open oven door, her face completely drained of color, her hands fluttering at her throat.

"What's *wrong*?" Pandora demanded, aware that something must be very amiss to cause the normally unflappable Mrs. McLachlan to react in such a fashion.

"Where . . . where did you *get* . . . this . . . this *thing*?" the nanny whispered, her voice sounding half strangled.

Alarmed, Pandora laid down the knife and came around to view the evidence. "It was . . . it was in the meat drawer in the fridge," she said. "I mean, I'm sorry I've made such a mess of it, but I'm sure I followed the recipe properly." Turning, she fumbled for her cookbook. "Look. It was this one. Roast Leg of Lamb, here . . ."

Mrs. McLachlan removed the roasting tray and contents from the oven and dropped it onto the warming plate with a dramatic *clanggggg*. Pandora stared at her in some confusion.

"That is *not* a leg of lamb," Mrs. McLachlan said through clenched teeth.

"Then what *is* it?" Pandora whispered, her skin breaking out in gooseflesh at the prospect of finding out the answer. To her mixed relief and frustration, the nanny didn't reply, but instead crossed the kitchen to open the fridge door and peer inside.

"What are you doing?" Pandora begged, by now somewhat unnerved, as Mrs. McLachlan sniffed once, twice, and then slammed the fridge door shut with a decisive thud.

"Pandora, my dear child . . . ," she began, and then, aware that the roasting pan and its grisly contents were still in evidence, crossed to the range and mercifully covered the mystery meat with a dishtowel. As she turned back to Pandora, it was immediately obvious that no answers would be forthcoming. Not now. Probably not ever, Pandora realized, recognizing Mrs. McLachlan's closed and nailed-down expression as one barred to all attempts at inquiry.

"Lamb is off the menu, I'm afraid," the nanny said with a grim little smile. "So we're going to have to come up with something to replace it. I shall dispose of this . . . thing, and while I attend to that, perhaps you would be kind enough to grate some Parmesan, put a pan of water on to boil for pasta, and we'll put our heads together and come up with something we can use to make a sauce. . . ." Bearing the dishtowel-veiled roasting pan, Mrs. McLachlan headed out for a word with Tock, leaving Pandora none the wiser.

Later, sitting in pride of place at the head of the table, Pandora had cause to give thanks to her own lack of culinary talents meatwise, be it lamb, beef, or whatever. For, as Zander cleared his plate of his third helping of Pandora's hastily assembled *penne bianche*, he dabbed his lips with a linen napkin, raised his glass to the cook, and said, "With food as good as *that*, it's a wonder anyone bothers to eat meat."

Pandora's breath caught in her throat.

"Does that mean you're a vegetarian?" Luciano inquired, his voice betraying his dismay at the prospect of such culinary monotony.

"Absolutely," Zander affirmed, adding self-righteously, "I never eat anything that has a face."

Wondering if the three tins of anchovies in her pasta sauce qualified as faceless, Pandora blushed, hoping no one would take it upon themselves to enlighten Zander as to the ingredients of what he'd just devoured.

"What about fish?" Titus asked. "I *hate* fish. Can't stand all the bones . . . I *never* eat it."

Please . . . no, Pandora begged silently, praying her father wouldn't rise to the bait.

"You just did," Luciano said baldly.

"Did what?"

"You just ate fish, Titus. Loads of them. You too, Zander. Both of you with every evidence of enjoyment. Oh, for heaven's sake, don't look so *stricken*. Pandora has been working all day to make this meal; the least the pair of you can do is not pick it apart and accuse her of corrupting your sacred palates. Sometimes"—Luciano stood up and began to clear the table—"it's just far better *not* to know what you're eating."

Amen to that, Mrs. McLachlan silently vowed, briefly allowing herself to imagine Zander's expression if Pandora had presented him with her original menu: roast leg of deceased gangster in a blood *jus*.

The Witness in the Moat

✳ ver Argyll, apparently unaware that the weather forecast had promised weeks of unbroken sunshine, a vast blanket of gray clouds rolled in from the west, skidded to a halt over the peaks of Mhoire Ochone, and settled down to the business of soaking every square centimeter of land between Auchenlochtermuchty and Lochnagargoyle. Digging in his drained moat, Tock dropped his shovel, covered his eyes in despair, and moaned. Overhead, silhouetted in a lit window on the first floor, Mrs. McLachlan tucked Damp into bed and fleetingly observed that the patter of the rain outside sounded like a perfect lullaby.

Tiptoeing into the nursery to kiss her youngest daughter

good night, Baci Strega-Borgia peered through the window at the gloom beyond and heaved a deep sigh. "So much for my plans for a picnic tomorrow," she said wistfully. "Honestly, Flora, I only have to *think* picnic and the rain starts. . . . Horrible weather."

Mrs. McLachlan looked up from sorting out Damp's clothes for the following day and smiled. "Some would say there's no such thing as horrible weather, madam—only inadequate clothing."

Under the quilt, Damp stiffened. Mrs. McLachlan was placing a *woolly cardigan* on top of the pile of her clothes for tomorrow. This was not to be tolerated.

"Hobibble scratchy," she decided, bringing her brows down with a finality that she hoped the nanny would understand to mean that no negotiations were possible cardigan-wise. In case of misinterpretation, she added, "Don't like it, that one."

Signora Strega-Borgia closed the curtains on the dismal evening outside and crossed the nursery to bend over Damp, enveloping the little girl in her familiar scent of lilies. Damp's arms came up around her mother's neck, hugging her so tight that Baci lost her balance, toppling over to land face to face on the bed with her daughter. Their breath commingled and their noses touched.

"Oh!" Baci gasped, her eyes widening in surprise.

"Madam?" Mrs. McLachlan turned and saw Baci sit upright, both hands on her stomach, her attention focused on something as yet invisible.

"I felt the baby kick," she explained, a smile breaking out across her face. She hugged Damp and stood up, eyes shining. "I must go tell Luciano. He'll be thrilled. . . ."

"Damp *not* frilled," the little girl decided, her bottom lip quivering dangerously as Baci blew her a kiss and glided serenely out of the nursery.

Mrs. McLachlan sighed. Do I have to do *everything* around here? she wondered, hearing Baci's footsteps recede downstairs as she rushed off to give Luciano the glad tidings, blissfully unaware that she'd left Damp on the verge of tears. Oh pet, not tonight, the nanny thought, praying that the little girl might somehow telepathically understand that Nanny McLachlan was Otherwise Engaged on Important Business. . . .

"Rrright, wee lassie, I'll make a bargain with you," she said, plucking the offending cardigan off the pile of clothes and coming over to take Baci's vacated place on Damp's bed. "If you go to sleep right now, Nanny'll put this hobibble scratchy away."

"New baby wear it?" Damp asked hopefully.

"Probably only once"—Mrs. McLachlan smiled—"then new baby will refuse to wear it ever again, just like you." Wedging the vexed item of knitwear into the back of a drawer, Mrs. McLachlan restacked Damp's Russian dolls in ascending order of size, their painted expressions seeming to indicate that no way, not even in the depths of Siberia, would they be caught dead wearing a cardigan like *that*. Crossing the room, the nanny turned out the main light, wound up Damp's moon-and-stars mobile, and tenderly tucked a stray strand of hair behind the little girl's ear.

"Sleep now, pet. Sweet dreams."

Popping the dingy paw of a much-loved small velvet fox into her mouth, Damp closed her eyes, falling into sleep secure in the knowledge that the Dread Scratchy would not be out there, lurking in the darkness, waiting for her to wake up.

In her bedroom adjoining the nursery, Flora McLachlan paced the floor, waiting for the house to fall silent. Footsteps sounded on the stairs and the sound of laughter echoed down the corridor. Just as the Strega-Borgias had been blissfully unaware of their near brush with cannibalism at the dinner table, so, too, were they ignorant of the real danger closing in on StregaSchloss. A very real danger that had crushed poor Latch, temporarily wiping his memory and leaving him comatose and reeking of sulfur.

Mrs. McLachlan shuddered. The smell of sulfur would have immediately alerted her to the presence of a demon, but Latch wouldn't have known what was going on. Not at first. And by the time he'd realized that he'd unwittingly invited a demon into StregaSchloss, it would have been too late. . . . He wouldn't have been able to protect himself. Until the butler recovered sufficiently to confirm what had happened to him, Mrs. McLachlan had to assume the worst and take measures to protect StregaSchloss from further demonic visitations. Locking the doors was pointless, as was phoning the police.

Telling the Strega-Borgias that they were under threat of invasion by the powers of darkness was likely to achieve little other than hysteria, followed by denial that such things were possible. Mrs. McLachlan gazed unseeing at the darkness beyond her windows. She had to act now. Swiftly and secretly, she needed to use all her skills to protect those she loved.

Rain smeared the windows, pattering on the leaves of an ancient chestnut tree, the roots of which resembled a tangle of pleading, outstretched fingers reflected in the vast puddle at the bottom of Tock's moat. The rush and babble of rainwater pouring through gutters and downpipes sounded like distant voices; to Tock's ears, the water sounded more like a mocking gabble, wet and gleeful as it rose steadily in his no-longer-drained moat.

Normally, on a night like this, the crocodile would have pulled his lily-pad comforter over his head and swum away to the dark and reedy end of the moat in order to sleep. Normally, the moat would have been three meters deep in water. . . .

Two centimeters of muddy slime dotted with marine hazards do not a cradle make, Tock decided, gripping a borrowed golf umbrella in one forepaw and glaring up at the house, where Mrs. McLachlan's bedroom window shone its solitary light into the darkness. Please, Tock begged silently, his eyes slitted against the unaccustomed brightness, turn that light *off*. Without the lightless sanctuary of water lapping all around, the crocodile felt as if he were stripped of a layer of protection. Water, for Tock, was pillow, sheet, and quilt in one. Mud and rain were simply not the same at all. Wondering if the Strega-Borgias would mind if he spent the night in one of their bathtubs, he folded the umbrella, picked his way across the bone-strewn moat floor, and was halfway out when a noise from above caught his attention.

Mrs. McLachlan's window opened a crack, then, very slowly, was drawn carefully upward until it stood wide open, spilling light into the darkness. The light attracted the attention of some of the insect population of Argyll, which, despite the rain, never could resist such an invitation. Then the light was abruptly extinguished and something large flew *out* of the window, hovering over the meadow just long enough for Tock to identify what he'd seen before the object appeared to gather such speed that it literally dematerialized over Lochnagargoyle.

"Whaa . . . ?" Tock honked in alarm. Had he really *seen* that? Surely not, his rational reptile mind decided—must've been something you ate giving you nightmares. *Oh, but Tock*, a small snappish voice informed him, *you're not asleep. You're awake. You're knee-deep in primal ooze and you certainly could use a bath but trust me, you're* not *dreaming.*

"But . . . but . . . but," Tock squeaked, dropping the golf umbrella in alarm.

No buts, Tock, the small inner voice continued. *Face it, you did just see Mrs. McLachlan, She-who-must-not-be-eaten, sitting on top of a flying carpet, long silver hair spilling out in the slipstream; and yes, she did fly out over the meadow; and, yup . . . she's gone.*

"Waughhhh," wailed Tock, diving headfirst into the safety of his moat and remembering half a picosecond before his snout embedded itself painfully in the mud that the concepts of "moat" and "safety" were, in all probability, history.

The Witness in the Ashes

Mrs. McLachlan was unaware that she had a stowaway on board until she touched down outside the library and began to roll up her flying rug. A peevish voice squawked, "Do you *mind*?" and a tiny hairy leg poked out from between the knots of the rug's fringe.

"Oh, for heaven's *sake*," Tarantella complained, scuttling up the nanny's arm and halting on her shoulder. "Don't look at me like that and don't give me a hard time. I was doing you a favor, actually. If it wasn't for *moi*, your precious carpet would have more holes in it than a colander. . . ." Holding up a partially digested moth as evidence, the tarantula continued, "I cannot begin to tell you how *disgusting* these things taste. And fat-

tening? Eurghhh, they're right off the scale. Anyway. Here we are. Wherever *here* is. Not exactly a home away from home, is it? I mean, for goodness' sake, what sort of a neighborhood *is* this?" She waved a dismissive leg at the darkened street in which they stood. All around lay torn scraps of paper, broken glass, and discarded cigarette butts, as if someone had emptied their dustbin outside the library. This squalor was illuminated by a single gaslight burning over the graffiti-daubed door that stood ajar in front of them.

"*Tchhhh,*" Tarantella tutted disgustedly. "Look at that. DETH 2 CENTRES. Lordy, if only vandals would learn to write properly, we'd get a far better class of graffiti. 'Death' isn't spelled like *that*."

"Nor are 'centaurs,' " muttered Mrs. McLachlan. She took a deep breath before pushing the door fully open and entering the ruins of the library.

Her shadow stretched crookedly ahead, swallowed by the deeper darkness of the farthest corner of the room where, in a marble fireplace, flames had burnt ever since she could remember. . . . The fire had turned to cold ashes now, as had everything it had consumed, for the entire library appeared to have been gutted by flames—charred timbers and fused metal lay zigzagged from floor to ceiling as if tossed carelessly about in a vile parody of pick-up sticks. The little lion's-head fountain had been shattered, leaving a naked metal pipe spewing water over the ashes, turning the floor underfoot into a carbon-flecked porridge of devastation.

"Tell you what"—Tarantella broke the silence—"this was

no accident. Check out that wall over there." Spray-painted in something red and viscous, glittering in the shards of light filtering through from the door, was the message:

UR 2 L8 4 ACORY.

Mrs. McLachlan closed her eyes, as if to erase the words from her memory. Darkness rose up inside her mind as the significance of the message struck home. You're too late, it gloated. Whoever had written those words had *known* she'd be along to read them.

"Eurrrghhh," Tarantella complained. "Writing on walls. How tacky can you get? It's a sign of a culture on its last legs, when they resort to debasing the language. Speaking as a disinterested witness, I'd say the writing's on the wall for mankind. . . . Think about it: when the ancient Romans started scrawling C U L8R @ C. MXMS sort of thing, it was time to pack up the chariots and kiss your kids *vale*. . . ." She peered at the wall, concentrating furiously. "What does it *mean*? 'You're too late for . . . a cory'? What's a *cory*? C'mon, team."

Mrs. McLachlan's eyes snapped open and she glared at Tarantella. "There are times, *dear*, when your flippant attitude is singularly inappropriate. This is one of them. 'A' is for Alpha, the first letter of the Greek alphabet; 'C' is 'cent,' that's Latin for a hundred, Alpha Cent-ory."

"Alpha Centauri? The star?"

"Also the name of the centaur, Alpha, who used to guard this library."

"You're talking about him as if he's dead," Tarantella observed, looking away from the gloating epistle on the wall. "D'you think he was murdered? Here?" She gulped, and edged closer to the collar of Mrs. McLachlan's blouse, her voice dropping to a wobbly whisper. "Um . . . tell me, how exactly do we know that the murderer isn't still around? You know, lurking wild-eyed in the shadows, ax in hand, that sort of thing? *Not* that I'm worried, speaking for myself, but who would look after my clutch of spider eggs if I were to meet with an unfortunate end . . . ?" This last query emerged as a squeak from somewhere around Mrs. McLachlan's armpit, since Tarantella had disappeared from sight down the inside of the nanny's blouse.

Carefully picking her way through the wreckage, Mrs. McLachlan searched for some clue as to what had happened to Alpha. Of the thousands of artifacts once held in safekeeping in the library, little remained. Gone was the meticulously cataloged seed collection harvested from every plant that had ever grown on earth. Gone, too, was the DNA locked in amber from every species that had ever lived here. The drawers and cabinets housing the library archives had been wrenched off their hinges and upended on the floor, as if whatever had swept through the building had discovered that what they sought was too precious, or too secret, to be listed in the library catalog. With a feeling of approaching dread, Mrs. McLachlan tried to recall the list of several items that the library would never allow to go out on loan, items that were simply too potent to be displayed in locked glass cases: the Portal Ankhs of Nemesis IX; the nine Ring Binders of

Darkness; the Brazen Head; and the Pericola d'Illuminem, commonly known as the Chronostone, the Stone of Time. . . .

"You've gone all goosefleshy," complained Tarantella. "Please . . . can we go home now?"

Ignoring this, Mrs. McLachlan crossed the room until she came to the fireplace, her attention caught by a small movement in its feathery ashes. Casting around, she found a charred table leg and used this as a poker, prodding systematically through the ashes until she met a slight resistance. Something gave a stifled sneeze and, hearing this, Mrs. McLachlan crouched down and blew gently into the fireplace, as if attempting to rekindle the flames. With each puff, ashes blew aside until a small shape was revealed, curled up into a little ball of terror, its brassy scales untarnished by the fires that must have recently blazed around it.

"It's a salamander . . . ," the nanny whispered, her breath misting the shiny scales across the creature's breast.

Its eyes remained squeezed shut, the lids so transparent it was possible to see the swiveling eyeballs beneath. It was very small indeed; a newborn, Mrs. McLachlan estimated. Tarantella emerged from the cuff of Mrs. McLachlan's blouse and regarded the little beast with revolted fascination.

"Ugh," she decided. "Um . . . d'you want to talk about this? Like, when there's probably a mad axman with several pressing literacy issues rampaging nearby, *why* are we wasting time gazing at a half-cremated lizard? Once more, with feeling: Please—can—we—go—now?"

One of the creature's eyelids scrolled upward, revealing an

eye the exact color of a tropical lagoon. The eye widened as its owner tried to make sense of the tarantula and the woman bending over it, and then, as if overtaken by melancholy, the eye flooded and a single tear rolled out and vanished in the ashes.

"Leaking, too . . . ," Tarantella groaned. "Oh, joy."

The ashes stirred as the creature struggled to its feet, its stubby tail flapping determinedly as it tottered out of the fireplace and hopped straight into Mrs. McLachlan's outstretched hands.

"D'you thmoke?" it inquired wearily.

"Only if some cretin sets my legs on fire," Tarantella snapped. "Honestly. What sort of a question is *that*? Only idiots smoke. . . ."

"And demonthhh," the salamander said firmly, both eyes wide with remembered terrors. "Demonthhh thmoke *all* the time. And *I* thould know."

"Have I missed something here?" Tarantella demanded peevishly. "Some vital bit of information? Like who am I speaking to? And why, pray tell, does a bonsai lizard speak with such authority on the subject of demons? In short, squirt, *what* are you, and why are you here?"

The salamander seemed to shrink slightly. "My name wath Orynx," it whispered.

There was a pause, during which both Tarantella and Mrs. McLachlan tactfully ignored the hiccupy sobs coming from the sad little salamander. Pulling itself together with an effort, it continued, "But my latht owner jutht called me 'Lighter,' ath in, 'Where'th that blathted lighter gone now?' or, 'Anyone theen my thigarth and lighter?' or even, 'Tell me where the Chronothtone ith, or I'll thet fire to you with thith here lighter.' "

Mrs. McLachlan flinched. "Orynx," she said softly, "who was your owner threatening to set fire to?"

Orynx blinked. "The horth. The weird horth with a man'th body."

Oblivious to the nanny's gasp at what she assumed was Alpha's fate, the salamander added happily, "The one that got away."

The Witness in the Thorns

Mrs. McLachlan was absent from the breakfast table the following morning, and thus Titus found himself alone in the kitchen. Seizing this as an ideal opportunity to devour the heavily rationed sugar-coated breakfast cereals and avoid the healthier cardboard-and-bran alternatives, Titus was applying himself to a fifth helping of Honey Nut Miserablios when first Pandora, then Luciano arrived in search of sustenance. Looking up from his brimming bowl, Titus gaped at his sister. What on earth was that *thing* she was wearing? And her *mouth* . . . she looked as if someone had punched her—her lips were all bruised. About to demand an explanation, Titus was beaten to it by his father.

"Pandora?" Luciano had turned his back on his daughter and was wrestling with a particularly ancient espresso-maker, trying to force its rusty top to part company with its equally distressed base.

"Dad?" Pandora smiled, walking past Titus and causing him to instantly lose his appetite as a cloud of perfume so intense he could almost *chew* it enveloped him, his breakfast, and everything within a three-meter radius of where his sister stood.

"Where did you get that lipstick?" Luciano demanded through clenched teeth.

"What lipstick?" Pandora's eyes widened in feigned innocence.

"*This* lipstick," Tarantella muttered from her perch on the cupboard. The tarantula waved a half empty tube of "Blood Lust" as evidence. "*My* lipstick, you thieving heathen."

Caught between her father and her beloved tarantula, Pandora blushed, unable to meet Luciano's gaze as he turned to stare at her.

"And your *eyes,*" he moaned. "Dear God. What have you *done*? They're purple, for heaven's sake. . . ."

Pandora's smile faltered. Blast, she thought. I'd hoped you wouldn't notice. With a toss of her head that released a fresh wave of perfume across the kitchen, Pandora sat down opposite Titus and, grabbing a bowl, helped herself to some virtuous muesli, then glared across the table at her gaping sibling.

"Don't you start," she warned, adjusting her off-the-shoulder T-shirt, which was threatening to expose her sur-reptitiously enhanced chest.

She's wearing a *bra*, Titus thought, aghast. But whatever *for*? This thought died unspoken as Luciano launched into orbit.

"Go! *Now!* Wash that muck off your face before anyone else catches sight of you looking like that!" he yelled, twisting the coffeepot so viciously that it yielded, its top parting company with the base, old coffee grounds spilling down his shirt and onto the floor.

"Looking like *what*?" Pandora said indistinctly through a mouthful of muesli, adding, "What *is* your problem, Dad?"

Titus gasped. Had Pandora lost the will to live? Everyone at StregaSchloss knew that when Luciano began to smolder it was vital not to inflame him still further. . . . Rolling his eyes, Titus concentrated on his breakfast.

"YOU'RE ONLY TEN YEARS OLD!" Luciano howled.

"Eleven next week, actually—" Pandora began.

"You're a *child*, *not* a grown-up. Children don't wear lipstick and paint their eyes. Not *my* children, anyway. Go on. Now. Do As You Are Told. And cover yourself up. This is Scotland, for heaven's sake, not some beach in Brazil."

"—so, since it's my birthday next week," Pandora continued serenely, "I'd like to have my ears pierced and then you can all buy me earrings as my present."

There was a shriek and a crash followed by stunned silence as the two halves of the coffeepot discovered the joys of being airborne. Zander, who had been trying unsuccessfully to use his cell phone in the privacy of the kitchen garden, ducked just in time to avoid becoming the unintended victim of one of Luciano's rages. The pot sailed on past, beheaded several stately foxgloves, and finally plunged into the steaming heart of the compost pile.

"I take it that now would *not* be a good time to ask if there's any chance of a cup of coffee?" Zander edged round the kitchen door and peered nervously at his employer and the children, all of whom were too embarrassed to reply. Luciano excused himself and squeezed past Zander to retrieve the coffeepot from outside.

"Sorry to interrupt your breakfast," Zander continued, "only, I'm a bit lost. I wonder, could one of you possibly give me a quick tour of the house? You see, I don't know where anything *is*. I've already found a crocodile asleep in the upstairs bathroom; I came down here to make some toast and nearly had my head bitten off by a very irritable Frenchwoman; there's a confused old lady dozing on the floor of the wine cellar; and to top it all off, I went for an early morning swim down by the jetty and, d'you know, I could have sworn I saw the Loch Ne—"

"Let me show you around," Pandora interrupted, leaping to her feet and propelling another tide of perfume around the kitchen. Titus coughed pointedly.

"Have you met the rats?" she inquired; then, unable to resist, she added, "I mean, apart from that one across the table, choking as it stuffs its face, or the big grumpy one outside digging through the compost heap. . . ."

Zander, catching on at last, burst out laughing. "Good

lord—for a minute there I thought you were *serious*. Rats? Yeurrrrrgh. Horrible creatures . . ."

Whoops, Titus thought, *wrong* answer. You just blew it, pal. Pandora *loves* her rats. Holding his breath, he waited for his sister to erupt, turn the hapless Zander into a heap of smoldering ashes, and storm out of the kitchen—

"Aren't they foul?" Pandora agreed, ignoring Titus's dumbfounded expression. "I've never understood why some people keep them as pets. . . . Titus, *do* stop making that dreadful face. Excuse my alien brother, Zander; he's just having a little difficulty adjusting to life here on planet Earth."

"What a total hypocrite," Titus muttered to himself, stomping along the rutted track leading from StregaSchloss to Auchenlochtermuchty. Turning around, he looked back to where the house sat outlined against the brightness of Lochnagargoyle, its honey-colored stone glowing in the sunshine, the loch a perfect cobalt blue. From this distance he could just about make out the tiny figures of Pandora and Zander, the smaller one waving its arms, the larger one less animated but walking so close to his sister that at times it was hard to tell them apart.

Waving his arms theatrically and adopting a falsetto squeak, Titus launched into a parody of the conversation he imagined was taking place between the distant figures.

". . . and here's the meadow, Zander, where I pick the flowers for my hair. . . ."

Titus's voice dropped an octave in imitation of Zander:

"Eurghhhh. Flowers. Can't *stand* them. Surely you don't like flowers, do you, Pandora?"

"Gosh, no. Only kidding, Zander dwahling.... I'd never have them anywhere near me. The only good flower's a dead flower—that's my opinion. Let's go stamp on some flowerbeds, shall we?"

The sound of an approaching vehicle interrupted Titus's attempts at satire. Stepping onto the shoulder of the road and avoiding the embrace of a particularly vicious bramble branch, he realized too late that the ground under his feet consisted of only a thin veneer of turf between him and a vast underground rabbit warren of unguessable dimensions, its tunnels probably stretching between where he'd been standing and the center of the earth. As the ground collapsed beneath his feet, he fell backward into the bramble thicket with a dismayed howl.

Thorns punctured Titus's exposed arms and legs, snagged his T-shirt, and pinned him in place like a museum specimen. So concerned was he with extricating himself from the clutch of the brambles that he briefly forgot what had caused him to hurl himself into the bushes in the first place. A blast from a horn reminded him. Rumbling down the track toward him was a huge articulated truck. Stones sprayed from under its tires as it slowed, brakes hissing as they brought the vehicle to a halt in front of where Titus stood coughing in the dust by the roadside.

The driver's window slid open and a man leant out, shouting to make himself audible above the din coming from the rear of the truck. Titus frowned, cupping his hands around his ears as he walked closer to the truck's cab.

"Sorry?" he yelled. "I can't hear you, you'll have to shout louder."

The driver tried again, but it was no use. The cacophony of squeaks coming from the tarpaulin-covered rear of the vehicle was now deafening. As Titus stepped still closer, his nostrils were assaulted by such an overpowering reek of stale urine that he could hardly breathe. Above him, the cab door opened and the driver grabbed a map from the dashboard before jumping down onto the track.

"Can't stop them making that racket," he yelled, adding, "Not since the refrigeration unit broke down. Sorry about the smell. . . ."

Titus smiled uncertainly. Sweat was running down the driver's face, and he fanned himself with his map before unfolding it for Titus's inspection.

"I'm looking for a place called SapienTech. Supposed to be somewhere outside Auchenlochtermuchty. You got any ideas, pal?"

"You need to turn around!" Titus yelled. "You're going the wrong way. Turn around, hang a right at the main road, and keep going till you reach the village. . . ." His voice trailed off as he spotted something moving in the deep shade beneath the truck. A small white shape scuttled into the grass on the side of the narrow road, followed by another . . . and another.

The driver was oblivious to Titus's distracted state. "Turn

around?" he roared. "Are you kidding? How am I supposed to turn my truck around without ending up in the ditch?"

More white shapes were flooding out from under the chassis, some bolting for freedom, others lying where they'd fallen, ignored by their fellow escapees. Muttering balefully, the driver climbed back into his cab, affording Titus a view of the logo printed on the back of his sweat-stained overalls. Titus automatically logged it into his memory, along with SapienTech, whatever that might be. The truck shuddered, a beeping sound emerged from its rear, and, ignoring Titus's advice, the driver began to reverse along the road, back the way he had come. Titus watched until the truck disappeared behind a row of oaks, the rumble of its engine fading into silence as it headed for Auchenlochtermuchty.

Then, and only then, did he bend down to examine the little bodies lying where they had fallen in the dust. Rodents had never really been his thing; Pandora's love affair with rodent-kind had provided enough pink-eyed squeaky things to last Titus an entire lifetime, but the sight of all those dead white mice filled Titus with a strange mix of pity and horror. Why white mice? And why so many? The rear of the truck must have held thousands of the poor creatures. What did SapienTech *do* that required the delivery of a truckload of white mice? Looking around for a suitable implement, Titus sighed deeply. Why, he wondered, when I don't even *like* mice, do I feel so obliged to do the decent thing? Gently lifting the corpses into the shoulder of the road, Titus wearily began to dig a mass grave with his bare hands.

A Spell of Good Weather

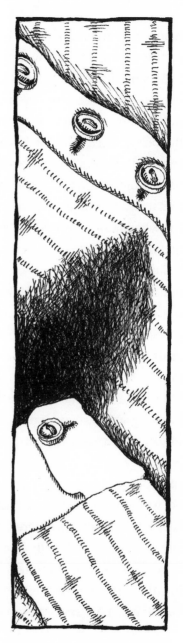

Signora Strega-Borgia dragged a mildewed picnic hamper through the kitchen door and hauled it onto the table, narrowly missing overturning Luciano's coffee cup as she did so.

"Darling, look what I've *found*," she said, blowing a cloud of dust off her discovery. "It was tucked away in a corner of the map room. It's the old picnic basket from the hot-air balloon. What a *find*. Just think, it must be *hundreds* of years old...."

Luciano looked up from his newspaper and winced. "It's an antique, Baci. It's probably riddled with antique bacteria, or perhaps they're fossilized by now."

Ignoring Luciano's health warning, Baci undid the leather buckles securing the hamper lid and muttered to herself as she began to pack a picnic for consumption down on the shore of Lochnagargoyle.

"Proper linen napkins, I think. And real wineglasses, since you object to drinking out of plastic cups, don't you, darling?"

Luciano concentrated on the newspaper, studiously avoiding being roped into Baci's plans for lunch. Undaunted by her husband's lack of reply, Baci opened the fridge door and continued determinedly, "Cold roast chicken, hummus, lettuce, tomatoes; I'll make a potato salad, the children can pick some strawberries—maybe Mrs. McLachlan could be persuaded to make a cake. . . ."

Luciano stood up and crossed the kitchen to turn on the lights above the table. "Maybe soup would be more appropriate," he muttered, returning to his paper.

"*Soup?*" Baci staggered from the fridge to the table, her arms laden with picnic ingredients. "Oh, for heaven's sake . . ."

Outside, the blue skies had turned dark gray. Moreover, a howling gale was whipping around the kitchen garden, tossing the bay tree back and forth as if trying to remove all its leaves by force. Somewhere deep in StregaSchloss, a door slammed.

"And don't forget to pack the thermal underwear," Luciano added as raindrops peppered the windows. "Plus the umbrellas, raincoats, and woolly hats . . ."

"Count me out," Tarantella said from her teapot on the cupboard. "I don't do rain, as a rule."

"Right," Baci said through clenched teeth. "This time, it's

personal. Something has to be done about this weather. I refuse to spend the remaining weeks of summer up to my eyes in mud and puddles, trying to squeeze in picnics between downpours." Dropping the lid of the hamper, she strode out of the kitchen and along the corridor, grabbing a golf umbrella from the hall stand before slamming out through the front door.

"Let me carry that." Tock vaulted out of the moat and gallantly waddled to his mistress's assistance, seizing the handle between his teeth and unfurling the umbrella with one expert thrust.

Peering out at the rain from the ground-floor window of the laundry room, Damp had been watching Mrs. McLachlan pull crumpled sheets out of a basket prior to flattening them with her hot, hot, burrrny—a procedure which Damp found to be singularly lacking in entertainment value. Turning to the window and pressing her nose to the streaming glass, Damp was mystified to see her mother crossing the meadow, followed at a distance by Tock, who appeared to be gnawing an umbrella which had turned itself inside out.

"Mama all wet," the little girl observed, watching as Signora Strega-Borgia waved a Disposawand around her head, her mouth opening and shutting, but her words lost in the steady babble of the falling rain.

"Poor Mama." Damp's breath misted the windowpane as a sudden gust of wind snatched the umbrella from Tock's jaws and bowled it across the meadow toward the loch, where it disappeared from sight.

"Damp get 'nother one," the little girl informed Mrs. McLachlan as she slid down from the window seat and headed off to her mother's rescue.

Absorbed in her thoughts of the previous night's events in the ruined library, Mrs. McLachlan failed to notice as Damp left the room. The nanny stood utterly still, oblivious to everything around her as she considered the fate of Alpha, the centaur librarian, now missing but just possibly still alive. Some months previously, Mrs. McLachlan had accidentally stumbled upon the Chronostone at StregaSchloss, and putting two and two together, had arrived at a reasonably accurate three and eleven-twelfths. She didn't know exactly *how* the stone had arrived in their midst, or even *why*, but when a demonically inclined houseguest of Baci's had made it exceedingly plain that she would destroy the Strega-Borgias to get her hands on the Chronostone, Mrs. McLachlan had been forced to intervene. Only seeking to protect those she loved at StregaSchloss, her main concern had been to remove the stone from the house to a place of greater safety. Lodging the Chronostone in the library for safekeeping had seemed like a good idea . . . at the time.

Now, with Alpha missing and his library in ruins, Mrs. McLachlan didn't feel quite so sure. By bringing the Chronostone to the library, had she unwittingly put Alpha in danger? Turned the Hadean radar toward the library? Alerted some devilish entity to the centaur? Mrs. McLachlan shuddered, her attention returning to the present, where, to her extreme annoyance, she discovered she'd made a large iron-shaped burn mark right in the middle of one of Signor Strega-Borgia's shirts.

"Oh, for goodness' sake, Flora! Get a grip," she muttered, turning around to check that Damp hadn't spotted her nanny cremating the laundry. The room was empty save for herself. Damp had disappeared.

Tock cowered behind a dripping oak tree, wishing his beloved mistress would just call it a day and accept that into each life some rain must fall. The crocodile peered around the tree trunk and sighed. Someone should tell his mistress that lying sprawled across the soggy grasses of the meadow with limbs extended like a mutant starfish wasn't going to make a blind bit of difference to the weather. He was just about to amble across to where Baci lay getting wetter by the minute and suggest that she consider emigrating to somewhere with less in the way of precipitation, when suddenly, as if some unseen hand had turned off a heavenly tap, the rain stopped.

"Excuse me?" he honked, wrinkling his eyes in the dazzling sunshine that, impossibly, was now painting the meadow in golden light. Squinting upward, Tock saw an unbroken expanse of blue stretching from Lochnagargoyle to the far peaks of Mhoire Ochone. Has ... was ... *did* she? his mind stuttered, finally clawing its way to the unlikeliest of conclusions. *My* mistress? Did *my* mistress do this?

Mrs. McLachlan raced around those parts of StregaSchloss frequented by Damp, barreling through doors, scanning rooms, calling the little girl's name over and over, but hearing nothing in reply. Breathless with anxiety, she ran out into the rain, searching for the littlest Strega-Borgia in the old icehouse, the greenhouse, and the potting shed, but all to no avail. Mrs. McLachlan was catching her breath under the partial shelter of an apple tree, debating whether to sprint down to the lochside or enlist the help of the beasts in aerial reconnaissance, when she heard Damp singing nearby: "*Rain, rain, go 'way, cummergenan other day.*"

Mrs. McLachlan's relief was short-lived. As Damp drew a breath and belted out another verse, the nanny caught sight of her, or at least she caught sight of the multicolored golf umbrella that the little girl was using to stunning effect as a wand.

"RAIN, RAIN, GO 'WAY..."

The umbrella spun around, faster and faster...

"CUMMERGENAN..."

... the colors blurring, merging to form a dazzling white circle of light...

"NO! DAMP!" Mrs. McLachlan screamed. "STOP!"

"OTHER DAY," Damp sang firmly, then hurled her umbrella-wand into the air.

Instead of falling back to earth, the umbrella appeared to gather speed, rising through the leaden skies like a reverse comet, ripping through the cloud cover as if tearing away the dull gray wrapping paper from a dazzling blue present.

"Oh *bother,*" said Mrs. McLachlan with feeling. The rain stopped, the gray fell away to the horizon, and the sun came out with an almost audible *ta-daaaa*. Mrs. McLachlan closed her eyes in despair; unwittingly, Damp had turned a vast spotlight on herself, the magical equivalent of Beauty inviting the Wicked Fairy around for a wee game of darts. . . .

"Och, my wee pet," Mrs. McLachlan whispered. "What *have* you done?"

Hell's Bells and Buckets of Blood

Reading a well-thumbed paperback novel to while away the boredom of the night shift, the duty demon was mouthing the trickier bits of the story under his breath when the Hadean search engine registered a hit. Barely lifting his eyes off the page, the demon reached out a nail-bitten finger and pressed the PRINT INCOMING MAIL button on the keyboard, before rapidly turning to the last-but-one page of his book.

Such are the deplorable lack of reading skills in Hades that it was a full two hours later that the demon closed his book with a feeling of acute dissatisfaction border-ing on acid indigestion, and turned his attention to the recent printout curled in his in-tray.

"*Loh—loh—location: Argyll,*" he read effortfully. "*Subject: unknown. Send on?*"

The demon scratched his head, his claws poised over the keyboard. SEND ON? blinked on and off, the screen demanding that he assign this unknown event in Argyll to some department of Hades for further investigation. The demon paused. How big an event in Argyll? he wondered. Was it just a wee squitty magical hiccup? A rabbits-out-of-the-hat trick, barely worthy of a two on a scale of one to ten? Or perhaps it might be a smattering of vengeful voodoo—say, a four for effort? His claws clattering on the keyboard, he typed in a query:

SCALE OF EVENT—ONE TO TEN?

Sitting back to wait while the computer replied, the demon was aware that he'd heard of Argyll before. The faintest bell of recognition began to chime far away down a dusty corridor of his memory; faint but persistent, it clanged repeatedly in his mind. The computer sprang to life and supplied the answer to his question.

SCALE OF EVENT—ONE TO TEN: THIRTEEN.

Behind the boarded-up door of a room in the basement of the demon's memory, something stirred, shook itself, stood up and hurled itself straight through the door, thundered along the dusty corridors, and arrived screaming blue murder in the middle of the gray porridge of the demon's brain.

"ARGYLL!" it shrieked. "CLASSIFIED INFORMATION.

SECURITY CODE: XXX. EYES ONLY. DO NOT, REPEAT, *NOT,* OPEN WITHOUT CLEARANCE FROM *BELOW.*"

Giving a little sob of terror, the duty demon picked up a cell phone and began to key in an unlisted number.

Stuck in traffic on the Hades Orbital, Isagoth lit his fortieth cigar of the day with an underpowered salamander and tossed the wriggling creature out of his window without a second thought. All roads into Hades were part of a colossal one-way system; the city planners reasoned that there would be little traffic heading in the opposite direction. Consequently, the motorways were designed to encourage easy access with no possibility of exit. A steady stream of battered white vans and bloated SUVs poured into Hades, their leaky exhausts belching fumes as they inched blindly forward, horns blaring, engines screaming, a tide of automotive lemmings rushing toward towns with names like Perdition, Purgatory, and, ominously, Evisceration (population 666 and falling). As traffic hit the Orbital, speeds dropped still further, to a pace equal to that achieved by a growing fingernail. Isagoth's blood pressure rose higher and higher as the hours ticked by, and when his cell phone rang, he could barely hear it over the hammering of blood in his veins.

However, replacing the phone in his breast pocket and catching sight of his gleeful reflection in the rearview mirror, he suddenly decided that Things Were Looking Up. If his informant had been correct, an event scoring thirteen on a scale of one to ten was cause for celebration. In fact, events scoring anything higher than nine allowed ministers such as himself to exercise privileges only permitted in full-on emergencies.

"I've waited an entire lifetime to be allowed to do this," Isagoth remarked, turning a dial on the dashboard and flicking a concealed switch below the steering wheel. A warning light flashed on the speedometer and a computerized voice informed him that his vehicle was now armed and had automatically initiated countdown.

"Excellent," Isagoth hissed. "I love playing dirty . . ." Removing a pair of armored goggles from the glove compartment, the demon secured them round his head, took a deep breath, and floored the accelerator.

Everything within a radius of twenty kilometers vanished in the blast from six chassis-mounted plasma cannons—cars, roads, houses, and their occupants. Blood, bone, and bitumen rained down on the ruined Orbital but, to his extreme delight, Isagoth made it to work in record time. Moments later, he strode across the metal walkway linking Administration with Wet Affairs, drawing respectful glances from the lesser demons who guarded the entrance to the Pit.

"Nice evenin', yer honorship," one of these ventured, bowing obsequiously as Isagoth swept past, and, on receiving no reply, muttered, "Snotty git," at the Defense Minister's retreating back. This was a mistake, an Absolute No-No, he realized, for as soon as the words had left his mouth, Isagoth stopped, turned on his heel, and rapidly retraced his steps to appear in front of the lesser demon like a bad case of acid reflux.

"I BEG YOUR PARDON?" Isagoth demanded, his voice loaded with the promise of future pain.

"I, erm . . . I, um . . . I, errr," the demon gulped. "I said, yer worshipful eminence, 'Mind 'ow yez go—there's a snotty bit.' I mean, look at it—*tchhhhh*, them sinners; once we've finished wiv 'em, they just leak and ooze and drip like you wouldn't believe. . . ."

"Nope, you're right. I wouldn't believe," Isagoth agreed. "GUARD! Take this one down. He's outlived his usefulness. Tongue, eyes, ears . . . you know the drill."

"Your 'ighness?" the demon quailed. "Mercy. What did *I* do? Why me? I was jis' bein' 'elpful, me. No, nooo, aaarghhh—" Enveloped in the massive arms of a guard, the demon's pleas for clemency were instantly muffled, as if someone had turned down his volume control. The guard impassively dragged his prisoner off in search of a rusty pair of shears, and Isagoth strode on until he reached his office.

Closing the door behind himself, he nearly screamed out loud when he realized Who was waiting for him, drumming His fingers on the obsidian desktop.

"CONGRATULATIONS, MINISTER," the Boss purred. "FINALLY, YOU MADE IT INTO WORK ON TIME. SHAME ABOUT THE COLLATERAL DAMAGE TO THE ORBITAL, THOUGH—IT'S GOING TO COST AN ARM, A LEG, AND SEVERAL EYEBALLS TO REBUILD WHAT YOU DESTROYED IN YOUR HASTE TO BEAT THE TRAFFIC, WOULDN'T YOU AGREE?"

"Yes, Your Foulness." Isagoth could barely force the words out through a throat so clenched with terror it hardly allowed the passage of enough air to breathe, let alone speak.

"SO ... WHY THE RUSH? WHAT'S THE EXCUSE? AND, BY THE WAY, *KNEEL*, SCUM. I LIKE MY MINISTERS TO KNOW THEIR PLACE."

Isagoth fell to the floor, noting that the cleaners hadn't been in his office for a while, judging by the litter of cigar butts and crushed salamanders strewn underneath his desk.

"Your Evil Eminence," he began. "Most Vile Viscount of the Verruca ..."

"CUT TO THE CHASE, WRETCH," the Boss commanded. "JUST CALL ME S'TAN AND GET ON WITH IT."

S'tan? Isagoth reeled inwardly. What kind of name was *that*? Swallowing with difficulty, he did as he was bid.

"Our man from Wet Affairs intercepted the centaur, Alpha, and began the usual ... procedures. I'm sure You don't need to hear the gory details. However, when he paused to allow the prisoner time to regain consciousness, our man was hunting for his lighter to rekindle the pyre under the prisoner—"

"UGH," S'tan moaned. "SPARE ME, PURLEEEASE. TOO MUCH INFORMATION."

"Indeed. My apologies. So, S'tan, as our man searched for this missing lighter, the centaur slipped his chains and escaped."

"HOW UNFORTUNATE," S'tan tutted. "DEAR, DEAR ..."

"Um, no. Actually, centaurs are half man, half horse; no Bambis in their genetic makeup whatsoev—" Catching sight of S'tan's expression, Isagoth flinched. "Anyway, S'tan," he babbled, "we're pretty sure the centaur had the Chronostone with him when he vanished. But he was somewhat damaged by that time—a bit of a crispy critter due to the . . . procedures used to extract information from—"

"HOW CRISPY A CRITTER? RAW? MEDIUM RARE? WELL DONE . . . OR BURNT?"

"Half burnt, your Satanic S'tan-ness. Probably in need of medical attention, if not immediate immersion in salt water, perish the thought—which brings me to—"

"I HAVE TO SAY YOU'RE SURPRISINGLY CHILLED FOR SOMEONE WHO'S LOST MY CHRONOSTONE THROUGH SHEER INCOMPETENCE." S'tan stood up and strolled across the office to where Isagoth knelt quaking before Him. "LET ME JUST REFRESH YOUR MEMORY. *YOU. LOST. MY. CHRONOSTONE.*"

Taking a deep breath and praying that for once his hunch was correct and he was speaking the truth, Isagoth said, "With all due respect, Your Stainless Steeliness, I am delighted to tell you that I have *found* the Chronostone."

Just then, a muted ringing tone came from S'tan's person. It grew louder and more insistently shrill until, emitting a hiss of frustration, the Boss rooted in His pocket and produced a personal organizer. Flipping it open, He sighed.

"A POX ON IT. I'M LATE FOR MY APPOINTMENT WITH MY AROMATHERAPIST, THEN I'M OFF ON TOUR FOR THE NEXT FORTNIGHT . . . WEEK AFTER, I'VE A PRODUCTION BUDGET COMMITTEE . . . EDITORIAL MEETING . . . BOARD OF GOVERNORS . . . BAND PRACTICE . . . CRIMINAL JUSTICE LAWYERS EXECUTIVE PAINTBALL WEEKEND . . . LOOK, SCUM—

HAVE MY CHRONOSTONE ON MY DESK BY THE STROKE OF MIDNIGHT OF THE AUTUMNAL EQUINOX—UNDERSTOOD?"

"Implicitly, Your Gruesome Greatness. Count on it."

"TWENTY-SECOND OF SEPTEMBER, AND NOT A NANO-SECOND LATER." And with this, the Boss swept out of Isagoth's office, His fur-lined cloak swirling majestically in His wake.

The Witness in the Water

Out in the glassy deep of Lochnagargoyle, the Sleeper surfaced, his head breaking water first, followed by three vast arcs, the only visible portions of the beast's massive body, the remaining ninety percent of it submerged and hidden beneath the water.

"Ochhh, ah'm no feeling very weel," he observed, giving a forlorn belch, which echoed off the distant shore. "Dearie me, was it something ah ate?" he wondered out loud, trying to determine which of the shoals of fish he'd recently devoured might have been responsible.

In the shadows beneath a cluster of scrub oaks clinging to the shore, the centaur Alpha struggled back to consciousness, a state he'd been keen to

avoid since fleeing from the library with his tail on fire. Now, all too awake, he dragged himself centimeter by painful centimeter across the pebbles of the foreshore and, giving a groan of agony, rolled into the healing chill of the loch. Aware that time was fast running out, Alpha lay in the shallows and curled around the Chronostone lodged deep in his belly. Bleakly, he considered what to do. One option was to take the stone with him into the realms of Death, but that offended his sensibilities as a librarian. That, he decided, was like burning all the books rather than allowing them to fall into the wrong hands. The only alternative was to pass the Chronostone on. Pass it on like an Olympic torch to the next in line. The trouble with *that* plan was the lack of suitable candidates. Any old mythical creature would do: a centaur, a dragon, a griffin . . . even an abominable snowman. Unlike humans, mythical beasts could withstand the power of the Chronostone, but, unsurprisingly, the lochside wasn't exactly thronged with wannabe Chronostone custodians, be they legendary, mythical, or otherwise.

High overhead, seagulls circled, their watchful eyes marking the movements of Alpha dying on the foreshore and the Sleeper feeling like he was dying out in the middle of the loch.

"Ah dinnae want to throw up, ken?" the Sleeper moaned to himself, for once wishing that his bride-to-be was around to hold his head, even if as she did so, she would be bound to nag him about her singular lack of an engagement ring. "Ochhh, ah reely hate throwing up, me, 'specially when ah haftae swim aroond in it efterward. . . ." With this in mind, the giant beast made for the shore in the hope of evacuating his stomach on land instead of water.

What he found, as he lunged out of the water and onto the beach, was so surprising that it quite overcame his temporary stomach upset.

"Whoor youse?" the Sleeper demanded, skidding to a halt in a shower of pebbles. A winged horse fluttered in front of him, its once-white coat covered in blackened patches, its outspread wings pitted with burn marks where entire layers of feathers appeared to have been consumed by fire. The horse turned its golden eyes on the Sleeper, blinked . . . and changed.

"Eh? Whit?" The Sleeper took several slithers backward, his initial surprise turning to feelings of unease, his stomach once more sending out a signal of deep disquiet. The burnt horse had been replaced by a charred centaur, its hooves clattering on the pebbles of the shore as it lurched toward him, its mouth effortfully framing the word, "Help." To the Sleeper's horror, the centaur's mouth opened still wider, and from it fell a shiny stone, a glittering gem that looked, to his inexperienced eyes, very much like an egg.

"Now, jist hang oan a wee minute," the Sleeper said in a shaky voice. "Dinnae give me yon egg, pal. Last time anybody gied me yin of those, it came attached to a paternity suit. That egg's no' mine. I'm no' its father."

In front of him, the centaur shape-shifted again, as if by changing form it could somehow escape the pain of its terrible burns.

"Tell me it's a' a bad dream," the Sleeper whispered, unable to tear his gaze away from the sight of the centaur as it became a burning wooden horse, its timber ribs exposed by the flames that licked greedily around its flanks. Unable to move on its rigid wooden legs, the horse burnt silently, and would have been completely destroyed by fire, had not the Sleeper finally decided to intervene.

"NO WAY, PAL!" he roared, dragging the blazing horse into the loch and holding it underwater until it was completely extinguished. "You're no leaving your egg an orphan, right?" he muttered, his coils unwinding to release the horse into the shallows, where it lay floating in the tidal ebb and flow of the water.

"Right?" The Sleeper's voice dropped to a whisper as the wooden horse shape-shifted for the last time.

It grew smaller and smaller, as if immersion in water had caused it to shrink. For a moment then, it lay still. Peering at the tiny blackened shape, the Sleeper was reminded of a twig, wizened and lifeless in winter, miraculously bursting into life by spring. From below the horse's neck, twin buds grew, swelled, and burst open. At first their crumpled shape did look uncannily like young leaves, but as they rapidly unfurled, they revealed themselves to be rudimentary wings. Simultaneously the creature's two hind legs melted together to form a long, extended tail. When the Sleeper leant down for an exploratory sniff, this tail rolled itself up into a tight coil, and its owner emitted a loud snort from flared nostrils.

"Two things, fish-breath," he muttered. "That stone I spat out is *not* an egg. Do I look like a chicken to you?"

"Um, ochh, weel . . . no. Ah'd say youse were mair like a sea horse, maself."

"Exactly." The reconstituted Alpha allowed a grim smile to cross his mouth. "However, no matter what form my body may take, my soul will always be that of a librarian, so . . . pay attention: that stone is the property of the library. You may not photocopy, scan, clone, or reproduce library property by means mechanical, digital, or magical without the express permission of the librarian—that's me, by the way. Furthermore, you may not use library property for the purposes of Black Magic, unlawful killing, or material gain. Library property should not be used in the furtherance of any criminal act or any attempt to reverse the laws of nature. If you agree to be bound by these conditions, say yes. . . ."

"Och, I . . . er, I . . . I, um . . ."

"Seeing as you're Scottish, I'll assume that 'I' means yes. Splendid. Consider yourself elected to the honorable company of mythical librarians."

"But, but . . . I dinnae understand . . . ," the Sleeper wailed. "Whit *is* a librarian?"

His voice echoed back at him across the loch. Whatever a librarian was, he realized, it *wasn't* anymore. The sea horse had gone, leaving behind its shiny stone, which lay gleaming and glittering amongst the pebbles on the beach, rather like a phoenix surrounded by battery hens. To the Sleeper's intense relief, upon closer inspection it looked nothing *like* an egg, but in every way resembled the diamond of his fiancée's dreams.

"Noo, if ah could jis' find a ring tae put it in, we'd be sorted," he decided, tucking the Chronostone into his abdominal pouch for safekeeping. Wondering if any suitably circular bits of metal had been washed ashore at high tide, the Sleeper scanned the beach for a while but, aside from pebbles and driftwood, the shore below StregaSchloss was remarkably litter-free. However, if he remembered correctly, the same could not be said for a fenced-off length of foreshore farther down the loch. From what he'd been able to see of *that* particular beach, it was covered in rusting oil drums, discarded plastic crates, broken glass, and mountains of old tires. To complete this picture of Highland charm, someone had thoughtfully bulldozed a deep trench along the high-tide line and filled it with what smelled like rancid fish parts. These had been decomposing spectacularly for the past two months, forming a malodorous barricade that nothing dared cross, a state of affairs heavily encouraged by the current owners of that stretch of Lochnagargoyle. Reminding himself not to *eat* his way past the barrier this time, the Sleeper swam off on a beachcombing expedition for Ffup's ring.

An Empty Net

For reasons undreamt of by Titus, the weather had taken a remarkable turn for the better; so much so that by eleven o'clock at night he'd been forced to open both his bedroom windows, allowing air and hordes of ravening gnats to circulate freely around his room. The only source of illumination being his laptop, the gnats clustered round its glowing light and discovered that, while they couldn't read what was written on the screen, someone had thoughtfully provided them with a large food source in its vicinity. Proboscises quivering with anticipation, they settled in their hundreds on the banquet laid out before them and helped themselves to the sheer abundance of Titus.

So absorbed was Titus with

what he'd found on the Internet that he didn't even notice as the gnats attempted to drain him of blood. Intent on discovering what manner of company would drive a truck full of white mice down a single-lane road in rural Argyll, Titus had trawled the Internet for signs of the name he'd spotted on the back of the driver's overalls. Then, the name "Corp-ex" had meant nothing. Nor had it meant very much when he'd found, in the dust of the track, some tiny plastic rings with SAPIENTECH printed on them in miniature type, followed by what looked like a bar code. However, several pieces began to fall into place when he'd discovered that similar tiny plastic rings had been fastened around the dead mice's front paws.

And now, eyes glued to the screen, occasionally gasping, "Wow," or "Heck," and frequently, "Are they *allowed* to do that?" Titus had hacked his way into the heart of Corp-ex.com and discovered a cesspit of exploitation, corruption, and pan-global multinationalism. This was a sprawling business empire that subjected people in the third world to slavery, destroyed swaths of virgin rain forest, emitted toxic fumes that fell to earth as burning acids, irradiated lakes in remote parts of the Russian wilderness, poisoned oceans by slipshod oil shipments . . . oh, and yes, drove truckloads of laboratory mice down single-lane roads in rural Argyll.

Titus sat back in his chair and groaned. *Now* what? Faced with the global span of Corp-ex.com's many dodgy business interests, he felt as confident as an anchovy about to declare war on an octopus. Well . . . perhaps *not* an anchovy, he amended rapidly. Maybe more of a gnat going after a rhinoceros? Whatever. A lone teenager with zero chance of stopping a vast corporation that, if previous performance was anything to go by, was probably intent on polluting one of the last unspoiled sea-lochs in Scotland. Brushing aside environmentalists, imposing media blackouts, lying to shareholders, and even shrugging off a series of devastating attacks on its research stations by a group of eco-terrorists intent on blowing it off the face of the planet—Corp-ex had ignored them all. Insulated by wealth, the company rolled on, blinkered, deaf, and utterly immune to public opinion. Like they were going to pay any attention to one Titus Strega-Borgia, outraged resident of Argyll?

I mean, get a grip, he thought. Just what exactly am I going to do? March up to their no-doubt heavily guarded entrance gate and demand that they cease trading immediately or I'm going to the police? Yeah, right. Like *that's* going to work. Perhaps I could demand to speak to their leader? Failing that, I might try tiptoeing around to their chain-link perimeter fencing by dead of night carrying a set of bolt cutters. Snip my way in. And, if by some miracle their guard dogs don't deliver me back to StregaSchloss in the form of mince in a matchbox, then what? What am I looking for? What makes Lochnagargoyle an ideal spot for one of Corp-ex's business ventures?

Scrolling down the pages of information on the screen in front of him, Titus re-read the various names of companies sheltering under the Corp-ex.com umbrella. Several were pharmaceutical giants whose names were familiar; others he'd never heard of. His eyes skidded to a stop halfway down a page, his attention caught by a familiar name; a name last seen printed on a dead mouse's identification tag; a name last heard from the mouth of a driver trying to deliver said mouse to SapienTech of Auchenlochtermuchty. Oh yes, Titus breathed, *now* we're onto something. . . . SapienTechnologies Inc. had a Web site, the hyperlink for which was printed in blue, signaling that it was live. It read:

http://www.sapientech.co.uk/homepage/url

More than slightly curious, Titus clicked on the link and waited to see what would happen. In the silence, he could hear something moving outside. It sounded like hesitant footsteps on the rose-quartz drive, as if whoever was out there didn't want to be discovered tiptoeing outside StregaSchloss at this late hour. He peered at the screen, but the laptop was still engaged in the cyber equivalent of tapping politely on SapienTech's door, checking its watch, squinting through the mailbox, and wondering when someone was going to invite it in. Against the hideous possibility that behind the door lay a cyber-plague, Titus had installed virus-checking software, which, he fondly imagined, also stood on SapienTech's doorstep, armed to the hilt, bristling with menace, and even now picking its teeth with the business end of a cyber-machete. Understandable, really, Titus thought, that the door was taking so long to open. . . .

Sighing with impatience, he stood up, stretched, yawned so widely his jaws almost locked, and crossed to an open window to see if he could spot whoever had been tiptoeing across the drive. To his surprise, he saw the distant figure of Pandora sprinting across the open fields toward the dark mass of the forest skirting Mhoire Ochone. In the moonlight, her shadow looked like a giant daddy longlegs, her scissoring legs skimming over grassy hummocks as if, any minute now, she might achieve liftoff and flutter into the night. What on *earth* was she doing? A metallic *chingg* came from his laptop, alerting Titus to the dialog box that had popped up on his screen.

WARNING: THIS SITE IS NOT SECURE AND INFORMATION YOU SEND CAN BE READ IN TRANSIT. DO YOU WISH TO CONTINUE?

In the time it took Titus to read this and press ENTER, Pandora had vanished from sight, but by then Titus had other things on his mind. His virus-protection software had swung into full-on defense mode and was rapidly deploying its virtual troops, booting them into the front line and passing around the Kalashnikovs. The laptop chittered and clicked, its hard drive spinning in an attempt to cool itself down as something out there on the Internet, hidden behind the door of SapienTech, stretched out a long cyber-probe, reached down the telephone line past the paralyzed server, hurled itself along underground cables, and, with deadly accuracy, attempted to plunge straight into the brain of Titus's laptop. Blissfully unaware that his defenses were under attack, Titus gave a snort of disgust. In front of him, a new dialog box read:

ERROR TYPE: KLZ2.

THE SPECIFIED SERVER COULD NOT BE FOUND.

This being the computer's way of saying, "Gosh and golly, I *tried* to visit those nice folks at SapienTech, but d'you know, when I got there, not only had they moved the premises, but some thoughtless cretin had demolished the building after they'd gone. . . ."

Wearily, Titus returned to the previous screen, only to find it blank. Scroll and click as he might, he found himself utterly unable to access anything to do with Corp-ex.com or its many subsidiaries.

It was as if it had never existed.

A Walk in the Woods

The forest floor was dappled with moonlit patches, their irregular shapes reminding Pandora of a jigsaw, a vast puzzle requiring some even vaster hand to reach down and reassemble the scattered pieces into an illuminated whole. The air was so still it appeared to be holding its breath, the silence so deep and velvety she could almost feel it caress her skin. Admittedly, she was covered in gooseflesh, which couldn't be blamed on the ambient temperature, since she was damp with sweat after sprinting across the fields. I'm *not* nervous, Pandora told herself, ignoring her pounding heart, I'm...uh, just a bit puffed after all that running. Ahead lay the dark forest of Caledon; behind her, moonlit fields, StregaSchloss, and safety.

Unable to decide whether to turn back or carry on, Pandora weighed her options. Turning back and heading for home did have a lot to recommend it: a warm bed, soft pillows, a vast book she'd hardly been able to tear herself away from—not to mention the sure and certain knowledge that no orcs were likely to leap out from behind a tree if she was safely tucked up in bed. On the other hand, fear of fictional characters was no reason for turning back home. She'd come too far to give up now. Half-smiling to herself, Pandora felt she'd stepped between the pages of a book. As if she was on a quest. She was the huntress; and out in the darkness lay her unsuspecting quarry. Although this was really just a game, there had been enough of an edge of danger to set her heart racing. She felt electric, alive, and deliriously grown-up.

What was it Zander had said earlier? He'd turned to her, halfway through their tour of StregaSchloss, and she'd realized how very blue his eyes were—so blue, in fact, that she hardly listened to what he was saying. "You have an old soul, Pandora," he'd whispered, sending an agreeable shiver running through her body. She'd frowned, not having the foggiest idea what he was twittering on about, but perfectly happy to stand there and listen to him read her the telephone directory if necessary, if only it meant she could continue to gaze into his blue, blue eyes. . . .

He'd reached out then, patted her on the shoulder, and said, "We're two of a kind, you and I. . . . D'you know what I mean?"

"Um . . . yeah. Sort of. Absolutely."

"I sense that we've known each other before. In a previous life, perhaps. Maybe we were brother and sister, maybe even comrades, brothers-in-arms."

"Gosh. I . . . er . . ."

"What star sign are you, Pandora? No, hang on, don't tell me. I bet I can work it out. I see you as brave, fierce, loyal, passionate—the vibe I'm getting off you says Scorpio. Am I right, or am I right?"

She should have stopped him right there and then. He was so *wrong* and, as a dyed-in-the-wool Leo, she was on the point of roaring her defiance when he leant forward and *kissed* her on the top of her head and carried on as if nothing had happened, as if she hadn't turned into a human lobster, for heaven's sake.

"Don't look so shocked. I can always tell these things. I'm a Pisces—my intuition is never wrong. . . ." Then he'd burst out laughing, even though it wasn't at all funny, and flung his arms wide, as if embracing all of StregaSchloss, the gardens, and the loch. "This place is just so full of energy, it's almost *alive*." Zander inhaled, looking as if he was trying to absorb Argyll through his nostrils alone. "Can't you feel it? Like an electric current running through your body? No, don't say a word. Twin souls have no need for language. I know you understand me. Let's just be still and absorb the essence for a moment."

To Pandora's acute embarrassment, he'd turned his face up to the sky and begun to breathe loudly, all the while muttering, "*In* through the nose, two, three—imagine a stream of positive earth energy filling every cell of your body; *out* through the mouth, two, three, releasing all that negativity, emptying your body of toxins; *in* through the nose, two, three . . ."

Politely, Pandora had tried to look rapt with wonder.

". . . *out* through the mouth, two, three, becoming at one with the mystery . . ."

Pandora had fixed an expression of deep concentration on her face.

". . . two, three, opening your channels to the goddess . . ."

Biting her bottom lip, Pandora had desperately attempted to tune him out. No. It was hopeless. She had to stop him, otherwise she was about to burst into hysterical laughter, and *that*, she sensed, wouldn't go down at all well. Despite it all, she still wanted to impress him. Clearing her throat, she aimed for a light, conversational style—anything to make him stop *breathing* like that.

"Ah . . . so . . . why are you *here*? Is being a butler something you've always wanted to do?"

Zander's head had snapped around to face her, and in that moment Pandora had felt her blood turn to ice. As if a mask had fallen away, his face was filled with hate, his mouth twisted into a snarl of contempt—then, just as abruptly, the moment was gone. He'd given that slightly hysterical laugh again, and, looking away from her, had swooped down, plucked a dandelion head out from the path at her feet, and begun to puff it to pieces, blowing the tiny seeds into her hair.

"Apologies, Miss Strega-Borgia, I forgot myself. Let's see if *butler* is my true destiny. What have we here? A tinker, a tailor, a butler, a sailor—"

"It's *soldier*, not butler."

"Never fancied the army, myself. Real warriors don't wear uniforms, and they fight their own battles, not other people's. . . . Rich man—*puff*—poor man . . ."

". . . beggar man, thief," she'd added.

"The seven ages of man," Zander observed, gently picking dandelion seeds out of her hair.

"But there's *eight*," she had mumbled, face aflame.

"Rich men and thieves are the same thing," he'd said, turning away and gazing down Lochnagargoyle before crushing the denuded dandelion underfoot and walking on so quickly she'd had to run to catch up with him. . . .

He wasn't walking quite so fast now, she decided, her eyes growing used to the darkness in the forest. Up ahead she could make out the glow of his flashlight as Zander climbed the tree-lined western slope of Mhoire Ochone. He appeared to be making for Star Wood, a little clearing in the forest of Caledon that, according to local rumor, was formed when debris from a comet had peppered Scotland in the early part of the seventeenth century. Nothing had ever grown in Star Wood until recently, when a sturdy example of a cell tower had sprouted out of the soil and sprung to a height of a hundred meters in approximately two days flat. Unsurprisingly, this tower didn't put out leaves or flowers, but it did emit microwaves, supposedly enabling the residents of Argyll to use cell phones. Unfortunately, this improvement had the opposite effect on the area immediately surrounding StregaSchloss, blanketing everything around in blissful, beep-free silence. Not possessing a cell phone herself, Pandora had little sympathy for Titus's frustration when he discovered that his newest toy still didn't work unless he made the effort to carry it beyond the dead zone of StregaSchloss.

Watching from behind a nearby tree, Pandora saw Zander halt in the center of Star Wood. He switched off his flashlight, presumably because sufficient moonlight was pouring into the clearing to allow him to read the map he held folded in one hand. He turned around to face Lochnagargoyle and pulled a small object out of his pocket. Pandora was disappointed to see that this was nothing more exciting than a cell phone; she realized that after their conversation she'd been unconsciously expecting him to produce something far more bizarre—a ceremonial dagger, an astrolabe, or an aura detector at the very least. . . . Slightly appalled at herself, she crept closer, all the better to eavesdrop. This is *not* good, Pandora, she thought. Skulking around in the darkness is very bad indeed. If he finds you spying on him, he'll never speak to you ever—

"Yeah, I've got a clear signal," Zander said, his voice breaking the breathless silence of the woods. "Took me a while, huh? Right, let's keep this brief, before anyone can get my coordinates off the phone. I'm in, the hosts don't suspect a thing, and I can probably stay at least a month, which gives us more than enough time to set up. . . . What? . . . You're never going to believe this. A butler . . . Yeah, OK, very funny . . . No—I don't iron. . . . Look, just shut up and listen."

Pandora noticed that Zander's English accent had slipped

somewhat, developing a pronounced American twang the more he spoke. Puzzled, she tried to concentrate on what he was saying.

"Take the boat to the dilapidated old jetty twelve miles up the loch from the target. You can't miss it, since there's the most over-the-top bloated monstrosity of a house right behind it. . . . No, that's *not* the target, but, yeah, if we'd more time, I'd blow it up as well. . . ."

Pandora felt her heart stop. Now just wait a minute, she thought. That's *my* house you're talking about. But unable to tear herself away, she listened with a sinking feeling as Zander continued.

"Look for something with about fifty chimneys and you can't go wrong. It's tied to the jetty, right? . . . No, not the chimneys, you moron, the package of *plastique* that's going to blow the target out of existence. Right? . . . Yeah, *exactly* the same way we did it in Panama, then in Angola, and that freezing dump in—what was it called? Uh . . . Archangel. Except this time, they won't be expecting us. They've only got minimal security at this factory. I tell you, they're so confident, they're not even bothering to cover their tracks. The beach is awash in dead mice. I guess they must think the locals are too stupid to notice. Anyway, I say we do it sooner, rather than later. Listen carefully: if I haven't heard from you by midday tomorrow, I'll assume it's set up to rock and roll for, say, two p.m.? Are we clear on that? . . . Good. One last thing—don't, for God's sake, attempt to land at the jetty and go walkabout. The hosts have got all manner of things guarding the house; compared to these guys, the target's a complete cakewalk—"

As Pandora reached out to scratch a gnat bite on her leg, her balance shifted from one hip to the other. To her utter horror, something tiny beneath her feet gave way with a loud crack out of all proportion to its size. Across the clearing, Zander spun around, snapping his cell phone shut and staring in her direction. Oh no, no, no, she thought. What do I do *now?*

Run, her mind informed her, just as Zander broke into a sprint up ahead.

A Brush with Greatness

In the nursery, moonlight shone through a gap in the curtains, illuminating Damp's bed in a pool of silver. The little girl had woken to the sound of footsteps on the rose-quartz drive outside, and now, with her thumb jammed firmly in her mouth, she lay wide awake in the darkness wishing she had someone to play with. Hanging above the chest of drawers was a framed repro-duction of *La Giaconda*—Leonardo da Vinci's painting of the Mona Lisa—which had graced the nursery wall for the past thirteen years, ever since Luciano Strega-Borgia had ban-ished it from his study, claiming he couldn't stand looking at that enigmatic smirk for one moment longer. The fact that Baci Strega-Borgia was heavily pregnant with Titus at the time

and had taken to wearing an identically enigmatic smile as she approached Titus's birth might have had something to do with Luciano's loathing of the Leonardo. In truth, unsettled by the prospect of his approaching fatherhood, terrified that his slender wife would be unable to withstand the rigors of childbirth, and praying that he wouldn't faint dead away on the day itself, Luciano felt that the last thing he needed to be surrounded with was enigmatically grinning women. Hence, the picture ended up in the nursery, where it hung, for the most part unobserved, in the shadows of Damp's room.

Damp gazed at it, her eyelids flickering as sleep stole across the bed to claim her. The quilt settled its feathers around her, the air hung still and quiet, and Damp was just on the point of blissful surrender, when . . .

. . . an unfamiliar female voice rang out.

"Leo, for God's sake, where did that child spring from?" The woman shifted impatiently on her seat, her limbs cramped from attempting to hold the same pose since daybreak. Sancte Spiritus, *she thought, but he's a right slave driver, this one. No coffee breaks, no pauses for a little* vin santo *and* panforte . . . *no conversation,* nada. Just the *swish-swish* splot *of brushes on canvas . . .*

"I said, Maestro, there's a child in your studio. One of yours? Or not, since you appear immune to a woman's charms . . ."

Across the dusty studio, the painter gave an exasperated pfff *and looked up from a table where he'd been trying to mix a color similar to the ochre of his sitter's skin.*

"In the name of the Redeemer!" he shrieked. "What are you

prattling on about now, woman? At daybreak it was "Oh, Leo, I'm sooo tired, can't we just go for a little lie-down?" and then we had, "Leo, wasn't that the bells of the Angelus? Elevenses? I'm so famished I could eat a wild boar panino, *and now you tell me there's a child. . . ."*

Damp gazed up at the wildly gesticulating figure and risked a smile. "Hello, Man," she said, unsure if this was indeed the case, since Signor Leonardo da Vinci was sporting a rather abbreviated dress, tights, and pointy shoes in fetching shades of rose madder. The long pointy beard was a bit of a giveaway, though. So, too, was his deep male voice, raised in anger. *Sounds like Dada,* Damp decided, her bottom lip automatically wobbling in a learned response to Italianate hysterics.

"What? Are they now sending me babies as apprentices?" Leonardo glared at Damp and, correctly assessing that this one was on the verge of tears, relented somewhat. Passing her a tiny sable paintbrush, he said, "Here, bambina, take this little brush. You can start by stirring together two parts of burnt umber to one part of ultramarine. Surely even a complete beginner can manage to mix me a decent black?"

"Not like black," Damp stated firmly. "Want pink."

"PINK?" Leonardo shrieked. "Are you insinuating I'm some kind of painter of fluffy bunnies? An illustrattoria?"

"Suddenly I'm absolutely starving," Mona complained. "Must've been the mention of trattoria that did it. C'mon, Leo, it must be lunchtime by now."

"Why am I so plagued with imbeciles?" Leonardo roared, hurling his brushes aside with such force that they bounced across the dirt floor. "If it's not the postman ringing twice on my doorbell, it's

the infernal din from the bells of the cathedral; if it's not the putta
wanting pizza *in the* piazza, *it's the infant apprentice demanding
access to my most precious pigments.* . . . *How am I, Leonardo da
Vinci, supposed to be able to hear my Muse when she whispers her
inspirations in my ear? Surrounded by the din from a thousand
bells and lungs, will my Muse need a megaphone to make herself
understood?" He stopped abruptly in mid-flow, slapped himself on
the forehead, and grabbed a stick of charcoal in one hand.
Scribbling feverishly on a fresh canvas, Leonardo began to outline
the first sketch of a device to magnify sound: da Vinci's* magna
voce, *or megaphone. The Muse had spoken, and for the time being
at least, the painter was deaf to all but her voice.*

*Waving the tiny sable brush in the air, Damp seized this as an
opportunity to make a couple of magical adjustments to the half-
finished portrait on the easel.* Pretty pink, *she decided, absurdly
pleased with herself and wondering if the Man in the Dress would
admire her efforts. So absorbed was Leonardo in his outline of the
megaphone that he didn't notice Damp's interventions; nor did he
spot his sitter sneaking outdoors in search of a decent roast lark* cia-
batta, *an item that would prove impossible for her to chew, given the
parlous condition of what lay beneath her lips. When* La Giaconda
*smiled in farewell to Damp, the little girl recoiled in horror, unac-
customed as she was to being grinned at by ladies with brown rotting
stumps in place of pearly-white twenty-first-century teeth.*

*"Go 'wayyyy," she wept, stepping backward with a howl of ter-
ror and falling . . .*

. . . into the embrace of something soft, warm, and, to her
relief, intensely familiar.

"Och, wee pet," Mrs. McLachlan whispered. "What are you doing out of your bed? It's past midnight—time you were tucked up and fast asleep. . . ." Scooping the little girl into her arms, the nanny carried her off to the comforts of cot, pillow, and feather quilt, unaware that in one chubby fist Damp was clutching a souvenir. Attracted to anything remotely resembling a wand, Damp had hung on to her battered antique sable brush, given to her courtesy of Signor Leonardo da Vinci, who, across the canyons of Time, was standing in a studio in sixteenth-century Florence, wondering what angel had guided his newest apprentice's hand. No answer was forthcoming from the finished portrait in front of him; for, still wet, the freshly applied pigment smiled back at him, silent, knowing, and utterly enigmatic. The Mona Lisa's mouth was painted shut; there would be no telling . . . and no teeth, either.

Assault and Battery

Ahead of Pandora, the path divided in two. The right-hand track led back home, twisting and winding down Mhoire Ochone, and, ultimately, to StregaSchloss. To the left was an overgrown footpath, wound about with rampant honeysuckle, following the flow of a series of waterfalls and streams and culminating in a deep pool cut into the middle of a coire that defied all but crampons to scale its steep sides. However, next to the pool was a hidden cave that might afford her the perfect sanctuary in which to hide from Zander.

Twenty minutes later, Pandora wasn't so sure that she'd made the right choice. Lying on the ground and rolling into the darkness, she'd discovered that a recent rockfall had almost entirely filled her hideaway; there was just enough space for her to lie flat inside the mouth of the cave and pray that Zander wouldn't look down. Grabbing handfuls of last autumn's leaves, Pandora tried to camouflage herself, her ears tuned for his approaching footsteps, her heart hammering with terror.

She knew now that she should never have followed Zander into the woods. What had started out as a game, a joke, really, had turned deadly serious. That's the problem with adults, she thought miserably, no sense of humor whatsoever. . . . She'd never seen anyone quite *that* angry before. Zander had been incoherent with rage, swearing and shrieking like a madman. To her immense relief, he appeared not to know who exactly he was threatening to tear limb from limb and baste in sump oil, and in his fury he'd tripped and fallen, which had allowed her to put a considerable distance between them; but judging by his approaching footsteps, she'd failed to lose him entirely. Lying in the darkness, Pandora didn't want to imagine what would happen when he found out that it had been her following him. Or what her parents would say when he told them. Oh. My. God, she thought. I'll be grounded for . . . *months*.

Suddenly such homely concerns fell away. Parental disapproval was infinitely preferable to what lay ahead. He'd turned his flashlight on again, and its beam came closer and closer now, sweeping the path over by the pool, its light dancing across the swirling water.

"You may as well show yourself!" Zander yelled, his voice echoing weirdly off the walls of the coire. "I know you're here, because there's nowhere else to go, *is there?*"

Pandora swallowed, the sound her throat made so loud, she was sure he could hear her.

"You're finished, d'you know that?" Zander continued, his voice closer now as he turned to face the cave, his back to the rock pool. The flashlight beam was dazzling, searing her eyes, destroying her night vision, and pinning her in place like a rabbit caught in headlights.

"I've followed the trail your company has left across the planet. Yes, it was me. In Archangel. Me in Angola and Panama, too. Just little old me destroying your factories, putting out your lights, one by one. Did you really think you could hide from *me*? Surely you must know by now that *nothing* will stop me?"

He's insane, Pandora told herself. Who on earth does he think I am?

"I can't let you go back now, can I?" Zander added conversationally, his voice tinged with faint regret. "You know too much."

I'm going to die, Pandora realized, a glacial calm settling over her entire body. Here, now, in a dirty cave in Coire Chone . . .

"It's 'Crone,' actually," a whispery voice informed her.

Whatever, she thought. It doesn't matter. It could be in a bed of roses in the middle of a moonlit loch for all I care—

"Nice imagery," the voice said encouragingly. *"Do go on. Can't tell you how much we've all been looking forward to meeting you. What took you so long, child?"*

"I'm getting a little *impatient* out here!" Zander shrieked. "I'm going to count to ten and then—"

137

"*Oh, ignore him,*" the voice snapped. "*Ssso tedious, these little tin-pot terrorists; what the world needs is less of them and more storytellers like you, m'dear.*"

Huh? Pandora's mind stalled, crashed, and then rebooted rapidly. I *beg* your pardon?

"*No, no, don't beg. Just get on with the story. The moonlit loch— tell me more. Were there stars in the sky? A crescent moon? We love crescent moons, don't we, sisters? We call them the Luminous Toenail Clippings of the Divine. . . .*"

Pandora heard a sound like thousands of leaves beginning to stir. Her skin broke out in gooseflesh. She'd been so sure the cave was empty, but *now* . . .

"Three . . . four . . ."

"*Don't worry about him,*" the voice insisted. "*We'll deal with him in due course.*"

Pandora froze. Was it her imagination, or were there dim shapes moving in the darkness? The voice sounded closer, as if its source was creeping nearer.

"*There's nothing to fear, child. We would never harm a witch, or her kin.*"

"Five . . . six . . ."

"*Your ancestors offered sanctuary to my kin. In return, we gave you the gift of our loyalty. We've been your familiars for hundreds of years—*"

"Seven, *eight* . . ."

Something infinitely soft brushed Pandora's arm so gently, it felt like a breath. The sound of rustling grew louder still, but Pandora could clearly hear the voice whispering, "*When you need us, we will come. . . .*"

I'm sorry, Pandora thought. You've lost me. . . .

"On the contrary, you've found us, but you need to lose him.*"*

"*Nine, ten* . . . Don't say I didn't warn you!" Zander's sneaker-clad feet appeared outside the mouth of the cave, but far, far worse was the appearance of the glinting, steely head of the ax he was swinging from one hand.

"Oh, puhleeease," the voice sighed. *"How he does go on. If there's anything worse than ax-toting psychos, it's morons who insist on interrupting the first decent conversation I've had in years. Excuse me, I'd love to stay and chat, but, regrettably, I have business to attend to—"*

And in front of Pandora's astonished eyes, the image of Zander, feet, ax, and all, was obscured by a blanket of fluttering fragments of black. Masses of crumpled wings beat a whispery tattoo as, in their hundreds, the bats of Coire Crone rose out of the cave in a synchronized exodus of rabid outrage.

"Get off me! *Aughhh!* No! Get back—*ugh.* Filthy creatures. Help—*help*, my *eyes.* M*ffff, Hell. Nooooaaaarghhhh*—"

Pandora's view of events was severely limited, which was probably just as well since the image of Zander smothered in demented bats would have fueled her nightmares for the rest of her life. Mercifully, all she could see was his feet kicking and flailing as he attempted to hold his ground against the onslaught of claws and teeth. Then he was gone, fleeing for his life, roaring and crashing along the overgrown path; in his wake, the insistent beat of bat wings rose and fell as they circled their prey.

Zander's shrieks grew fainter and more distant until, finally, silence fell in Coire Crone. Pandora rolled back out of the cave

and slowly climbed to her feet. On the path ahead lay an abandoned ax, its handle pointed accusingly to where, far off in the
moonlit distance, a black tornado of bats spiraled behind
Zander, marking his frantic retreat to StregaSchloss. Bending
down to pick up the ax, Pandora found herself shaking so badly
she almost fell over. She felt as if she were about to suffocate
out of sheer terror, her eyes riveted to the ax head, which had
been meant to close her mouth forever. . . . She realized the
squeaky voice repeating "Helphelphelp" was hers and, gasping
for air, she commanded herself to get a grip. Close your eyes,
Pandora, she ordered herself. Don't look. Now, stand up—no
wonder you can't breathe curled up like a pretzel. She straightened up, forced herself to take several deep breaths . . .

. . . and wished with all her heart that Mrs. McLachlan
were beside her in Coire Crone, dressed in sensible tweeds
and stout shoes and effortlessly taking charge of the
situation. . . .

"Och, you poor wee soul," would be her introduction, swiftly fol-
lowed by a hail of tsking sounds when she caught sight of the
weapon lying glinting on the path. "The things people leave lying
around the countryside. Really. Someone could do themselves an
injury with that thing. . . ."

Mrs. McLachlan was very good at being tactful, too—so good
that she'd pretend to ignore the fact that Pandora was now sobbing
hysterically, and would simply take her by the arm and lead her
gently back home, all the while maintaining a flow of light, non-
threatening conversation.

"Isn't that honeysuckle a bonny flower? Such a lovely perfume.

Reminds me of my wedding day . . . Mind your step here, pet. We're coming up to a very boggy patch. . . . No, don't open your eyes just yet; not far now, and we'll make a nice cup of hot chocolate and send you straight to bed. . . . Heavens, I simply must remind Tock not to trail mud across the hall floor and into the kitchen—would you just look at the state of that rug. . . . Och, lassie, you're asleep on your feet. Drink up now, and off to bed with you. . . ."

Pandora's eyes sprang open. In front of her, Mrs. McLachlan's face swam into focus.

"Be careful what you wish for," the nanny said firmly, her eyes fixed on Pandora as Zander crashed into the kitchen, hair awry and face covered in tiny red bite-marks. Mrs. McLachlan glided across to stand directly between Pandora and Zander, keeping him at bay while guiding Pandora out of the kitchen, tutting mildly as she took in the butler's disheveled appearance.

"You'll find the antihistamine cream in the middle drawer of the china cupboard. Those gnats are quite *brutal* after dark, but you weren't to know, were you, Mr. Imlach? Fishing, were we? My husband used to go night fishing, too. Up at Ballachulish. Or was it Altnaharrie? Och, no, wait a minute, Mr. Imlach, it's coming back to me now—it was the wee lochin by Castle Clachan at Strathlachlan. Silly me, I get so mixed up—it was that long ago. . . . He'd come home with so many fish, my heart would sink. Not the salmon *again*, I'd say. Did you have any luck, tonight, Mr. Imlach? Catch anything?"

By now, Pandora was safely in the passageway outside the

kitchen, but she heard Zander's muttered reply, his American accent now replaced by one of impeccable English parentage: "Nearly landed one, but it got away at the last moment."

"Och well. Never you mind, Mr. Imlach. Plenty more fish in the sea . . ." And as Mrs. McLachlan closed the kitchen door, she whispered, "Night-night, sleep tight. Watch the bats, these ones bite." And pressing a finger to her lips, the nanny propelled Pandora upstairs to bed.

A Ring of Spells

Clutching an overnight bag containing his pajamas, toothbrush, steam iron, and a battered copy of *The Gentleman's Gentleman,* Latch hailed a taxi from the rank outside the hospital. There was little, if anything, that the medical staff could do to help him now. Latch's memory was returning, and with it came a clear sense that he had to warn Mrs. McLachlan before it was too late. . . .

Climbing into the rear of the taxi and fumbling with his seat belt, Latch recalled that in his time as butler at StregaSchloss he'd encountered talking beasts, deep-frozen ancestors, Mafia invasions, cloned homunculi, and even monsters dropping in for after-dinner drinks—all of which were par for the course when one was in the employ of a student witch.

Over the years he'd grown to *expect* strange happenings at StregaSchloss but— He clutched his seat belt as the taxi driver braked hard for a suicidal ram, which ambled witlessly across the road in front of them.

"Get oot ma road, y'old de'il," the driver bawled, swerving to avoid a collision.

Indeed, Latch agreed. There's the problem in a nutshell, as it were. The old devil. Though not so much of the old. The devil he'd met the night the Strega-Borgias were due to fly home from Milan had been middle-aged, slightly balding, blandly dressed in a dark suit, and leaning insolently on the doorbell at StregaSchloss. . . .

"What, now?" Latch muttered, on the verge of lowering himself into a blissfully hot bath. Downstairs, the front doorbell rang once more, demanding an answer.

"It's eight o'clock," Latch groaned. "I'm due at Glasgow Airport in three hours' time and— Oh, for heaven's sake, I'm coming!" And grabbing his clothes as he hurtled downstairs, he'd just fastened the last buckle on his kilt when the front door flew open by itself, revealing a man standing on the doorstep.

"Ooopsss," the stranger said, his voice like nails being dragged across a blackboard. "Tssk, tsssk. Naughty boy, Isssagoth. Ssso impatient."

Beneath his kilt, Latch's stomach announced its intention of vacating itself by all means possible.

"No, no, no," the stranger murmured. "Not on my shoessss, puh-lease. Ussse the bathroom. Behind you, firsst door on the right."

Latch bolted for the bathroom, emerging minutes later, empty and ashen, utterly convinced that Death himself was sitting on the hall settle, drumming his manicured fingernails on his knee.

"There you are," the stranger said blandly.

"H-h-how did you know where the bathroom wa—wa—is?" Latch quavered.

"I know everything about thisss house. Every last nook and cranny. Every last crook and nanny, too. All I have to do isss read your mind, my dull little friend. I know all your secretsss." The stranger gave a repulsive snicker and snapped his fingers in front of Latch's eyes. "Now, let'ss not wassste time, shall we? Three words: Where. Is. It? The stone. Comprenez? The Chronostone—capisce? The diamond, Mr. Butler. Where is it?"

Latch's heart squeezed itself into a rigid pebble of muscle and attempted to hide itself behind his tonsils. The diamond? He dimly remembered finding a vulgar gem in the shattered remains of an old grandfather clock several months before . . . but jewelry not really being his thing, he'd passed it over to Mrs. McLachlan without a second thought. He had the vaguest recollection that she'd said something then about a library, but maybe he'd misheard her.

"Reeeeally," the stranger murmured. "The library. How parochial. How frightfully small-minded of her. . . . Tell me, Mr. Butler, where exactly isss dear Mrs. McLachlan at present?"

Latch stared. He—it—this thing was inside his mind, probing around in his memory, helping itself to whatever it chose . . . and he was powerless to prevent it.

"Shame. She didn't leave a forwarding addresssss, then? So, Mr. Butler, let's just fry a few synapses while we're here, shall we?

Nothing permanent. Jussst enough to make sure you can't go blab-bing to your preciousss Mrs. McLachlan right now, hmmm?"

The demon reached out and seized Latch's face in its hands, star-ing into his eyes. Immediately, Latch snapped his eyes shut.

"Oh, come on, you ssstupid little man. Don't make thiss any harder than it has to be."

Fingernails scraped at Latch's eyelids, peeling them apart. Latch struggled in the demon's grip, opening his mouth in a scream of outrage.

"That'll do nicely," the demon remarked, and the last thing Latch remembered was the vile taste of sulfur as the demon Isagoth slipped inside his skull.

"Stop the car!" Latch begged and, well-used to such demands, especially after last call at the Auchenlochtermuchty Arms, the taxi driver did as he was bid.

"Are youse sure youse're a' right, big man?" he inquired as Latch, pale and trembling, crawled back into his seat after a noisy communion with the rhododendrons of Argyll. No answer being forthcoming, the driver pressed the pedal to the metal in the fervent hope of delivering this fare to his desti-nation without further mishap.

Flora McLachlan carefully drew back the covers from her side of the bed and eased her legs onto the floor. She hadn't slept at all, spending the night propped upright on pillows, fending off sleep in order to maintain a guard on Pandora. Pandora, who despite the horrors of Coire Crone had instantly fallen into a deep and dreamless sleep the moment her head had touched the pillow . . .

Wee *girls,* Mrs. McLachlan thought, regarding her reflection in the bathroom mirror as she brushed her teeth, washed her face, and reached for a dry towel. Och, honestly, she continued, if it's not one, it's the other, slipping out of bed and getting up to all sorts in the middle of the night.

"Wee *girls,*" she whispered, conjuring up the image of Damp and Pandora before her, visualizing the girls standing in the exact center of a sunlit lawn, surrounded by an unbroken daisy chain of spells, one enchantment seamlessly linked to the next, the whole forming a perfect circle of light that was designed to keep them safe from whatever lay in the shadows beyond. Utterly still, Mrs. McLachlan reached out with her mind and scanned the circle, checking and rechecking the hidden joins where Old Norse melded with Sanskrit, where rune flowed into hieroglyph, and where corruption might sniff and lick and try to force a way through. . . .

"Flora?" She heard a hoarse whisper at the bathroom door. "Flora, it's me, Latch. I've got to tell— It's *important*— Oh, for the love of heaven, woman, would you *stop* powdering your nose and let me in?"

He sounded so normal, huffing and shuffling his feet on the other side of the door, unable to disguise his impatience. Mrs. McLachlan wrapped a dressing gown around herself and undid the lock, her eyes shining as she opened the door. Perhaps she'd jumped to conclusions about what had happened to Latch, wrongly assuming that he'd been damaged by a close encounter with a demon. . . . After all, she scolded herself, what evidence did she have to back this up? A stench of sulfur and a temporary memory loss? Maybe both could be explained by a bacterial attack rather than a demonic one?

One glance at Latch's face dispelled such thoughts, for Latch looked as if he'd gazed into the abyss and the abyss had gazed back into him. To Mrs. McLachlan's raised eyebrows, Latch merely nodded, closing his eyes briefly to erase the memory of what he'd seen.

"It . . . I . . . he . . . ," he stammered.

"Hush, dear. I understand."

"It wanted something, Flora. It's going to come back for it. A stone—a diamond. I had no idea. . . . I couldn't stop it. . . . It was stronger than anything I've . . . I've . . ."

"Hush, dear. It's all over now." Mrs. McLachlan stepped forward and wrapped her arms around Latch, her mind a thousand miles away from the shuddering man in her embrace. *Already?* She hadn't expected it would all start so *soon.* She marveled at how calm she felt. Oh, my poor wee girls, she mourned, I had hoped we might have had more time. . . .

Ring of Iron

Feeling immensely pleased with himself, the Sleeper returned to his favorite spot in Lochnagargoyle and lolled in the warm shallows near the jetty. Removing the centaur's stone from his pouch, the Sleeper was delighted to find that it was a perfect fit for the metal ring he'd found lying outside the SapienTech building. Held snugly in one half of an illegal iron trap, the Chronostone now looked like part of an engagement ring made for a Tyrannosaurus. The Sleeper had used his brute strength to bend the trap's wicked teeth inward to form a perfect cage for the gem, and the hefty spring-loaded mechanism designed to cause the trap's jaws to snap shut had been permanently disabled with one swift jerk.

Twisting one metal jaw back upon itself, the Sleeper had created a semicircular aperture which would, he hoped, allow the passage of one dragon's talon. One dragon who would be in a state of utter bliss when she caught sight of the vast diamond her fiancé had found for her. . . .

Where *is* that wumman? the Sleeper wondered, undulating closer to the jetty and scanning the shore for signs of Ffup. Or, noo, hing oan a minute, he thought. Is this no yin of those days she brings ma breakfast and then does a disappearing act? He checked beneath the jetty for evidence of Ffup's loving kindness, and indeed there it was. Or rather, there *they* were: five waterproofed slabs of plastic explosive, hidden there by Zander and awaiting pickup according to his cell phone conversation of the night before.

Mmmmm . . . The Sleeper sighed appreciatively as he unwrapped the final breakfast parcel and slipped it delicately down his throat. Verry nice, hen, he decided, giving a discreet belch. A wee bit chewy, mind, and it didnae taste o' very much at a', but it filled a hole, and in ma book, that's whit's important. Blissfully oblivious to the fact that plastic explosive is normally used for *creating* holes rather than filling them, the Sleeper sank beneath the surface of the loch to digest his dangerous breakfast.

In the kitchen at StregaSchloss, Tock unrolled a large sheet of paper in front of his fellow beasts and stepped back to allow them space to admire it. Busying himself with opening a tin of prunes and slopping them over his breakfast muesli, the crocodile turned back to the company in time to witness

Nestor regurgitate a clot of porridge straight onto the middle of the kitchen table. This gobbet landed on Tock's carefully drawn plans for the remodeling of the moat, thus adding an unplanned three-dimensional aspect to the original design.

Clasping a claw over his yellow eyes, Tock gave a small moan. The drawing had taken him *ages*; many nights of hunching over a blank sheet of paper, followed by days of frenzied scribbling, measuring, rubbing out, and redrafting in order to arrive at this perfect design for a twenty-first-century moat . . . a twenty-first-century moat that was in danger of being buried beneath a volcanic eruption of porridge-lava. Dribbling with anticipation, Knot leant across the table, opened his mouth, and neatly removed the porridge, unfortunately obliterating a yeti-tongue-shaped section of Tock's original draft and leaving a gleaming saliva trail in its place.

"Nooooo," Tock breathed, aghast, while Ffup compounded the damage by dabbing the wet patch with a scented baby wipe, then drying the resultant smear with a quick blast of dragon fire.

"There you are," she said, adding inaccurately, "good as new."

Tock clamped his jaws shut on the scream that threatened to erupt from his throat. His companions gazed at him expectantly, drooling, snorting, and breathing noisily through their mouths, waiting for him to explain what his beautiful drawing signified.

"Let me see now—is it a . . . bracelet?" Ffup guessed, her mind, as ever, full of girly ornament.

"I think I'm trying to see it upside down," Sab said,

standing up to come around the table, forgetting that he was over four meters tall just as he crashed into the hanging pot rack over the range. The beasts waited until the din of clashing casseroles died down before continuing.

"S'like I Spy," Knot mumbled, a steady drip-drip of saliva obliterating yet more of Tock's design. "No. Hang on. *I've* got it. It's a half-eaten doughnut!"

"Spåre me," hissed Tarantella, who'd been following this exchange with thinly veiled irritation. "Did Gaudí have to put up with this? Oh, Señor Gaudí, ees eet a beeg wedding cake you are beelding for Barcelona? Did Sir Christopher Wren lay his designs in front of dribbling half-wits, only to have them compared to partially masticated pastries?" Launching herself off the cupboard and into the air, the tarantula landed in the middle of the beasts, produced a miniature walking stick from some internal cache, and limped carefully to the edge of Tock's drawing. Using her walking stick as a pointer, she began to explain the design for the new moat in the tones of a weary tour guide. "Your attention, please. *Tap, tap.* Here we have the water-lily collection—*tap*—and over here—*tap*—we envisage putting the Japanese water garden. However, the main thrust of the design concerns the solar-heated swimming pool—*tap, tap*—which you will note is tiled throughout in lapis lazuli, a design feature that, regrettably, will push the construction costs into the thousands . . . uncompromising elegance—*tap* . . . architect's   vision—*tap* . . . unique . . . cultural heritage . . . financing this project entails . . . funding not forthcoming from Strega-Borgia bank accounts . . . forced to explore other avenues for raising money . . ."

At some point during the spider's long lecture, Knot must have fallen asleep, because when he awoke, things had moved on somewhat. The kitchen was empty of beasts, Tock's drawing had been put away, and in its place lay a newspaper with something outlined on it in red pen.

"So glad you could join us," Tarantella said, adding, "Here's the plan," and, bending closer to the newspaper, she read out loud: " 'Volunteers wanted. SapienTech has vacancies for individuals who are willing to assist in scientific trials of a new product. Remuneration in the region of €2500 per diem. No medical certificates necessary. A full examination will be given by our qualified medical personnel prior to the implementation of any procedures.' "

"Sounds pretty dodgy to me," Tarantella advised, "but compared to robbing the bank in Auchenlochtermuchty, I think it's got a lot going for it. Admittedly, 'The Five Volunteers' doesn't have the same impact as 'The Three Musketeers,' but how else are you going to raise the money for the moat extension, hmmm?"

Arriving at last in the SapienTech parking lot, Tock turned to face his fellow volunteers with a broad smile across his jaws.

"All for one, and one for all?" he inquired hopefully.

"I didn't really understand the last bit," Knot confessed. Then, seeing Tock's smile fade slightly, he added, "But . . . uh, yeah. The money's really good. Isn't it?"

Ffup adjusted Nestor's sling on her shoulders and shrugged. "Ah . . . guys . . . I'm not so sure Nestor's going to be able to pass an examination. I mean, the poor wee lamb can't even *read* yet. . . ."

Tock's smile vanished.

"This medical trial business," Sab murmured, "I've been giving it some thought. If we have a trial, don't we need a lawyer? Should I give my solicitor a ring? Just to make sure?"

"Look"—Tock sighed—"far be it from me to force you all into doing something you don't feel too sure about. It's my moat, and my problem. I'm the one who needs the money. Why don't you all just go down to the lochside and wait for me. I'm sure it won't take too long, whatever it is. . . ."

Peering at the visitors through the one-way glass of a window on the second floor, Dr. Penn Umbra felt as if her heart had stopped. Were these *more* giant eels? Like the one that had slithered out of the lake last night? Reaching out a shaking hand for the telephone, she forced herself not to faint as one of the hideously mutated creatures waddled across the parking lot and through the main doors into the reception area of SapienTech.

"Security?" Dr. Umbra squeaked. "There appear to be intruders in the staff parking lot. One of them has entered the building. Use all means necessary to intercept them. Tranquilizer darts, Tasers, whatever. Just do it. And don't let them get away this time. Understood?"

Dr. Umbra grabbed a nearby pencil holder, opened a drawer, poured herself a stiff measure from her reserve supply of bourbon, and drank it down in one gulp. Pausing only to remove a paper clip from between her teeth, she made a mental note to drink the stuff straight from the bottle next time . . . if there was a next time.

This latest series of drug trials at SapienTech had been dogged by disaster right from the start. Despite tight security, someone had leaked information to the media, and when the first stories began to surface about cancer clusters in remote Russian archipelagos, tourists trampled by winged rhinos in Africa, and severed heads that retained the power of speech in South America, it was only a matter of time before bands of eco-warriors began to pay close heed to what SapienTech was up to. Accustomed to battling off such unwelcome attentions, SapienTech prepared itself to repel the usual guitar-strumming, placard-waving, tree-hugging hippies. However, recently the eco-warriors had been replaced by something far more dangerous. SapienTech found itself being stalked by a new, improved species of eco-warrior, one that used guns, not guitars, to underline its message; a streamlined and deadly strain of eco-warrior that didn't pause to hug trees, but burnt whole forests to the ground in the pursuit of some lofty ideal. It appeared that the eco-warriors had evolved into eco-terrorists, declaring that banner-waving was for wimps and adopting far more extreme methods of persuasion.

Over the previous twelve months, a succession of explosions had destroyed SapienTech's high-security facilities around the globe and forced them to relocate to this dump in Argyll. Not that Argyll was so unpleasant when compared to, say, Archangel, but the main problem with Scotland was the difficulty in finding enough human tissue for proper research.

Unlike in Angola or Panama, no one here was desperate enough to volunteer themselves for medical trials, and Dr. Umbra had been forced to limit her experimental efforts to laboratory mice, stray dogs and cats, and, all too infrequently, the odd tramp or derelict who had the misfortune to cross her path.

Taking a fortifying swig from the bottle of bourbon and chasing it with three extra-strong mints to disguise her whiskey breath, she wondered if this was the day she'd been dreading most of her adult life. The day when the evidence of her scientific sins came back to haunt her. And judging by the massive monsters in the parking lot, there was evidence aplenty. . . .

She risked another look through the window, down to the tarmac, where one of the "visitors" was apparently wrestling with a smaller version of itself and producing an alarming quantity of green slime in the process. . . . What on earth *were* they? Mutations from the fatally irradiated lake in Archangel? She was so sure they'd all been eliminated, along with the human by-products of the chimera fiasco in Angola. Perhaps they were escapees from the Panamanian mind-canal disaster . . . but that didn't bear thinking about. Didn't they still have a death penalty in Panama? Half choking on a mint, she realized that she could speculate endlessly, but it was utterly pointless to do so. Whatever the things in the parking lot were, she vowed, by tomorrow they'd be yet more toxic sludge to fly-tip into the lake. Too much was at stake now. The drug trial had reached critical mass and was hurtling toward completion like a deranged snowball, rolling over people and places with ruthless velocity, flattening everything in its path.

Roars of outrage came from the parking lot below, agonized shrieks and screams that didn't cause so much as a frown to cross Dr. Umbra's brow, although, she had to admit, the smallest monster did have an excellent pair of lungs, which it was using to deafening effect. . . .

Picking up her phone, she redialed. "Security? Me again. Let's not be *too* brutal, shall we? Take the intruders to the containment area. Not the incinerator, no. I'd like to run a few tests before disposal." And snapping on a pair of disposable rubber gloves, Dr. Umbra headed downstairs to greet the beasts.

Out to Lunch

W"here *is* everyone?" Luciano muttered to Damp as they came downstairs into a deserted kitchen. Helping his daughter into her high chair, Luciano grumbled to himself as he plucked cereal packets from the pantry and laid them out for Damp's approval.

"This is the height of madness. . . . We shell out a king's ransom in staff wages, and in return we get a cook who won't cook, but can sulk for Scotland, we get a nanny who's spread so thin she's invisible, a butler who's forgotten who he is, and a replacement—" Luciano broke off and checked the view through the kitchen window down to the loch before continuing, "A replacement who eats like a rabbit, speaks in conundrums, and spends

every morning communing with Lochnagargoyle instead of doing his job."

"That one," Damp said, pointing to her breakfast of choice. "Want it, Dada."

"That's *not* how to ask properly." Luciano frowned through the window, distracted by Damp's lack of manners. "Come on, *bambina*, you know better than that, surely? What's the magic word?"

"Abracadabra," Damp replied automatically, before remembering that this was perhaps, on reflection, not a good idea, and rapidly amending it to, "Please," for her father's benefit. Recalling the abracadabra invocation required enough energy to fuel a small electrical substation, and to Luciano's alarm, when he turned from the window to grant Damp's request, he saw his daughter facedown in her empty breakfast bowl, fast asleep.

"Cara mia," he breathed, "are you unwell?" She was so small and vulnerable it hurt him to look at her. Nearly paralyzed by a sudden fear, he gathered Damp's unresisting body in his arms, stroking her forehead and smoothing her hair away from her eyes. "Wake up, my little one," he begged, struck by how limp she felt in his arms. "Damp? Open your eyes. Speak to me! *Wake up!*"

The child's eyes fluttered open, their vast dark pupils shrinking against the light. "Go 'way, Dada," she mumbled, her eyelids barely able to resist the pull of gravity. "Night-night."

Luciano panicked. Having spent huge periods of his life as

a parent cajoling his children to bed and then persuading them that sleep was A Good Thing, it felt totally wrong to find himself trying to do the opposite.

"BACI!" he shrieked, running out of the kitchen with Damp flopping like a rag doll over his shoulder. He took the stairs three at a time, arriving breathless and incoherent in the master bedroom where, judging by the trail of sheets, pajamas, discarded clothing, and shoes of varying heights and repair, Baci had locked herself in the bathroom to have a wardrobe crisis of epic proportions. Indeed, through the door, he could hear his wife bawling at her reflection.

"Nothing to *wear*...*Hate* my clothes...*Fat* and *horrible*...nothing *fits* anymore...hideous mumsy tents... *Eughhhh*—I look like a bloody *whale*...." And in response to Luciano's knock on the door, she howled, *"Go away!"* loud enough to make his teeth rattle. Looking down at his daughter, he noticed that the little girl was smiling....

Laying her in the middle of the bed, Luciano whispered, *"Precioza*...my *principessa*...will *you* speak to me? Just one word? Let your dada know if you're OK?"

Damp's eyes opened. To her father's immense relief, she looked straight at him, yawned cavernously, and, stretching herself in all directions, lolled across the sheets, perfectly at home, luxuriating in the huge space of her parents' bed, wriggly, giggly, and, thankfully, awake. From behind the bathroom door came a despairing wail followed by a crash.

"Horrible stuff. It's bringing me out in *spots*! Like some ghastly *adolescent*. I can't *stand* it. How on earth did I manage

to forget this bit? Tired, spotty, sick as a parrot . . . I *hate* being pregnant, horrible, horrible, horrblurrrgh . . ."

Damp and her father winced simultaneously, wishing that somehow they could muffle the ghastly eruptions now coming from behind the bathroom door. Four months into her nine-month stretch, Baci still couldn't believe that she had to go through this every morning. Each day she would wake up feeling perfectly normal, but ten minutes later she'd be draped over the bathroom sink moaning fitfully as her previous night's supper popped back for a gruesome encore. Morning sickness was one of the little clauses in teeny-tiny print at the bottom of the child-rearing contract that few, if any, parents stopped to consider in the heady rush of baby-creation. Fortunately, morning sickness wasn't fatal, no matter how much its sufferers might have desired it to be so. It was also curable—in a hundred percent of cases, the birth of the baby could be guaranteed to produce a full recovery. Aware that this information would provide scant comfort to his tear-stained, pale wife, Luciano waited until she'd staggered out of the bathroom and pitched facedown on the bed before he suggested a spot of retail therapy by way of distraction.

"Let's go and buy you something beautiful to wear," he murmured, stroking Baci's heaving shoulders. "Something really special. Something to make you feel good . . ." Not being a natural-born shopaholic, Luciano was unsure what exactly this something might be. Shoes? A dress? A handbag? He patted Baci silently, wary of suggesting anything that might cause offense and bring about a renewed fit of prenatal hysterics. Jewelry? Perfume? Flowers? What did she *need*? His eyes roamed desperately around their disheveled bedroom, alighting on their huge cedar-lined wardrobe. The doors to this lay wide open, exposing the colossal acreage of Baci's garments—countless laden hangers marching along the rails . . . and, in a tiny monochrome huddle, his own meager selection of clothes, completely overwhelmed by the volume of his wife's collection. Blinking rapidly, his eyes skidded across their dressing table, where the same rules applied, except his presence there was confined to a single bottle of cologne, surrounded by the superior number of Baci's unguents. There simply isn't *room* for another moisturizer in her life, he decided. One bottle more and she'd slither out of his life entirely, her passage lubricated by this cosmetic oil slick. . . .

"Luciano."

"*Cara mia?*"

"D'you know what would really cheer me up?"

"For you—anything. Say the word and we'll move heaven and earth to find it for you."

"Um. You won't be able to buy it in Auchen-lochtermuchty."

Since you could hardly buy *anything* in Auchen-lochtermuchty, this statement came as no surprise. Sensing an impending assault on the family finances, Luciano braced himself. Baci was sitting up now, a strangely enigmatic smile on her face. . . . Let it not be *too* expensive, he begged silently. What did she *want*?

"Damp, sweetheart, *not* the lipstick, please. Put it back, darling. Mummy needs it, yes, and Mummy needs those ones, too." Baci leapt to her feet with surprising speed for someone who'd spent the previous half hour prostrate over the basin. Marveling at his wife's powers of recuperation, Luciano suddenly remembered he'd been in this situation before. Three times before. Two years ago with an unborn Damp, eleven years past with Pandora-as-a-bump, and thirteen years prior with Titus in her tummy. Like many women, Baci was prone to food fetishes while pregnant; but unlike most women, her cravings ran to dishes so spicy and hot they required fire extinguishers to be placed on the table next to the salt and pepper. . . .

And Baci was quite right—the shopkeepers of Auchenlochtermuchty were united in their loathing of any food they perceived as "foreign." The local population's desire to remain untainted by twenty-first-century food fashion was best summed up by a conversation Luciano had overheard in the village store. One grizzled ancient clutching a basket laden with frozen meals had inquired where he might find a tin of chicken korma, only to be met with a walleyed stare from the shopkeeper, followed by, "If God had meant the likes o' us tae eat yon curries, he'd hae made us wi' asbestos tongues."

So. Not Auchenlochtermuchty, then. Luciano smiled, half watching as Baci buttoned up a large linen shirt over a pair of elasticized maternity tents, items of clothing for which the word "mumsy" might have been invented. Temporarily substituting greed for vanity, Baci reeled off the dishes of her choice.

"Vindaloo or Gulnar's Rooflifter would be my first

thought. But if you prefer Mexican, I'd love *huevos rancheros,* *salsa muerte con quesadillas,* or even a humble *carne con jalapeños.* On the other hand, if you want to eat Italian, I could cheerfully choke down *penne diavolo, rigatoni puttanesca,* or even *orrecchiette arrabiata....*" And Luciano was so happy to see his wife thus transformed, it wasn't until they were standing outside on the rose-quartz drive that he remembered the rest of his family.

"Are we just taking Damp?" Baci asked, opening the car door and lifting the little girl into her car seat. Guiltily, Luciano squinted upward to where Titus and Pandora's bedroom curtains were closed to the possibility of daylight. Like most adolescents, once woken up they would require two full hours to wash, brush, dress, eat, pack, eat some more, repack, change outfits at least once . . .

"*Yes,*" Luciano said, with rather more force than necessary. "Just Damp. Titus hates curries and we can't take Pandora if we go and buy her birthday present after lunch, can we? Quick, get in the car. I'll leave a note for them on the fridge— that way they'll be bound to see it . . . once we're gone."

A Silent Proposal

The rattle of the departing family car woke Titus from a sleep so deep, he found it almost impossible to bring his eyes into focus. StregaSchloss was unusually quiet; most mornings he would awake to clanking plumbing, footsteps thundering up and down stairs, the din of Nestor demanding breakfast . . . all accompanied by the background chirruping of birdsong. What time *is* it? he wondered, rolling onto his side and looking for his watch.

Ten seconds later, he was in the shower, cross at himself for sleeping in. Last night, when he'd finally put his laptop to sleep and crawled beneath the covers, it must have been three—four o'clock? I'll have missed breakfast, he thought gloomily; the milk will all be gone and Pandora

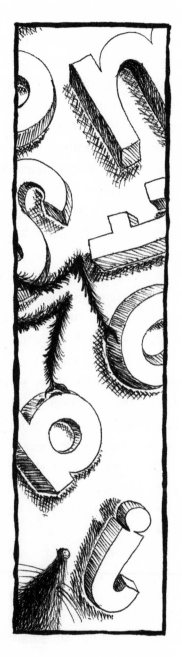

will have Hoovered down the last bagel and—Catching sight of his reflection in the steamed-up bathroom mirror, he gave a roar of alarm. *What on earth?* In the misty blur of his face, strange red blotches had appeared overnight. Touching his cheek, he found it to be covered in hard little lumps. Frantically wiping the mirror clear, Titus regarded the alien landscape of his face in appalled silence. *It was bad. It was . . . very bad. In fact, it was utterly, totally, absolutely catastrophic.* Titus closed his eyes and emitted a small moan. *Nope, enough,* he decided. *I can't bear to look anymore. I have metamorphosed into a pizza. I look like I've had the bubonic plague. . . . I am a human pustule, and thus will have to spend the rest of my life with my head inside a brown paper bag. I'll have to get a guide dog . . . no, I just won't ever go out except when it's dark. Oh my God, my life is in* ruins. . . .

Still, he decided, throwing on some clothes, there's no point in starving to death as well. Praying that no one would be around, Titus headed downstairs, aware for the first time exactly how many reflective surfaces there were between his bedroom and the kitchen. His hideously altered face swam out at him from suits of armor, shiny dark oil paintings, and highly polished banisters and newel posts, each bearing a scowling variant of Mr. Zitty, the world's first pimple persona. . . . Hearing a door close on the landing above, Titus raced for the kitchen.

"Vaw—vawl—vawlunt—vawlunt-ears wanted," Multitudina pronounced triumphantly, her whiskery nose pressed against the newspaper on the kitchen table, her pink eyes blinking rapidly with the effort. "Phewwww, *that* was a tough one. Er . . . what's a vawl-unt-ear, Tarantella?"

"A volunteer is someone who doesn't want to do something, but ends up being morally blackmailed into doing it anyway." Tarantella tapped the magnetic letters on the fridge door with ill-disguised impatience. "Leave the newspaper *alone*. Or else read it quietly to yourself. I'm sick of hearing stuff about LOCAL MAN BREEDS CHAMPION PIGEON or WEATHER FAIR FOR SHEEP TRIALS or even TEMPORARY TRAFFIC LIGHTS INSTALLED IN AUCHENLOCHTERMUCHTY. That newspaper's got as much in the way of dramatic tension as a shopping list."

"But I need to *learn*," Multitudina said, sitting back on her haunches and clawing at an itch behind her ear. "How am I supposed to become a litterat if I can't read?"

"*Literate*, not a litter-rat."

"Whatever. I want to read. I want to learn. You said you'd teach me, but all you ever do is give me *children's* picture books to read. I'm *not* a child."

"No. You're a rat," Tarantella pointed out unhelpfully. Then, relenting when she saw Multitudina's whiskers droop, she dragged a blu-tacked note off the fridge and handed it across to the delighted rat.

"Wow! Excellent!" Multitudina squeaked. "*And* some blue chewing gum as well? Yum. My lucky day." And popping the blu-tack into her mouth, she settled down to read Luciano's note to Titus and Pandora.

Walking across the meadow, Zander was too absorbed in his own thoughts to notice that he was being observed from a first-floor window of StregaSchloss. As he disappeared into the shadows of the house, a lace curtain twitched as it swung back into place, and Mrs. McLachlan turned to Latch with an unreadable expression on her face.

"Your thoughts?" she said.

"That wee laddie?" Latch snorted dismissively. "I could eat ten of him for breakfast and still have room for a dish of kippers."

Mrs. McLachlan smiled sweetly. "I don't *think* that will be necessary, Latch. Just keep an eye on him. I'm not sure what he's doing here, but I'm positive it has little to do with furthering his career as a butler in domestic service."

"Him? He wouldn't know a butler if one bit him in the leg. I mean, look at him—sitting on the grass and doing that yo-yo nonsense—"

"Yoga." Mrs. McLachlan's eyes twinkled. "Oh, Latch, dear—we've missed you so much. I'm *delighted* you're back."

A deep crimson blush suffused the portion of Latch's neck visible above his crisp white collar. The blush raced across his cheeks like a flash flood of embarrassment, the biggest wave flooding his face all the way up to the high-tide mark of his hairline before mercifully receding, ebbing away and leaving the butler damp with self-consciousness.

"Ah . . . um . . . Flora, I've been meaning to . . . I, er . . ."

Mrs. McLachlan laid a gentle hand on his arm. "Hush, dear," she murmured. "This isn't the right time."

"Ever since I saw you . . . ," the butler babbled, unable now to stop himself, "it's as if I've always known I . . . you . . . we . . ." He looked down into her face, his expression that of a man who cannot believe what is issuing from his mouth.

"Latch"—Mrs. McLachlan's voice was no louder than a whisper, but the grip of her hand on his arm spoke volumes— "this *isn't* the right time. I know what you're going to say. I think you might even be about to ask me something very important, indeed . . ."

Latch lowered his eyes, unable to meet her bright gaze.

". . . to which, after due consideration, I would reply in the affirmative . . ."

"*Flora?* You would?"

". . . however, my dear, you and I are professionals. And, as such, we know that no matter how pressing our . . . personal circumstances might be, we must always put our employers' well-being first."

"But yes. *Yes* would be your answer?" Latch persisted, adding for clarity, "To my question? Which you won't allow me to ask . . . yet."

"Och, my dear Latch"—Mrs. McLachlan smiled wistfully and shook her head as if to clear her thoughts—"there is something I must do first. In order to protect us all. The man you told me about—the one you thought was Death himself come to claim you—he will not rest, nor leave us be until he finds what he came for."

Latch's gaze drifted down to the herb garden, where Zander was now working on a series of t'ai chi exercises. Choosing his words carefully, he turned his full attention to Mrs. McLachlan and said, "Promise me something." Laying one hand on top of hers, he repeated, "Promise me you'll not go without saying good-bye—no, don't pretend, Flora. I can see it in your eyes. You're afraid, but you're going to do it anyway. Just do me the kindness of not pretending anymore. And when you do go . . ."

"Yes. I promise I'll say good-bye."

"Good lass," Latch said firmly, his expression resolute, his entire body language radiating quiet efficiency. Taking a deep breath, he said, "Right. Let the day's work begin, Mrs. McLachlan. To our duties."

And holding the door open, he almost broke down when she whispered, "And as for your very important question, dear"—she paused and looked up at him, her eyes even brighter than before—"if I cannot answer you in person, because I am . . . otherwise detained, I will find a way into your dreams, and you'll have your answer there." And slipping past him, she ran down the corridor like a schoolgirl, fleet of foot and laughing as she left him beached, blushing, and terrified on her behalf.

A Demon Disguised

Isagoth stood in the arrivals area of Glasgow Airport, waiting for his luggage to appear. He'd decided against wearing the bland business suit, and for today had gone for the rumpled chinos with Goretex jacket combo; anonymous with a faint hint of Action Man. In keeping with this, he'd razored his hair to two millimeters all over and covered his chin with spray-on designer stubble in a selection of colors from youthful black to pushing-fifty gray. His eyeballs smarted beneath the green contact lenses he'd been forced to adopt to disguise his state of permanent red-eye. As a final precaution, he'd showered till his skin almost bled, slathered himself in pungent aftershave, and marinated his

teeth in such industrial-strength mouthwash that his eyes watered. No trace of his normal sulfurous stench remained, which was just as well, for Glasgow Airport had employed sniffer dogs ever since nine naked stowaways had appeared off a flight from Milan. Consequently, the arrivals area was full of patrolling Alsatians, which set up a furious barking each time they heard a cell phone launch into a mangled version of the overture from *William Tell*. Furthermore, the airport was undergoing a major refurbishment, so from behind a screened-off section of the arrivals lounge came a continual din of badly tuned radios, sporadic bursts of hammering, and the deafening *screeeee* of power saws on metal.

Isagoth retrieved his luggage off the carousel and headed in the direction of the rental-car desk, where to his frustration he found himself waiting in line behind a large party of Japanese tourists whose command of Glaswegian was understandably nonexistent. Behind the disguised demon, a man and a woman joined the queue: their overladen luggage trolley and matching brand-new sneakers marked them out as visitors from America. Unable to avoid overhearing their conversation, Isagoth rolled his eyes and hissed as the couple loudly discussed the lamentable lack of facilities in this primitive country, the general surliness of the native population, and their concerns regarding the mental health of their only son and heir who, if Isagoth had understood correctly, had flown the parental coop to join a commune in Scotland.

"He's probably grown his hair right down his back by now," the man observed, morosely kicking the brake bar of his luggage trolley. "How're we supposed to recognize him, looking like some kind of hippie flower child?"

"Aw, sugar," his wife replied, accidentally nudging the trolley against Isagoth's ankles, "I'd know my baby boy anywhere. He can run, but he can't hide from his ever-loving mommy."

Ahead, the Japanese party were dispersing, smiling and bowing, their faces lit up like sunflowers as they spilled forth to conquer Scotland by camera. Isagoth stepped forward, placed the relevant paperwork on the desk before him, added a credit card like a cardsharp producing a hidden ace, and stood back, every inch the world-weary frequent flier.

"How long would you like the car for, sir?" The girl barely looked up from her computer screen, her long nails tippy-tapping on the keyboard.

"A week," Isagoth replied. That ought to be plenty of time, and besides, he thought, I've got no intention of returning the car anyway. *Not* that I'm about to mention that.

"Would you like a map, sir?"

A map. Not a bad thought, actually. He'd been driven by a minion last time, so he hadn't really paid any attention to where he was going. He nodded, his eyes hooded, his fingers drumming on the desk as the girl processed his details.

"We've got the Western Isles, Argyll, Perthshire, the Lothians, the Borders. . . ."

Behind him, Isagoth could hear the Americans go into raptures over this litany of Scottish place-names.

"Oh my gosh," the woman gasped. "It's just so romantic, isn't it, hon? Like something out of the movies—all those locks and brocks and islands—d'you think if we can find our boy, then we could maybe take some time to explore?"

"Well, Jolene, honey, if you've set your heart on seeing Scotland, I'm sure we could take a few hours off to tour. I mean, it can't take more than three hours to drive all the way around—you could fit this entire country into the state of Arizona and still have room for a coupla Grand Canyons. . . ."

"Argyll," Isagoth said firmly, his voice raised in competition with a resurgence of the din from the builders behind the screen. *"Argyll,"* he repeated, realizing the girl behind the desk hadn't heard.

"Say, mister . . ." The man behind broke off his discussion of Scotland's tiny acreage and muscled up to the desk. "Couldn't help but overhear you mention Argyll to this young lady here—'scuse me, ma'am, for butting in like this, but see, thing is, my wife and I are heading for Argyll ourselves."

Like I care, thought Isagoth, giving the American a dark stare before turning back to the girl, who had paused to examine her manicure in minute detail.

"And we're strangers in these parts ourselves, but when I heard you speak I knew you weren't from here, neither. Say, mister—'scuse my big mouth—my wife here's always chewing my ahh—giving me a hard time about doing this, but I always say, Jolene, how in tarnation are we ever supposed to make new friends if we just keep our mouths shut? And yeah, mister, you probably think I'm a fool, muscling in here, but, like I said, we're heading for Argyll too."

Isagoth turned to face his tormentor. "And your point is?"

"My point?" The American smiled broadly and threw his

arms outward in a gesture clearly intended to convey surprise at having to explain such a blindingly obvious concept. "My wife's just like you, mister. She likes things to be spelled out. Jolene, I say, sometimes it's good to circle around something before nailing it to the floor. Sometimes, Jolene, I say, it pays to take your time. Like hunting. Ever go hunting, mister? You get that critter right bang in your sights—a deer, say, pinned on the crosshairs of your big old rifle—and—"

The girl behind the desk seemed to awaken from a long sleep and spring back to full efficiency. Passing Isagoth his credit card, a sheaf of paperwork, and a set of car keys, she smiled coldly and turned her attention to the Americans.

"Next?" she said, with little enthusiasm.

"Not so fast, ma'am. Just hang on, mister." The American laid one meaty hand on Isagoth's arm and then, catching the expression on the demon's face, withdrew it instantly. "Now I can tell you just think I'm a gigantic pain in the fa—"

"*Lex!* Will you shut right up and let me handle this? Go and sit quietly over there and take your medication while I speak with Mr.—ahh . . . I don't believe I caught your name, sir?"

Isagoth turned to leave, but Jolene had blocked his escape with her vast trolley.

"Mister. What my poor fool of a husband was trying to say was: you're headed for Argyll and so are we. What d'you say we hook up? Share a vehicle? Save time, money, and—who knows?—we might end up sharing something more . . . ah, meaningful besides."

Isagoth pushed the trolley clear with such force that it barreled straight across the concourse, ripped through the screen hiding the building work from public view, and embedded itself on the business end of a circular saw. Interrupted in the middle of their tenth coffee break of the morning, several men wearing dirty jeans slung halfway down their buttocks rose to their feet in protest.

"Oh my goodness!" Jolene squeaked, then, recovering rapidly, added, "So I guess that means your answer is no?"

"Madam"—Isagoth bared his teeth—"frankly, I'd rather stick pins in my eyes." And, stalking out of the airport, he realized to his annoyance that for once he'd spoken the truth.

Zander Smells a Rat

Titus sidled into the kitchen poised for flight in case anyone was in there to witness his ruined complexion. Thank you, thank you, thank you, Great Spot Deity, he thought. They've all gone, leaving me to suppurate in peace. Carefully avoiding the possibility of encountering his reflection, he fumbled blindly in the fridge, producing a lump of dried-out cheddar, an unopened jar of pickled gherkins, and the scrapings at the bottom of a jar of mayonnaise. Better and better, he decided. Things are definitely looking up; all I need is bread and I'm in business.

Minutes later, carrying a quintuple-decker cheese-and-pickle toastie over to the table, he forgot to avoid the pot rack and consequently found himself mirrored tenfold in the polished steel of the many dangling casseroles. The distortion effect of these—spotty *and* bloated—caused him to lose his appetite altogether. Collapsing onto a chair and sinking his head into his hands, Titus failed to notice the presence of Multitudina next to the packet of Honey Nut Miserablios. The rat observed Titus with interest, wondering if she had been responsible for the plague of buboes marching across his face.

"Shame," she said, exercising all her reserves of compassion in a process that took approximately two seconds and returning to her forbidden reading matter. "Sap—sappy—sappy-ent—sappy-ent-ech have vac—vacan— Oh, for Pete's sake, why can't they write this stuff in English?"

Titus's head rose from the table and, to her credit, Multitudina didn't remark on his altered appearance.

"What *are* you reading?" he demanded, his attention caught by this reference to SapienTech.

"I wish I knew," Multitudina sighed, patting the newspaper under her belly. "I think I'll just go back to eating these things instead of reading them." And as she was about to sink her yellow fangs into the newspaper, she looked up to see Zander strolling into the kitchen from the garden. "Uh-oh," the rat whispered. *"Trouble."* And in front of Titus's astonished gaze, she leapt into the open box of Miserablios with a discreet crunch, leaving her bald tail dangling conspicuously over the edge of the package.

"Morning," Zander said, causing Titus to wish he could slip down a crack in the flagstones and disappear into a zit-zone where no one would notice or care about his spotty appearance.

"Lovely day," the proto-butler continued breezily, adding, "especially since it's my day off. D'you fancy a wee spin on the bike? We could take off down the shore, have a bite to eat in Auchenlochtermuchty.... What d'you think?"

I think I want to die, Titus decided. Now? Please? Before he notices that he's being matey with a human pustule. Oh, sigh. Better get it over with . . . and gritting his teeth, he looked up into Zander's face and—

Zander's identically pitted, bat-bitten, red, blotchy, hideously altered face looked back at him.

Titus's thoughts did an abrupt 180 degree turnaround and he managed to say, "Yeah, great, give me ten minutes," before realizing that now he was utterly *starving*.

A little later, flushed with the sudden chumminess that comes from discovering that one's companion is in an identical mess as oneself, Titus pointed to the newspaper ad and mumbled through a mouthful of cheese sandwich, "D'you know anything about these guys?"

Zander's eyes flickered. Oh yes, he thought, I know everything there *is* to know about SapienTech. Including the exact time they'll cease to exist . . .

"Nope," he lied, "not a thing. Why d'you ask?"

On the point of blurting out the details of his attempts to gain access to the SapienTech Web site, Titus became aware of two things at once. One, Pandora was standing at the kitchen door, her face ashen and her eyes widening as she saw who was sitting at the kitchen table; and two, Multitudina's tail was flicking back and forth in ecstasy as the rat discovered just how good Miserablios tasted.

Act normally, Titus told himself. Zander hasn't seen it yet.

Calm down, Pandora told herself. Zander doesn't know it was you—

"AUGHHHHHHH!" Zander roared. "It's a *rat*! On the *table*!"

"So it is," Pandora remarked, stepping to one side as Zander stumbled into the safety of the corridor. Hearing the voice of her trained human, Multitudina climbed back out of the cereal box, her whiskers glittering with sugar. Pandora crossed the kitchen, stroked the rat's head, and peered at her brother in some confusion.

Here we go again, Titus thought, zit city, not to mention rat planet. . . . Don't react, don't react, don't react.

"Heck, Titus, what were you *doing* last night? You've been eaten *alive*. I've never seen so many gnat bites on one person ever before. Yeurrrrch, you look *awful*."

Gnat bites? Titus felt like sobbing with relief. Only *gnat bites*? In a week's time he'd be back to normal? He was so delighted at this reprieve he wanted to *kiss* his sister. However, this was out of the question, so instead, grateful and babbling, Titus opened his mouth and inadvertently popped both feet straight in.

"Uh, yeah—by the way, Pan, I don't think it's a good idea to wander around the hills on your own at night."

Pandora's head jerked upright, away from her reunion with her pet rat.

"I mean, all sorts of weird stuff goes on after dark. . . ."

Despite the presence of a rodent on the table, Zander edged back into the kitchen, causing Pandora to clutch Multitudina so tightly, the rat gave a squeak of indignation.

"All I'm saying is, like . . . next time you fancy a walk in the dark, I'll come with you, OK? Just ask. I saw you out there last—"

"AOWWWWWWW! You wee *beast!*" Pandora dropped Multitudina onto the table and howled, "OUCH! That *hurts. Ow. Ow.* OWWWWW!"

"*What?*" Titus was utterly at sea. What *was* she on about now?

Pandora stood up, glared at him, and fled into the garden, leaving Titus staring at Zander in embarrassment. Unjustly slandered, Multitudina disappeared back into the cereal box in disgust.

"Phwoaaaah," Titus groaned. "What was *that* all about?"

"I haven't the faintest idea," Zander lied, stuffing his hands into his pockets to stop them shaking. They knew. Both of them. Her, in the woods, hiding in the coire; him, asking questions about SapienTech. What a mess. How much Pandora had overheard didn't matter. Not now. The main thing was to silence them. Quickly. He didn't have much time. Zander looked at Titus and smiled. "Grab your stuff—I'll be waiting outside."

Dragon Agony

Tarantella hid beneath a dandelion leaf and waited till the danger had passed, keeping one eye on the seagull wheeling overhead, while the others scrutinized her reflection as she applied lipstick to her mouthparts. Determined not to turn into a raddled frump after the efforts of spiderbirth, Tarantella was the arachnid equivalent of a yummy-mummy: fragrant, groomed, and impeccably made up. Day after day she'd commute down to the loch, tiptoe into the nursery she'd created under a seat in Titus's rowboat, gently kiss each of her tiny daughters, straighten the egg sac, and then settle down for some quality time with her unhatched children. Overhead, the seagull cawed, and then, performing one last

orbit in search of the outsized spider, the bird gave up and headed out over Lochnagargoyle toward the sea.

Tucking her lipstick and tiny mirror in a hidden cache under her belly, Tarantella hooked one leg onto a dangling length of spider silk and pushed off into the air—Lochnagargoyle's very own Tarzanella, queen of escapes.

Landing on the jetty, Tarantella scampered along its wooden planks and vaulted into Titus's rowboat. To her annoyance, she realized that she was not alone. Just offshore, out in the deeper water, the giant Sleeper was shaving barnacles off his chin using a razor-clam shell. He turned one vast eye in the tarantula's direction and flipped the end of his tail by way of greeting.

"Your wee gurrls are jis' fine," he roared. "Ah checked oan them this mornin'."

As a babysitter, the Sleeper left a lot to be desired, but as a nursery bodyguard he was unsurpassed. Tarantella tiptoed along the wooden seat and dropped underneath, hanging upside down and regarding her daughters with devotion. This bit was easy, she reminded herself. All that was required at this stage was for her to show up, make the appropriate maternal clucking sounds, check that her babies were warm and dry, then head home to put her feet up, safe in the knowledge that she'd done her duty. But all too soon, all three hundred sixty-five of them would hatch, look around, and demand room service. . . . Tarantella poked the silk-wrapped egg sac. Soon, she thought, very soon indeed. Then she could commence her plans for her daughters' education. Her babies were going to hit the ground running. To this end she had woven a "To Do" list into the silk of the egg sac. The list ran thus:

1. ELEMENTARY SPIDER SURVIVAL:
   Birds, bats, and big brutes: how to avoid being eaten or flushed down drains

2. BASIC TABLE MANNERS:
   How to eat like a goddess 24/7

3. INTERMEDIATE WEB DESIGN:
   Sticky feet and other weaving tips

4. ADVANCED LIPSTICK APPLICATION:
   Glossy or matte? Become friends with your mouthparts

and, ominously,

5. POST-GRAD SEX AND THE SINGLE SPIDER:
   Staying unattached: how to eat your husband

A shadow fell across the rowboat and the air filled with the smell of fish. Tarantella looked up to where the Sleeper's gigantic head blocked the sky from view.

"Huv youse seen ma wumman today?" he inquired, his ghastly teeth bared in a grin.

"Briefly," Tarantella admitted. "She's gone out for the day."

"Did she say whit fir? It's jist . . . weel . . . I've a big surprise for her and ah kin hardly wait to see her wee face when I gie her it."

"She's gone with the others to offer up her body on the altar of scientific discovery. For money."

The blank look of incomprehension on the Sleeper's face prompted Tarantella to try again.

"Oh, sigh. I forgot you don't do words of more than one syllable. Let me rephrase this. She has gone to the big factory down the loch. To earn money. As a sort of lab rat and guinea pig type of deal. Not a very good plan, I would say, but when did she ever listen to me . . . ?"

The loch was silent, its surface glassy-calm save for a whirlpool marking where the Sleeper had gone. A vast underwater shadow arrowed down the loch, heading for SapienTech. Tarantella watched for a moment, until the Sleeper's shadow had vanished from sight and then, hearing the distant scream of a shore-bound seagull, she made herself scarce.

In a cage in the containment facility of Room 101, the beasts huddled together, shivering. During the scuffle in the SapienTech parking lot, Ffup had accidentally torched a row of trash cans in an attempt to escape and Sab had turned himself into an immovable lump of stone and had needed to be forklifted into the building. Meanwhile, Knot had been copiously sick all the way through reception, inside the elevator, and along the corridors, and on arrival in Room 101, had suffered the further indignity of being forcibly washed with high-pressure hoses before being cattle-prodded into the cage with Tock. Throughout this sorry episode, Nestor had clung to Ffup and wailed inconsolably before falling asleep in her arms.

In the subsequent silence, the beasts held a whispered conference out of earshot of the security guards flanking the only exit.

"Any ideas?" Tock muttered, rubbing his stinging tail where a particularly vicious blast from a Taser had thrown him across the cage in response to his request for a bathroom.

"Just do it on the floor," Ffup suggested. "That'll teach them."

"That's not what I meant," Tock sighed. "I meant: any ideas about how we get out of here?"

"They do seem awfully keen to keep us here," Ffup said. "I know the welcoming committee left a lot to be desired, but hey—I think we've got the job, guys. Um . . . Tock, what d'you think they use that circular saw for? That one with the bucket under it . . . and what's with all the rubber beds? And all those piles of scalpels and big black paddles with sparks coming off them? And why so many mice in cages?"

"Feel sick . . . ," Knot whimpered.

"Listen," Tock hissed urgently. "We have to escape. This isn't what I thought it was going to be. We're *prisoners*, not employees. Check out the saw if you don't believe me. It's got red stuff dripping off its blade. . . ."

Ffup swallowed, took a deep breath, and said, "I'm going to

die! We're all going to *die! Aaaaaaaargh,* HELP, HELP, HELP. SAVE ME! I don't want to *die!* YEEEEEEARGH, *somebody* DO something!"

The beasts cowered in a corner, out of range of Ffup's fiery hysterics. The bars of their cage clanged and clashed as the demented dragon hurled her vast body against the reinforced steel, trying unsuccessfully to force her way through.

Across the room, one of the security guards levered himself to his feet and, grunting with exertion, lurched toward the cage, an aerosol can dangling from one apelike arm. Ffup's efforts redoubled, her deafening screams causing Nestor to run for the safety of Knot's woolly embrace before adding his own contribution to the general cacophony.

"*Waaaaaah,* Mumma, *waaaaaa!* NO WANT IT, *waaaaah!*"

"I'm going to *die!* Let me OUT. Let me OUT!"

"Listen, pal"—the security guard's voice was flat and monotonous—"cut that out, or we'll go get Dr. Umbra. And we wouldn't want *that,* would we?"

Across the room, Tock noticed the caged mice executing a synchronized wave at the mention of the good doctor.

"I WANT TO GO NOW!" Ffup shrieked, beyond reason or sense.

"Have it your own way, pal. I'm going to have to give you a wee squirt from ma wee can of tear gas and then you might have a wee think about whether we need to bother the doctor, eh?"

This time the mice did a synchronized throat-cutting mime.

"LET ME OUT OR I'LL—"

A *pssscht* sound came from the security guard's aerosol can. For such a small noise, its effect was spectacular. Ffup yelped and contorted herself into a ball of dragon agony, clawing at her eyes as tears sprayed from between her talons, while the tear gas lived up to its manufacturer's promises as a powerful weapon for riot control.

"My *eyes*," Ffup whimpered. "I can't *see*! I'M GOING BLIND! Get me a doctor—I NEED MEDICAL HELP!"

The door to the corridor opened and a woman entered the room. From the respectful salutes and flurry of activity around her, Tock knew that this must be the dreaded Dr. Umbra. His heart sank as he realized she was wearing surgical gloves and a rubber apron and was thoughtfully testing the edge of a scalpel against her thumb.

"Let's just have a little peek at your poor eyes, shall we?" she murmured, stepping forward.

Tock's horrified gaze skittered away from her across the room, skirted the rubber examination tables, avoided the dripping saw, and at last alighted on the cages of mice. The mice were now huddled in the shadows at the rear of their prison, their paws in their ears and their pink eyes firmly shut.

They didn't want to know.

Fire and Ice

Ⓧ nce an essential part of life at StregaSchloss, the old icehouse had overlooked the kitchen garden for hundreds of years. Previous generations of Strega-Borgias had cause to be grateful for its existence: the icehouse's thick stone walls, perpetually damp interior, and shadowy position had proved to be ideal for storing vast slabs of ice carried down from the frozen hillochs of Bengormless. Before mankind had invented freezers, deep-frozen grandmothers like Strega-Nonna had taken up residence in their icehouses, lying in state like marble effigies, oblivious to the traffic of maids and housekeepers who had been trained not to disturb the slumbering wrinklies while they stealthily chipped off fragments of ice for household use.

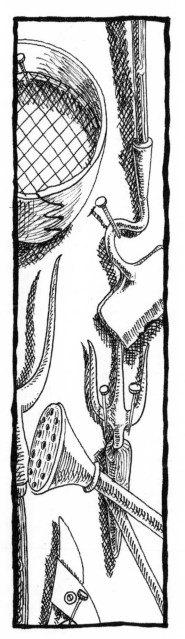

Now the icehouse lay semi-derelict and was home to field mice and pigeons rather than preserved persons. In her defrosted state, Strega-Nonna found the icehouse's damp silence oddly soothing, and took to spending hours within its walls, idly cataloging the Strega-Borgias' vast collection of rusty garden tools and thus avoiding some of the noisy chaos of life in twenty-first-century StregaSchloss. The icehouse also offered sanctuary from murderous trainee butlers, or so Pandora had thought. Now she wasn't so sure. Although no ice had been stored within its walls for nearly a century, Pandora couldn't stop shivering. She was crouched in the icehouse loft, surrounded by the sleepy cooing of several dozen pigeons and watching in terror as a shadow fell across the straw-littered floor six meters below.

Please, Pandora begged silently, let it be Strega-Nonna, nostalgically revisiting her old icehouse like a geriatric homing pigeon . . . please?

Dust motes danced in shafts of sunlight, which highlighted precariously balanced piles of redundant lobster creels, broken wicker crates, and shredded nets from some long-dead angler ancestor. In the deep silence, Pandora heard footsteps cross the floor below and then pause beside the wooden ladder to the loft.

It wasn't Strega-Nonna, she realized. She was in trouble now—deep, deep trouble—and Titus had dropped her right in it. Not his fault, of course; *he* didn't know what he'd done . . . but she'd seen the look on Zander's face when he worked out who had really been in the cave in Coire Crone. . . .

Next to where she was hiding, a pigeon popped its head out from between its wings, gave an inquiring *"Tuu-tuu?"* and waddled off across the loft to investigate.

"Who's there?" Zander hissed, the sound of his voice causing the pigeon to flap its wings in alarm.

Pandora held her breath, willing her nose to stop sending itchy signals to her brain.

"Dumb birds," Zander muttered, squatting on the floor and digging his hands in a mound of straw. He pulled out a plastic-wrapped bundle and stood up, giving a quick glance over his shoulder to confirm that he was alone. Ripping open the package, he produced several sticks of demolition-grade dynamite and carefully tucked each of these into a series of pockets sewn into the lining of his motorcycle jacket. With an efficiency born of years of practice, he wired the explosives to a radio-controlled detonator and then turned his attention to a slim device that would allow him to activate the detonator from a safe distance.

Crouched six meters above him, Pandora paid little attention to the sounds filtering up from below. Her concerns were more immediate: her nose was on the point of exploding, her eyes streamed, and her left leg had passed through the pins-and-needles stage into full-on cramp.

A series of clicks and beeps from below was followed by a shrill mechanical voice intoning, "T minus one hour and counting . . ."

This proved to be the final straw for the pigeon. Wings beating frantically, it flailed blindly across the loft, causing the other pigeons to cease cooing and wonder if they, too, were obliged to join in the hysterics. Dust and feathers rose into the still air, and Pandora's nose gave a warning squeak. The original pigeon fluttered down on top of a mountain of lobster creels, then overbalanced, overcorrected, and brought the entire edifice crashing down onto the floor. Immediately the loft filled with terrified birds flapping into the air and battering their wings against the roof, the walls, and each other. Amidst the utter pandemonium, Pandora heard the creaking approach of Zander scaling the ladder to the loft. With nowhere to hide, she looked around for something to use in her defense, but she could barely see past all the pigeons. She stumbled across the floor, fumbling blindly for the top of the ladder, hoping she might get there in time to push it off balance and send Zander crashing back to earth. She had nearly reached her goal when, to her horror, a hand reached through the rungs and fastened itself around her ankle.

Titus stood squinting into the sunlight, avoiding his reflection in the gleaming chrome of Zander's motorcycle and feeling decidedly nervous. There was *nothing* to hold on to, he realized, his stomach giving a slow lurch: no seat belts, no air bags, no crumple zone. . . . And, he thought, peering down at his T-shirt and shorts, these things offer zero protection. Overhead, a huge flock of pigeons clattered into the sky, their wings sounding like impromptu applause.

Have I got time to change? he wondered, this thought immediately followed by, Into *what*? A suit of armor? Aaargh—what do I *do*? Zander'll think I'm a complete numpty. . . .

Titus was halfway back up the front steps when a voice stopped him in his tracks.

"Forgotten something?" Strolling around a corner of the house was Zander, helmet under one arm, the other arm carrying a black leather motorcycle jacket and matching pants. Titus thought he'd pass out with relief as these were slung in his direction. Zipping up the dauntingly heavy jacket, he felt immediately invincible. Awash with gratitude, he turned to where Zander was removing a spare helmet from a locked box behind the passenger seat and muttering something about scaring the living daylights out of Strega-Nonna.

"She's probably never seen a motorcyclist before," Titus explained, well accustomed to Strega-Nonna's hissy fits and bizarre behavior. "What did she do?"

"Screamed like a banshee and swore at me in Latin," Zander replied, omitting to mention that she'd also tried to brain him with a lobster creel after he'd set the icehouse on fire, and had cursed him in five languages upon discovering that he'd barricaded the exit, thus condemning her and Pandora to death.

"She's quite harmless, really," Titus said, his words muffled inside the helmet as he climbed onto the passenger seat behind Zander. He was unable to hear Zander's reply over the roar of the motorcycle, and was too busy hanging on for dear life to notice the telltale cloud of smoke rising into the sky above the old icehouse.

Crash and Burn

Titus, dear?" Mrs. McLachlan stood outside Titus's bedroom, her voice echoing down the corridor. "I'm about to do a mixed-color wash, dear. Any contributions? Socks? T-shirts? Festering piles of damp towels?" Surely he wasn't *still* asleep? She knocked on the bedroom door and waited a moment before walking into the empty bedroom.

"Oh, for heaven's sake," she muttered, rolling her eyes and breathing through her mouth as she bent to gather several socks which had been widely distributed across the bedroom floor. "High time that young man learned that dirty laundry does not walk to the washing machine by itself...."

Repeating this procedure in Pandora's room, which was

similarly unoccupied and decorated with discarded clothing, Mrs. McLachlan *tssk*ed and looked at her watch. Wherever Titus and Pandora had gone, they'd be back soon, hovering vulture-like in the kitchen and demanding lunch. Sighing, the nanny headed downstairs, bearing her malodorous bundle in her arms.

Sorting through socks in the kitchen, Mrs. McLachlan sniffed, frowned, and sniffed again. What *was* that burning smell? She jammed a molding pile of bath towels into the washing machine, switched it on, and headed off to check that she hadn't mistakenly left her iron on in the linen room. Puzzled, she returned to the kitchen and opened each oven of the range in turn, making sure that no carbonized horrors lurked within, then she sniffed once more . . . and froze. Through the window, the kitchen garden had all but vanished, obscured by smoke drifting across it, escapee tendrils curling round the door into the kitchen like beckoning fingers.

"TITUS? PANDORA?" she yelled, praying for an answer that did not come.

Opening the washing machine in midcycle and flooding the kitchen floor with hot suds, she grabbed a wet towel and ran coughing into the garden, blindly following the chamomile path until suddenly she was confronted with the heat of the blazing icehouse.

"Merciful heavens," she heard herself say. "What madness is this?"

Wrapping the wet towel around her head, she tried to

reach the charred wooden door, but was overcome by the intense heat and had to retreat, choking and spluttering, into the relative cool of the smoke-filled garden. Ahead, the icehouse glowed like a beehive made in Hell; flames shot through gaps in the roof and glowing lines of angry red flared between spaces in the masonry. Already half-derelict, built to withstand extremes of cold, not heat, the icehouse looked as if it was on the verge of total collapse. From outside Mrs. McLachlan could hear ominous crashes and small explosions as the overheated stones cracked apart. Even the surrounding trees were affected; they shrank away from the blaze, their leaves shriveling and falling to the ground as gray ash.

Mrs. McLachlan ran for the house to summon help, aware that with the best luck in the world, a fire engine would take at least twenty minutes to negotiate the narrow track between Auchenlochtermuchty and StregaSchloss. One last glance behind her confirmed what she already knew: nothing living could survive such an inferno.

Clinging to Zander's back in a rigor of terror, compounded by a pressing need to use the bathroom, Titus was so convinced he was going to die that he didn't notice the bike was slowing down until it had stopped completely. Turning around with some difficulty due to Titus's limpet grip, Zander removed his helmet and tapped on Titus's visor.

"Hello? Anybody home?"

Titus opened his eyes and realized that he still had his arms wrapped round Zander's waist. Pink with embarrassment, he sprang off the passenger seat and somehow managed to miss his footing, falling facedown on the road and banging against the mesh of a chain-link fence that he hadn't realized was there. Somewhere nearby, several dogs barked in stern disapproval. Titus climbed to his feet, removed his helmet, and gazed around, somewhat at a loss to understand where he was.

"Er . . . I don't . . . um . . . ," he managed at last, catching sight of Lochnagargoyle through a cluster of strangely melted trash cans and assorted cars parked in front of an anonymous gray building. He couldn't see a single sign telling passersby what this particular blot on the landscape might be. Turning to Zander, he saw that the off-duty butler had parked his motorcycle next to a gate in the chain-link fence and had dismounted, presumably *without* falling on his face.

"Where *is* this?" Titus asked, hoping that wherever it was, the owners might allow him to use their toilet.

"I must have taken the wrong turn," Zander muttered, his face hidden behind the mirrored Perspex of his visor. "Look, er, do me a favor? Go ask if we've missed the turnoff for Auchenlochtermuchty somewhere back there? I'd go but . . . I, ah, want to check out the bike. It's . . . running a bit rough for my liking." And having got this lie out of the way, Zander bent down to examine a part of the engine that he was barely able to identify, let alone repair.

"Maybe you've picked up dirt in the spark plugs," Titus suggested helpfully, coming over to peer manfully at the bike alongside the butler.

"Look, *kid*," Zander snarled. "Just go ask, would you? Let me sort my bike out in peace, all right?"

Tempted to tell Zander exactly where to stuff his precious bike, Titus stormed off across the parking lot and pressed the doorbell outside what looked like a reception area, before his brain finally processed the letters embossed in the aluminum plate below the bell. SAPIENTECH UK, he read, just as the barking dogs skidded into the parking lot behind him.

"Ah . . . Zander?" Titus called, spinning around and forgetting his earlier desire for the butler's death by insertion of motorcycle.

"*Zander?*" he yelled as the dogs fanned out in a slavering line in front of him.

"ZANDER—I'M IN TROUBLE HERE!" Titus's voice had risen an octave in his haste to summon help before the snarling guard dogs came any closer. They advanced one yelp at a time, affording Titus glimpses of their hideous yellow incisors as they assessed his calorific value.

Titus couldn't believe his eyes. Zander was turning away, one foot balancing the weight of the bike as he slowly wheeled it around to face the way they'd come. With a loud roar from the perfectly tuned engine, he opened the throttle and was gone.

"You complete and utter *toad*! You piece of *scum*!" Titus shrieked. "I hope you crash and burn, you *bastard*!"

The dogs snarled as if in agreement. Then they licked their lips and inched closer, anticipating the unexpected pleasure of having Titus for lunch.

Ring of Dank Water

Pandora tried to focus on the gnarled face swimming up at her out of the fog. It was trying to communicate, attempting to say something. This much she knew, since its mouth rapidly opened and closed, occasionally pausing to stretch its wrinkled folds into a gummy grin. No. It was no use. She simply couldn't understand what it was saying, and besides . . . ever since she fell out of the loft, she'd been so . . . tired she just . . . couldn't manage . . . to stay awake. Her eyes rolled shut once more, causing Strega-Nonna to emit a string of curses that would have shamed a Sicilian *capo*. Wondering where on earth she'd picked up such unladylike language, Strega-Nonna

slapped Pandora's wrists and pinched her cheeks in an attempt to bring her back to consciousness.

Pandora's eyes flickered open. "Not *you* again. Go 'way. Too tired," and then, "What's burning?"

"We are," Strega-Nonna informed her with a deplorable lack of tact. "Or at least we *will* be soon if we don't get a move on."

Pandora lurched upright. The icehouse was ablaze, and as memory came crashing back, she realized that Zander must have been pretty hacked off with her to drag her out of the loft; then as the grimness of their present situation sank in, she upgraded "hacked off" to "murderous." For some unaccountable reason, this made her feel utterly calm. She'd arrived in some chilled, languid space, a place where panic might well have been clawing at the entrance, demanding to speak personally with Miss Pandora Strega-Borgia; but whoever was on doorman duty was having nothing whatsoever to do with *that* kind of lowlife gate-crasher. Miss Borgia isn't receiving visitors today. Thank you for your interest. . . . In front of her, Strega-Nonna frowned, her face surrounded by a wreath of white smoke drifting down from the burning loft. She looked like a shriveled angel, Pandora decided. Minus the wings.

Strega-Nonna rolled her eyes and snapped her fingers under Pandora's nose. "I'm not immortal, you know," she scolded, "and neither are you, child. We're going to be spit-roasted if we don't hurry up."

Hurry up? Pandora rolled this interesting idea around in her mind like a boiled sweet, using it as a distraction from the distressing clamor inside her head, where panic was trying to bluff its way past security with a false pass. Hey, buster, just where d'you think you're going? Miss Borgia is not to be disturbed. Now just back up, buddy, nice and easy, nobody do anything hasty. . . .

Strega-Nonna shook her. Hard. Slapped her face, one, two—

"*Aowwwww.* That *hurt.* What'd you do that for?"

She flinched as the antique woman patted her cheek fondly. "No harm done, child. You must wake up. I need your help. Come on, stop drifting off or you'll float away forever. . . ." Strega-Nonna knelt on the straw, oblivious to the burning flakes of ash sizzling in her hair. Despite her age and general decrepitude, she was attacking the floor like a thing possessed, sweeping aside bales of musty straw and clawing at the earth with her bare hands. Wary of being slapped again, Pandora bent to help, trying not to scream as burning roof beams creaked and sagged overhead. The old lady's efforts had uncovered a rusting iron ring set into a metal plate on the floor. She was hauling on the ring, her Herculean efforts producing little more than an almost invisible movement of the plate beneath. Given that Strega-Nonna was practically prehistoric and was attempting to lift a chunk of metal about a meter wide, her lack of progress was hardly surprising, but to Pandora's amazement, she saw that *something* was happening. With each demented tug on the ring, water was beginning to seep around the edges of the metal plate. Water that swelled up and immediately soaked into the parched earth around it.

Water that hissed and bubbled, as if under some subterranean pressure.

Temporarily defeated, Strega-Nonna fell backward, her hands slipping off the ring. "Can't manage on my own," she gasped. "Here, you. You're young and strong. You heave and I'll go and find us something to use as a lever." She looked around the icehouse, where shadows of ancient lawn mowers danced in the red glow of the flames. Up against the walls stood a row of antique hoes and rakes, mute witness to the Strega-Borgias' inability to throw anything out, no matter how useless it appeared to be. Consequently, the lower floor of the icehouse had become a retirement home for genteel gardening equipment deemed too rusty to use, but too well loved for disposal. Tottering across the floor, Strega-Nonna seized a rake, its fanned-out tines crumbling with age, and returning to the task at hand, jammed the handle of the rake through the iron ring.

"Right, Flora," she croaked. "Over to you."

Flora? Pandora didn't correct the old lady. Plainly she was losing what few marbles she had, but given the extreme nature of the circumstances, it was to be expected. A blazing chunk of timber crashed down behind Strega-Nonna, sending sparks flying all around. Little flames appeared as the sparks found new fuel in the straw-littered floor. Pandora leant on the rake handle and prayed that it wouldn't snap.

"Put your back into it!" Strega-Nonna shrieked, batting at the flames licking around her feet.

"I *am* . . . it's too heavy . . . it won't shift."

A low rumble came from beneath where Pandora stood, and water oozed out from the rim of the metal plate.

"KEEP GOING!" Strega-Nonna yelled, but Pandora needed no encouragement.

The metal plate shifted . . . shuddered . . . then rose up and teetered on its edge for a second before crashing backward in a shower of sparks. At first Pandora thought all her efforts had achieved nothing, for at her feet now lay a pool of liquid fire. Then she realized it was *water*. A dark pool of water reflecting the burning roof of the icehouse . . .

"What are you waiting for, child? A round of applause? GO. GO. GO!" And with this, Strega-Nonna pushed Pandora headfirst into the pool.

Pandora's scream turned into a series of choking sounds as she plunged below the surface. Strega-Nonna followed behind, propelling them both deeper into the darkness. The last clear thought that went through Pandora's mind was that they'd managed to avoid burning to death by drowning themselves.

Raining Dogs

The Sleeper paused on the sand above the high-tide mark to remove something sticky from his tender underbelly. Shells and seaweed were all very well, he thought, but he'd never before come across a beach quite so littered with dead animals. Several meters away, a seagull eyed him warily before bending its head to something lying on the sand. The bird's cruel beak dipped and tore into whatever it was, rending and gouging with every evidence of enjoyment. Dogs barked in the distance, and the seagull looked up again, its beak draped in what appeared to be red spaghetti, but which was, the Sleeper realized—

"AWWWWW, NO! Yon's disgusting. Leave that puir

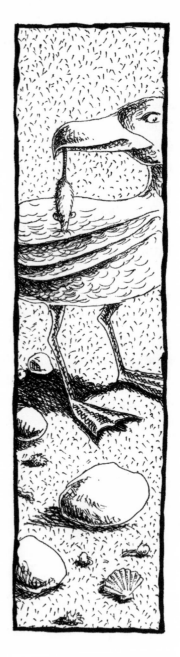

wee moose alane, ye big vulture. Go pick on somethin' yer ane size!"

The bird needed no further encouragement. Lifting into the air with the disemboweled mouse still clamped in its beak, it flew up to what it judged to be a safe distance and began to swear in fluent Seagullese, unfortunately forgetting its table manners in the process.

"Did yer mammy no tell youse no tae speak wi' yer mouth full?" the Sleeper muttered, picking the remains of the white mouse off his forehead before continuing his gruesome journey up the beach.

Little had changed since his beachcombing visit the day before. The same rusting oil drums, discarded tires, and festering trench of dead fish ... He halted, listened carefully, then shook his head as if to clear it. "They big burds," he observed to himself, "they sound jis' like a cryin' wean."

He was picking his way around a charnel pit of assorted furry legs and tails, feeling distinctly nauseated, when a thought occurred to him. He could still hear the shrieks from the seagull, but when he looked up, there wasn't a single bird to be seen. But, if anything, the ghastly screaming sound was even louder than before. It was so like a crying infant that it sent shivers rippling along his entire body, and he found his eyes watering in sympathy with the unknown baby who was making such a racket.

"Kin somebody no dae somethin'?" he roared. "Yon puir wee bairn's greetin' its eyes oot and naebody's listenin'?"

As if in response to this, the noise redoubled, swelling into a whole opera of infant anguish, complete with choking sounds, hiccups, and now the occasional word . . .

"Want Dadaaaaa," it wailed, and with that the Sleeper suddenly felt as if a giant hand had reached inside him and twisted a knife in his stomach. Ffup's mystery breakfast gave a warning of imminent reappearance.

"NESTOR?" he screamed, sick with horror. "NESTOR? MA WEE MAN? HING OAN, SON, DADDY'S COMIN' IN!" And willing breakfast to stay where it was, the Sleeper hurtled across the beach to the gray building up ahead.

Ffup's nostrils were plugged with asbestos wool and her mouth taped shut as precautions after she'd roasted a security guard and melted Dr. Umbra's rubber apron. Despite her best efforts, she hadn't been able to protect Nestor, and it was this knowledge, not the aftereffects of tear gas, that was causing her to weep hopelessly. Chained and manacled alongside her on rubber-covered tables, the beasts wept and roared in sympathy.

"What is it *now*?" Dr. Umbra paused, looking up from her examination of the hysterical Nestor, who lay trussed on the table beneath the circular saw.

"It's this stone monster, Doctor. The Tasers cannae touch it. I just bent ma cattle prod out of shape trying to get it out of the cage." The security guard found himself having to shout to make himself heard over the din that Nestor was making.

"Perhaps you could try taking its head off with a power

drill," Dr. Umbra muttered, her rubber-clad hands running over the controls to the saw and starting the blade spinning slowly in front of her.

The security guard shook his head in disbelief. "Nawww. With all due respect, Doctor, there's no way I'm going in there." He waved a trembling hand in the direction of the cage where Sab sat, stone still, stone cold, a griffin carved in one hundred percent basalt. "You didn't see it in action in the parking lot. It wisnae stone *then*, I can tell you. It was *real*. Snorting and roaring, wi' big claws and teeth—"

"Are you refusing to obey an order?" Dr. Umbra glided toward the guard, one finger raised in warning. "I wouldn't, if I were you. . . ."

The guard gulped, clearly unsure which of the unpalatable options before him would be easier to swallow. He was on the point of steeling himself to argue with the griffin in preference to the doctor when matters were taken out of his hands.

There was a forlorn "Och *no* . . . ," followed by a colossal explosion from outside, and the wall behind Sab's cage appeared to dissolve under a shock wave of powdered bricks and atomized concrete. Then, coughing and spluttering, a gigantic creature straight out of a B movie crunched over the fallen bodies of Dr. Umbra and the security guard and began to apologize loudly.

"AWFY SORRY ABOOT YER WEE HOOSE," it began, and then, embarrassed by having to discuss such matters in front of a roomful of strangers, added, "Ah never really knew the meaning of *explosive diarrhea* before, ken?"

To the puzzlement of the slavering guard dogs closing in on Titus, their prey appeared to be removing his black outer skin and waving it all about. The dogs stopped and sank back on their haunches for a quick scratch while they considered this bizarre behavior. The prey's actions were highly confusing; all the dogs' previous victims had either tried unsuccessfully to run away, or had attempted (also unsuccessfully) to defend themselves with feet, bags, briefcases, or whatever came to hand. The end result—human sushi—was always the same. Licking their lips at the prospect, the dogs stood up and closed in for the kill. Titus responded by renewing his efforts with Zander's leather jacket, feeling like a doomed bullfighter as he did so. The deadly weight of explosives tucked into the jacket lining made it a surprisingly effective weapon, and Titus had batted two dogs across the parking lot before a third managed to fasten its teeth into a sleeve and yank the jacket out of his grasp. Victorious, the dog ran across the parking lot to devour it in peace. Titus watched with grim fascination as the pack descended on the jacket and demonstrated the ease with which they'd probably tear him apart after they'd finished devouring the tasty hors d'oeuvre he'd thoughtfully provided. Titus wondered if he stood a chance of running out of the parking lot while the dogs' attention was thus diverted, but his meditations were abruptly cut short when the dogs were flung into the air by the force of the exploding jacket. The noise was deafening, but not nearly as painful to the ears as the ferocious explosion that followed from somewhere to the rear of the building.

Caught in a downpour of ironically bite-sized portions of dog, Titus did not dare open his eyes to see what had happened for some time. When he finally risked a peek, he saw that the parking lot resembled the aftermath of a serial killers' convention, with every vehicle bearing gruesome evidence of just how lethal Zander's jacket had been. Titus began to tremble uncontrollably. He'd been *wearing* a bomb? If he hadn't taken off the jacket . . . if the dogs hadn't ripped it out of his hands and dragged it across the parking lot to devour it in peace . . . Titus was so dazed with horror that it was some time before he realized that he wasn't alone. Familiar voices came from across the parking lot, and he saw Tock waddling around from behind the building, followed by the Sleeper and the other beasts.

"Did you do a dump in the parking lot as *well*?" Tock was clearly aghast at the carnage all around. "I mean, not that I'm not extremely grateful for the explosive nature of your emissions, but why here?"

"Naw. It wisnae me, pal. And fir your information, ah've nae idea whit's gone wrang wi' ma bowels. Like ah said, ah didnae know whit explosive diarrhea *meant* till today, ken?" Turning to Ffup, the Sleeper roared, "Whit did youse pit in ma breakfast, wumman?"

"I didn't put anything in it." Ffup's tone was indignant. "I didn't even think about Your Breakfast this morning. What d'you take me for—a wife?"

On legs that could barely support his own weight, they

were shaking so badly, Titus staggered across the parking lot like a sleepwalker. Ffup was now clutching Nestor as if she'd never let him go, and somehow the sight of this made Titus aware that what he really needed right now was for someone big to hug *him* and assure *him* that it was all going to turn out just fine. He'd actually been thinking of his dad, but when the dragon reached over and wrapped a wing around him, he found himself almost weeping with an insane mix of relief, horror, and rage. He had to warn Pandora. She had to be told that Zander was mad, bad, and dangerous to know.

"Can we go home?" he mumbled from the depths of Ffup's underwing, too faintly to be heard above the beasts' raised voices as they assessed the damage lying all around them.

"What a *mess.*" Sab shuddered, fastidiously removing a lump of something from the underside of his foot. "Someone should inform the Department of Health and Safety about this place."

"I think *not,*" Tock decided. "Use your brain, for heaven's sake. In the space of a few minutes, our gigantic colleague over there has destroyed half a building, wrecked who knows *how* many hundreds of thousands of pounds of equipment, and killed two people. . . . Where we beasts may regard such actions as heroic acts of liberation, the law in this country still takes a very dim view of such things—"

"Can we go home? Now?" Titus interrupted.

"—two counts of willful damage to property, plus two of manslaughter . . . ," Tock continued gloomily. "Plus heaps of witnesses. D'you think if we plead self-defense, we might get off with a fine?"

"I want to go home. . . ."

Sab snorted dismissively and extended his wings to their full span. "The boy's right. It's time to go home. This never happened. We weren't here."

"But . . . ," Tock bleated, "there's a pile of rubble and two dead bodies back there, plus several security guards who saw the whole thing from start to finish—"

"Correction," Sab said firmly. "Several security guards who're going to swear they saw the Loch Ness Monster demolish their workplace. That's not going to go down too well with the local constabulary, is it? Can you imagine? Oh, honest, officer, it was awful—massive big head and, gosh, pass the smelling salts, such *teeth*, and its body must've been about a thousand meters long—"

"Naw, only nine hunnert an' eighty-two," the Sleeper admitted sadly.

"What I'm saying"—Sab sighed—"is that we're free to go. Why are we hanging around the scene of the crime?"

"What crime?" Tock grinned. "What scene?"

"Honest, officer," Knot added.

"It wisnae me," the Sleeper roared. "A big boay did it an' ran away."

"You said it," Ffup muttered, flapping into the air with Titus and Nestor clinging to her back. "I'll just take the kids home, shall I, *boys*? Someone's got to act like a responsible adult around here, and it certainly isn't going to be one of you lot. . . ." Her voice tailed away as she flew off down the loch, heading for home.

"Whit have ah done wrong noo?" the Sleeper moaned at

Ffup's diminishing silhouette. "What mair d'youse want, wumman?"

It wasn't until he arrived back at StregaSchloss that he remembered he still had Ffup's diamond ring tucked in his pouch. In all the excitement, he'd simply forgotten to give it to her.

The Biter Bit

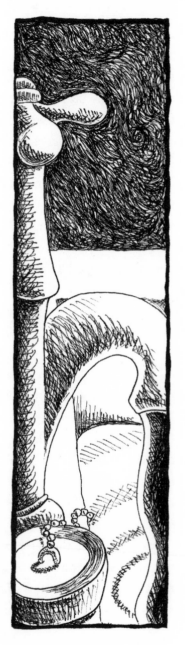

A motorcycle slowly pulled into the courtyard of a converted stable on the shores of Loch Lomond. Dismounting, the rider removed his helmet and checked his watch. Wondering if he had enough time to take a shower and wash the smell of smoke from his hair, he crossed the courtyard and bent down to remove the key from under a plant pot at the front door. He stood up, feeling slightly dizzy, then remembered he hadn't had anything to eat all day. In fact, he recalled he'd even turned down the kid's offer of a share in his cheese-and-pickle sandwich, since by then he'd decided it was the boy's last meal on earth. Opening the door, he noticed signs of recent occupation: a telltale wisp of steam coming from the kettle and an empty coffee cup on the table. She'd left her book lying spine up beside her cell phone, which meant she probably wasn't going to be long, but when he heard footsteps behind him, he spun around in alarm, only relaxing when he saw who it was silhouetted in the doorway.

"My God—what have you *done* to your face?"

He'd forgotten entirely, till she reminded him. His initial relief at seeing her turned immediately to annoyance. He'd just pulled off their biggest job yet, and she was giving him grief about his appearance! He was on the point of reminding her that he deserved respect for what he'd done, not comments about how he looked, when he realized she was genuinely upset.

"I've been sick with worry," she began. "When I found that you hadn't made the drop-off . . . I know I was at the right place—you said the jetty down from the huge house, didn't you? I hunted all over, sure that I hadn't gone to the wrong place, wondering why you hadn't left it, wondering if the police had picked you up—"

"What d'you mean I hadn't made the drop-off? Of course I did. That's why I phoned you last night. I told you I'd left it wrapped in plastic under the jetty. Remember?"

She stared at him, frowning in confusion. Gritting his teeth, he tried again.

"I tied it under the jetty two days ago. I phoned you last night to let you know it was waiting for you. Look, it doesn't matter. It came up as a news flash while I was getting gas. I'm waiting in line to pay, and there on the TV overhead some bloke's announcing to the world that 'explosions have just destroyed the U.K. headquarters of biotechnology giant SapienTech, burying years of research under a mountain of rubble, yadda, yadda, yadda . . .' " He stepped forward to grab her by her shoulders, his face lit by a manic grin. "Don't you see? We did it! WE DID IT!"

She wriggled out of his grasp, pushing him violently away from her. "This time, *we* didn't do it!" she yelled. "Don't you hear what I'm saying? I didn't lay the explosives at SapienTech. It wasn't *me*. The explosives weren't under the jetty where you said they'd be. Don't you get it yet? Can't you understand—it wasn't *me*. I didn't *do* it."

"So who did?" he screamed. "*Somebody* did. Someone picked the parcel up at the jetty. Someone took it to SapienTech, just like we'd intended to do. Someone must have known exactly what we were planning. . . ."

She closed her eyes and turned away, going upstairs to pack, as the enormity of what he'd said hit him with such force it nearly caused his legs to give way beneath him. Sinking into a chair, he put his head in his hands and yelled out loud with the pain. His entire face felt as if it was on fire, each bite-mark a separate pinpoint of agony. He stood up and ran for the sink, meaning to splash his face with cold water to soothe the hurt, but when he turned on the tap, he almost fainted at the sight of what came pouring out.

A tiny, still-functioning part of his mind told him that it was only water; clear, pure, West of Scotland H_2O.

"Water . . . ," he croaked in agreement. "It's only water."

He tried to scream for help, but his throat had seized up.

Something was terribly wrong—he was ill . . . very ill . . . or going mad. . . .

He tried to turn the tap off, but his hands were shaking so much he couldn't get a grip on the spigot. Water poured down the drain, the noise filling him with the worst fear he had ever known.

Unperturbed, the rational part of his mind was calmly dissecting the situation.

I'm afraid of water, he thought. Afraid of water? Hydrophobic?

His mind skittered to a standstill, impaled on that one word.

Hydrophobia.

It was then he realized he was in deep trouble.

He was still clutching the edge of the sink and making little whimpering sounds when she reappeared, her face pale but determined.

"What's the matter with you?" she demanded. "You look *awful.*"

He could hardly reply, his throat felt so constricted with terror. All he could manage was a feeble croak followed by the unwelcome discovery that he'd dribbled a mouthful of saliva down his chin. Wondering what was going on, he looked up and found that he couldn't see her properly—she kept going in and out of focus, her voice echoing weirdly in his ears.

"Come on. Get a move on. I've got the passports, laptops, credit cards—everything's packed. It's a short drive to the airport." She was walking around the kitchen, checking they'd left nothing behind. She picked up her cell phone, tucked it in a pocket of her leather jacket, and pushed past him to the sink to rinse out her coffee cup. The sound of running water was so unbearable that he had to bolt out of the kitchen and stand gasping for breath outside in the courtyard, making a determined effort to pull himself together. Spitting out a mouthful of frothy saliva, he was dimly aware of her locking up, replacing the key under a plant pot, and finally turning to glare at him as she climbed onto his motorcycle.

"I'll drive," she stated, pulling her helmet over her head and lifting the visor so that he could hear her. "All I ask is, don't throw up on me, all right? And, yeah, quit dribbling, would you? I know you don't feel too good right now, but if we get through the next few hours, we might just manage to walk away from this one."

She turned the engine over and dropped her visor. On legs that were suddenly three thousand miles long, Zander lurched onto the seat behind her. Just get through this, he told himself. Hang in there. It'll all be fine.

It wasn't until they'd stopped at the junction with the main road around Loch Lomond that he realized he wasn't going to make it after all.

A group of bikers looked up when the big Norton pulled up on the road near their lay-by. They listened to its thrumming engine with the same rapt attention normally given by opera buffs to passages of Wagner. Then, after a considered pause, they passed a verdict.

"Niiiiiice," one of the bikers growled, adding, "not a bad wee bike, either."

The bikers noticed that the bloke riding pillion was acting strangely: lurching back and forth on his seat, threatening to overbalance the bike, hauling at his helmet, and, it was agreed, behaving like a complete plonker. The bikers rose to their feet and ambled across the road, watching through narrowed eyes as the rider turned around and yelled at her passenger.

"Aye, that's right, then. Youse tell him," one of the bikers muttered encouragingly, as the woman pushed her companion so hard he slid sideways, out of sight on the other side of the bike. To unanimous disappointment, she then kicked off, opened the throttle, and turned left for Glasgow, leaving her ejected passenger coughing in a cloud of blue exhaust fumes.

At least, that's what they thought at first. That was before the guy dragged his helmet off and began to convulse, before they'd called the ambulance, and before they found out what was really going on.

"Never seen a bloke take it so hard," they told the ambulance crew.

"Bein' dumped isnae much fun, but all that frothin' and screamin's a wee bit o'er the top, eh no?"

"It's like he'd bin poisoned or somethin'. And when we tried to get some water don him, he acted like we were tryin' to *murder* him. . . ."

"He probably thought you were," the senior paramedic observed.

The bikers couldn't help but notice that all the ambulance

crew were now gloved up and wearing masks over their mouths and noses. "Hing oan a minute. What's going on . . . ?"

"Listen up." The paramedic held his hands up for silence. "We might have a problem here. We need to get this guy into that hospital and run some tests, pronto. If they come back with the result I'm expecting, you're all going to have to be quarantined in the Isolation Unit. . . ."

In the ensuing riot, the paramedic held his hands up once again. "It's a precaution, OK? There might be nothing wrong with him, in which case you'll all have had a wasted trip to Glasgow. But . . . if I'm right, there's the possibility that some of you might be infected, and if you are and you don't get immediate help . . ." His voice trailed off as Zander was lifted into the ambulance, trussed and wrapped in plastic like an oven-ready chicken. What little could be seen of his face was not encouraging.

"Aw nawwww. Tell me this isnae happenin'. . . . I don't want whatever he's got. What *has* he got?" The bikers were endeavoring to keep calm and not throw a synchronized wobbly, but when the paramedic gave his response, several of the big, bearded men had to sit down immediately.

"He's covered in bites, convulsing, hydrophobic, frothing at the mouth. . . . My guess is he's got rabies."

And as if this wasn't enough to tip the bikers right over the edge, as the doors of the ambulance closed, the paramedic added in a whisper, "By the time you start to froth at the mouth, there's nothing anyone can do. That guy isn't going to make it."

Through a Glass, Darkly

Sulking in an attic bedroom and poring over recipes so saturated with grease that the words almost slithered off the pages, Marie Bain was the first to hear the sound of an approaching siren. Her cookbook slid to the floor as she scuttled over to the window to find out what was going on. To the cook's considerable excitement, a large red fire engine was hurtling along the track to StregaSchloss, dust and gravel boiling up in its wake.

"Les pompiers!" she squeaked, hastily running a brush through her lank hair and wondering which of her two aprons would set off her washed-out eyes to best advantage.

By the time the fire engine

220

had *nee-nawed* to a stop on the rose-quartz drive she was ready and waiting on the front doorstep.

"*Mon Dieu,*" she gasped, wringing her hands. "Eet eees *tragique, non?* Terrible. *Incroyable.*" With little idea of what she was supposed to be talking about, she carried on dramatically, "How deed such a terrible theeng 'appen? *Moi,* I am *inconsolable, distraite. . . .*" And apparently overcome with anguish, she selected the most handsome fireman as the perfect candidate and, tottering down the steps, collapsed at his feet. Dashing around the house from the kitchen garden, Latch wanted to roar with frustration when he saw the firemen bending over the fallen cook.

"LEAVE HER!" he yelled. "The fire's here! Run your hoses around the back! Hurry up, it's an inferno back here!"

With her eyes squeezed tightly shut, Marie Bain sensed that all was not going according to plan. The diminishing thunder of footsteps made her risk a quick peek in time to see the last of the team of firemen running *away* from her, around the back of the house. Over the mechanical rattle coming from the fire engine parked behind her, she could overhear a conversation. Marie Bain propped herself on one scrawny elbow and looked around, but there was no one to be seen. The rose-quartz drive glowed in the afternoon sun, bees trawled the honeysuckle on the southern aspect of StregaSchloss, and overhead, a lone seagull rode the thermals, its cry barely audible.

"What are all these disgusting slimy things?" a voice inquired, following this query with a series of wetly slapping *schlupp-schlupp* sounds. "*Hundreds* of them . . . yeurchhh, it's like wading through jellyfish."

Schlepp, schluppp.

Marie Bain sat up, drew her gray cardigan tightly across her bony chest, and made a furtive sign to ward off the Evil Eye.

"Just keep going," another voice advised, "and mind the bones."

Crunch, crunch, schlepp, schlupp.

"Allo? Who ees there?" Marie Bain whispered, praying that this was a bad dream.

"Can you hear something?" the first voice said, and Marie Bain's nostrils were suddenly assailed by a strong whiff of swampy decay. "I'm utterly *covered* in slime," the voice continued, unaware that to Marie Bain, this sounded more like a threat than an observation. "Hey—Nonna, look. Daylight! Up ahead . . . we're nearly *out!*"

Marie Bain leapt to her feet, overcome by her imagination, which was telling her to flee before the bone-crunching, slimy Swamp Things appeared and dragged her off, *schlepping* and *schlupping* with glee as they devoured her entirely. Frantically turning her head from side to side to find out which direction they would attack from, she spotted movement down in the mud at the bottom of the moat.

"*Non, non, non . . . ,*" she sobbed, as the mud sucked and belched, throwing up the shapes of clawed hands and limbs, until finally a head emerged, slime dripping down its tentacled skull. The first Swamp Thing crawled out of the mud, blinking in the light as it removed a decaying water lily from its neck. Catching sight of the quivering cook, it waved a slime-slathered arm in greeting, a gesture that entirely failed to reassure Marie Bain of its good intentions.

For the second time that afternoon, Marie Bain collapsed in a heap on the rose-quartz drive, but this time her faint was genuine.

A little later, Mrs. McLachlan poured tea, passed around a plateful of lemon drench cake, and smiled serenely at the assembled firemen squeezed around the kitchen table. The blazing icehouse had been extinguished, mercifully revealing no charred bodies in the embers, and now, with their job done, the firemen were in a celebratory mood. One of them had even been kind enough to carry the unconscious Marie Bain into the house to recover, much to Mrs. McLachlan's amusement.

"Excuse me for a moment, gentlemen," she murmured. "Do help yourselves to tea and cake. I just have to attend to my duties for a wee while."

Across the kitchen garden, Pandora, Titus, and the beasts were regarding the hissing ruins of the icehouse with dismay.

"Dad's going to go ballistic," Pandora decided, awed by the scale of the damage. "First, he'll see this mess, and then we'll have to tell him about Zander. . . ."

"It's hardly *our* fault Dad hired a psycho butler, is it?" Titus said. "And when he finds out that his employee torched the icehouse and then headed off down the coast and blew up a research center—" Titus clapped his hands over his mouth and rolled his eyes apologetically. "Ooops. Sorry. Me and my big mouth. We're not going to talk about that, are we?"

"No, dear. We most certainly are *not,*" a voice said, causing everyone to jump guiltily, unaware that Mrs. McLachlan had slipped amongst them.

"Oh lord . . . ," Tock sighed. "D'you think if we amend our plea to 'guilty with provocation,' we might get off with community service?"

"Suddenly I have this overwhelming desire to turn back to stone. That way no one could put handcuffs on me . . . ," Sab murmured.

"Feel sick," Knot moaned.

"I don't want to go to *jail!*" Ffup squeaked. "I didn't do anything wrong. It wasn't *me!* A big boy did it and ran away. . . ." The dragon's voice trailed off, quelled by a glare from her fellow beasts.

"Indeed?" said Mrs. McLachlan, in a tone of utter disbelief. The beasts shuffled uncomfortably, trying to avoid meeting her eyes. "Now, dears," the nanny continued, smiling at Titus and Pandora, "it's a terrible shame about your poor icehouse, but it was an accident—"

"It wasn't!" Pandora yelped. "It was deliberate—" She stopped, aware that Mrs. McLachlan was holding something in her outstretched hand. "What's *that?*"

The nanny didn't say a word, just waited for Pandora to work out the answer for herself. The object she held was a small glass ball about the size of a marble, on the end of a melted metal chain. The glass had cracked, as if it had been subjected to intense heat, and, furthering this impression, it was so damaged by smoke that it was almost opaque. Feeling faintly sick, Pandora realized what she was looking at.

"It . . . it was Zander's . . . ," she whispered. "His dowser's crystal. The one Mum transformed . . ."

"The *Orba Occultis*," Mrs. McLachlan said, adding, "Honestly, the *things* some people leave lying around. I suppose it wouldn't have occurred to *him* that the combination of sunshine, glass, and tinder-dry straw might be quite so lethal. . . ." The nanny waved a hand at the smoking ruins of the icehouse and emitted a meaningful *tssk*.

"Oh, come *on*." Pandora's voice was indignant. "Why are you pretending it was an accident? Zander tried to *kill* me and Strega-Nonna—"

"Don't mind *me*," Titus said. "He only tried to blow me *up*. That wasn't an accident either, was it? I feel sick when I think how close we came to . . . I mean, we nearly—"

"Yes, dear." Mrs. McLachlan laid a hand on Titus's shoulder. "But it *didn't* happen. Trust me, your parents *don't* need to know how close they came to losing you both."

"But . . . but Zander's dangerous," Pandora insisted. "He's a *murderer*. Shouldn't we at least tell the police about him? Before he tries to kill someone else?"

Mrs. McLachlan peered into the *Orba Occultis* and sighed. Passing it across to Pandora, she said, "Take a good look at this and tell me what you see."

Shuddering at the thought of touching something belonging to Zander, Pandora reluctantly took the glass between her finger and thumb and gazed at it. "It's *darker,*" she whispered. "It's turned almost . . . black."

Mrs. McLachlan held out her hand and Pandora returned the glass, glad to relinquish it. For once, no one could think of anything to say. Taking a deep breath, Mrs. McLachlan slowly closed her fingers around the glass and looked straight into Pandora's eyes.

"The glass is now completely black. Young Mr. Imlach has no future, I fear. It's over, dear. We won't be seeing him again."

Something about the way Mrs. McLachlan said this made Pandora's skin crawl. On the brink of blurting out a question, she closed her mouth with a snap. Mrs. McLachlan looked at her watch and tutted.

"Just *look* at the time, dears. What an *exciting* afternoon we've all had, what with fire engines and . . . everything. I'm just so thankful that none of you were hurt. So fortunate you were out on the boat at the time . . . wasn't it?"

Titus gulped and looked down at his shoes.

"And Pandora, your parents might not appreciate seeing you dressed like a mud-maiden, dear. Why not have a quick swim while I get our supper ready?" Mrs. McLachlan reached out to pluck a decaying water lily from the front of Pandora's T-shirt. "What a state you're in, child. Your mother would have a fit if she saw you like this. . . ." Turning her attention to the beasts, she held them transfixed with a chilly stare. "Your mistress would make herself *ill* if she knew what really happened today. . . ." Holding her hands up to forestall objections, she continued, "No. I don't want to know. Next time you decide to go and volunteer yourselves as guinea pigs for medical research, don't leave the newspaper ad lying on the kitchen table for anyone to find."

Tock covered his eyes with his forepaws and gave a small honk of alarm.

"Yes, dear. You'd make a useless criminal mastermind. Just as well I burnt the newspaper before those nice men from the fire brigade caught sight of it."

Tock gazed up at Mrs. McLachlan, his golden eyes moist with embarrassment. "I'm sorry," he whispered. "It was all my fault. I thought we could earn some money to help with redecorating my moat. . . ." Struck by the thought that despite everything, his moat was still in a parlous condition, he groaned. "I wish I'd never drained it in the first place. If I hadn't pulled that stupid plug, none of this would have happened."

Pandora bent down, flakes of dried moat-slime falling off her arms as she wrapped them around the woebegone crocodile. "Pet lamb, if you hadn't pulled that stupid plug, Nonna and I would be dead by now. We couldn't have moved the plug in the moat ourselves, not from underneath. And if your moat hadn't drained out under the icehouse . . ." She shuddered at the thought of the fate she had so narrowly avoided. "I've never been so pleased to see mud and slime in my entire life."

"And I've never been so pleased to see anyone quite so filthy dirty as well," Mrs. McLachlan said quietly. "When I saw the icehouse was locked from the outside, and both you and Titus had vanished, I realized that none of this would have happened if I'd been paying attention. . . . My dears, I'm afraid I haven't been the most attentive nanny of late. . . ."

Mrs. McLachlan's eyes prickled as she felt Pandora's hand slip into hers, and when Titus patted her awkwardly on her back, she had to turn aside to spare them the sight of her tears.

In the embarrassed silence, they could all hear the murmur of voices coming from beyond the door to the kitchen. Pulling herself together, Mrs. McLachlan tucked Zander's black glass ball into her pocket and wiped the hand she'd clasped it in across her skirt.

"This conversation never took place," she said.

"What conversation?" the beasts said in unison.

"My woolly unwashed lips are sealed," added Knot.

Turning to Titus and Pandora, the nanny raised one eyebrow inquiringly.

"Um, yes. Absolutely," Titus gabbled. "In fact, I'm not even here right now."

Pandora jabbed him in the ribs. "Race you down to the loch, Invisible One?"

She looked for confirmation that this was correct behavior and was rewarded with a wink from Mrs. McLachlan, whose lips were not sealed, but curved upward in a wide and conspiratorial grin.

A Devil Dines Out

The dining room at the Auchenlochtermuchty Arms was full of guests and, to his disgust, Isagoth was forced to wait until a table became free.

"*How* long?" he demanded, leaning over the waitress with barely disguised irritation.

"Terribly sorry about this," she said, running a finger down the list of bookings. "We've had a wee bit of an unexpected rush tonight, sir. It's all those reporters up from London. . . ."

Isagoth suppressed a hiss of annoyance. He didn't want excuses, he wanted dinner. Right now. Then he wanted to get the job done.

"It'll be in all the papers tomorrow . . . ," the waitress added.

"What will? Dinner?" Isagoth snapped.

She looked up at him, then, realizing he didn't know what she was talking about, attempted to explain. "Och, sir, I'm sorry. Have you just arrived in Auchenlochtermuchty? You won't have heard about the accident at the research station?"

Isagoth toyed with the idea of turning *her* into the accident at the Auchenlochtermuchty Arms, then decided against it.

"Awful it was, sir. Sirens, police, ambulances . . . and they say some people *died*—"

"Indeed," Isagoth interrupted. "Tragic. Sorry to hear that." The demon's temper strained at the leash, growling to be released.

Something of this must have shown in his eyes, because the waitress bent to the bookings register and plucked out a time from its pages. "Nine o'clock," she said.

Isagoth was about to protest when a horribly familiar voice rang out across the dining room.

"Say, lady, could we have another jug of iced water over here? And what's keeping my steak? Has your maître d' gone to shoot it himself?"

Isagoth closed his eyes and wished himself elsewhere. Hopefully he hadn't been spotted yet. There was probably still time to slip out of the dining room before— A giant hand descended on his shoulder and spun him around into a wave of garlic so pungent, he could feel his skin shrivel.

"Say, Jolene, honey," the American tourist yelled. "Lookee here. Guess who I've just run into? Well, feller, looks like you picked the right time to roll into town. All these newshounds

buzzing around the big story, like a bunch of blowflies on—
Sheesh, I should've guessed you were with the media,
moment I clapped eyes on you."

To his utter dismay, Isagoth found himself being propelled
across the crowded dining room, observed by tablefuls of people who made it their business to notice everything, no matter how trivial. Feeling about as transparent as a crystal ball at
a psychics' convention, he fixed a rictus grin on his mouth and
sat down, pressed into a chair by the irrepressible Lex.

"Call me Lex, call me Sandy, call me anything you like, but
just don't call me late for dinner," Lex bawled, sloshing iced
water into a glass for Isagoth and summoning the waitress to
their table. "This one's on me," he roared. "Jolene and me,
we're celebrating tonight, so chow down. Have anything you
like, friend. No expense spared . . . Here—take some of this
garlic bread."

Isagoth nearly screamed out loud. Garlic? Was the man
insane? Offering a demon garlic was the ultimate no-no in
Hadean etiquette. It was about as welcome an offer as a
stake—of the kind usually driven through hearts.

"I'm allergic to ga-gag-garlic," he managed to gasp, turning
to the waitress and muttering, "I'll have the black pudding,
followed by the black-faced lamb on black rice and, uh . . .
black forest *gâteau* with black-currant ice cream."

"Will that be all, sir?"

"Fetch me a decent drink. Johnny Walker Black Label. Just
bring the bottle and a glass. I'll do the rest." Might as well
enjoy this, he thought, slumping resignedly in his seat and

nodding to his American hosts. "Sssso," he hissed, "what are we celebrating tonight?"

Lex took a large bite of his garlic bread and proceeded to spray crumbs across the table as he regaled everyone within earshot. "Jolene and I, we're over the moon . . . we found our boy. Well, not exactly *found* him, you understand, but we know where he's holed up . . . taken us months . . . private investigators . . . attorneys . . . he fell in with bad company . . . first it was tree-hugging hippies, then it was a bunch of criminals . . . get him back home . . . try to find the right medication . . . normal life . . ."

Isagoth wasn't paying attention. For one thing, Jolene's sneaker-clad foot was rubbing up and down against his leg, and for another, his cell phone was vibrating steadily in his breast pocket, so much so his left nipple was beginning to hurt.

"Terribly sorry." Isagoth stood up and pulled his cell phone from his pocket. "Excuse me for a moment while I take this call. Just, ah, start without me. I'll be back."

"Must be his editor," Lex mumbled through a forkful of shrimp cocktail.

"I just *knew* he was a reporter, moment I saw him," Lex observed, over a mountain of grilled steak and fries.

"Must be one heck of a big story he's working on. . . ." Lex sighed as the last morsel of cheesecake slid down his throat.

One hour later, as they paid the bill, Lex and Jolene had to admit that they'd been stood up. Isagoth's dinner *noir* still sat on the table—cold, congealed, and all too visible. Of the demon, there was no sign.

Pure Dead Romantic

The first stars of evening were shining over Lochnagargoyle as Ffup crept across the meadow with a large wicker basket tucked under her wing. Pausing every so often to move the load to the opposite wing, she hoped the Sleeper would appreciate the magnanimity of her peace offering. She also prayed that the Strega-Borgias wouldn't notice that she'd plundered their larder in order to make peace with her beloved.

Ten jars of anchovies, four multipacks of canned tuna, an assortment of sardines, pilchards, salmon, and mackerel (also in cans), and one can opener . . .

Ffup dropped the basket in the long grasses and suppressed a howl. She'd forgotten the can opener. She could even remember leaving it in the bathroom sink while she slapped some last-minute moisturizer on her scales . . . stupid, stupid, and stu—

"Could you hurry it up, please?" a peevish voice complained. "I don't have all *night*, you know." Tarantella clung to the lid of the picnic basket, her mouthparts gathered in a disapproving pucker. "At this rate," she continued, "my daughters will be having babies of their *own* before I ever see them. It's vitally important I'm there when they hatch; learning begins at birth, you know. Who they see when they first open their eyes will affect them for the rest of their lives, will be their primary role model, and I want it to be *me*, not some passing lobster or, heaven forbid, a seagull. . . ."

"Right, I hear you," Ffup groaned, heaving the basket aloft once more and striding down the little bramble-lined path while she muttered to the hitchhiking tarantula.

"A bit of gratitude would've been nice," she snorted. "It's not *every* spider that's allowed to gate-crash a romantic dinner for two."

Tarantella shuddered. "Oh, puhleeease, you dim dragoness. Tarantulas don't do romantic dinners for *two*. When will you get it through your scaly little head that we tarantulas only ever eat alone. When *we* invite a bloke over for dinner, we mean something completely different. When I say, 'Come for dinner, darling,' I'm implying I'm the one with the appetite and he's the appetizer. Owwwww—don't slam on the anchors without warning. I nearly fell *off*."

Ffup had skidded to a halt on the pebbly foreshore, her eyes

234

wide with wonder. All the way along the edges of the jetty were hundreds of lit candles, their flames burning steadily in the still air. A thick carpet of seaweed had been laid in a broad band along the shore and down the middle of the candlelit jetty like an illuminated runway leading out into the loch. The basket fell from Ffup's grasp with a crash, prompting a furious squawk from Tarantella. Oblivious, Ffup glided forward like a sleepwalker, the talons of her feet piercing the seaweed carpet and emitting faint squishing sounds as she walked. Giving a wail of horror, Tarantella tried to overtake the dragon, but by the time she reached her daughters, it was too late. All three hundred sixty-five of the tiny spiderlings were transfixed by the sight of Ffup and her Sleeper intertwined in the shallows by Titus's boat.

"Ahhhhh," they breathed as the dragon kissed her beloved.

"Awwww," they sighed as the Sleeper produced a vast diamond ring.

"Out of the way, Mum, we can't *see*," they complained as the Sleeper slid the ring onto the fourth talon of Ffup's left paw.

Even when the three hundred sixty-five spiderlings let rip with rapturous applause from their combined 2,920 legs, the sound was barely audible. It was the faintest of sounds, the whisper of tiny hairy legs clapping against other tiny, equally hairy legs. To a trained ear such as Tarantella's, it sounded like the quietest, most discreet hiss. Had she not been so wrapped up in the events taking place out on the loch, Tarantella might have heard an echoed hiss coming not from the loch, but from an area of deep shadow several hundred meters down the foreshore. The faintest hiss of a demon who has finally laid eyes on his quarry.

On the fourth talon of Ffup's left paw, the Chronostone shone like no diamond ever could. It glowed, it glittered, and it gleamed, but for the first time in its entire history, it was entirely outshone by the twin tears of sheer happiness that ran down Ffup's face and fell, unobserved, into the darkness of the loch.

When the Feeling's Gone

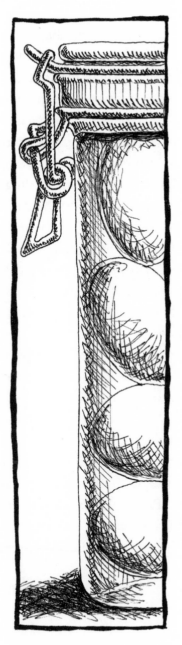

Damp's unbroken weather spell continued to have a magical effect on the climate around StregaSchloss. While the rest of Argyll bemoaned the mist and gnats, Auchenlochtermuchty baked under blue skies and sunshine that toasted plants and people alike. So unusual was this weather that it shared the front page of the local paper, alongside the shocking news of the explosions at SapienTech.

"Sometimes I despair of mankind," Luciano groaned. "Listen to this, Baci. How's this for sensitive reportage?" He gulped a mouthful of coffee and, clearing his throat, began to read out loud.

" 'AUCHENLOCHTERMUCHTY ROASTS IN HEAT WAVE. "It's not natural," complains resident, calling for local government to install air-conditioning across homes in the region. "If we'd been meant to roast like this, we'd have been born with cooking instructions tattooed on our bums." ' And then, Baci, right beside that piece of pointless reportage, we have, 'SEVERAL FEARED DEAD AS FIRE SWEEPS FACTORY. The charred remains of two bodies were pulled from the—' "

"Stop!" Baci shrieked, grabbing the newspaper out of Luciano's hands and hurling it across the kitchen. "I can't bear to think about it—what nearly happened *here* . . . the icehouse, our children . . ." Her words turned into choking sobs, and she collapsed onto a chair, overcome with horror.

"Cara mia." Luciano leapt to his feet and wrapped his arms around his wife in seconds flat. "Listen to me. Nothing happened. Titus and Pandora were nowhere near the fire. All that we lost was a building—which we can rebuild, if need be. You must stop blaming yourself for this. It wasn't *your* fault."

"But—but if I hadn't dragged you off to Glasgow for a c-curreeeeee," Baci wept.

"Just because you had a sudden yen for fiery food does not make you an arsonist," Luciano groaned. "That's a ludicrous idea, woman. It's as insane as saying . . . oh . . . like saying because you like blood sausage you must be a vampire."

Baci looked up, wiping her eyes and sniffing. "Did you say blood sausage?" She swallowed and managed a watery smile. "D'you know, Luciano, I could eat one of those raw, I'm so hungry. . . ."

Oh dear, Luciano thought, lord preserve us from pregnant women and their cravings. He was about to get up to make a token attempt at searching through the fridge, when the front doorbell rang.

"Zander'll get that," Baci decided, standing up and heading for the pantry. "Luciano, don't worry about the blood sausage. I've just remembered there's a jar of pickled eggs in here somewhere. I rather fancy a few of them with some ice cream if there's any in the freezer."

Pickled eggs and ice cream? Luciano grabbed the table for support. *That* was a combination he could hardly bear to imagine, let alone enjoy as a spectator sport. The doorbell rang again, this time in three peremptory bursts.

"Where is that butler?" Luciano demanded, peering at his watch. "It's ten o'clock. He should have been up hours ago. We don't pay him to sleep. . . ."

"Don't worry, darling, it was his day off yesterday. He's probably slept in." Baci reappeared, an open jar in one hand, half a pickled egg in the other. She chewed, swallowed, smiled blissfully, and opened her mouth to devour the other half. The doorbell began to ring without pause, and before Luciano had time to react, Baci dropped the pickle jar on the table, dumped the half-eaten egg beside it, and stormed off down the corridor.

"I'm *coming!*" she yelled, infuriated by the incessant ringing. Reaching the front door, she hauled it open with such force it flew out of her hands and crashed back against the umbrella stand, sending walking sticks flying across the hall. On the doorstep, two complete strangers regarded her with expressions of polite confusion.

"No thanks," Baci managed. "Whatever you're selling, we don't want it. Please be good enough to close the gate properly behind you as you leave." And, closing the door behind her, she'd just made it back to the kitchen when the doorbell rang once more. This time, Luciano answered, reasoning that it was better for all concerned to leave his wife guarding her eggs in peace.

Five minutes later he was back, this time accompanied by the two apologetic strangers, who smiled nervously at Baci and stood shuffling inside the kitchen doorway until Luciano invited them to take a seat. Baci mashed an egg on top of her chocolate-chip ice cream and raised a spoonful to her lips, before making an attempt to be hospitable.

"So sorry," she mumbled. "I'm always a bit of a witch before I've eaten breakfast. So . . . um, what *are* you selling? Double-glazing? Conservatories? Encyclopedias?"

"Baci, *cara mia*, they're not selling anything. Mr. and Mrs. McHail are trying to find their son, Alex."

Baci blushed deeply and stood up to apologize. "Heavens. Forgive me. I'm horrified at myself. What a complete *witch* you must take me for—yelling and shutting the door in your faces like that. It's just that we do so tire of people ringing our doorbell and trying to offload stuff we neither want nor need. . . ." Baci lifted a hot-plate lid on the range and put the kettle on to boil. "Can I offer you some tea? Coffee?"

"Baci . . ." Luciano closed his eyes and took a deep breath. "*Baci*. Would you hush one moment and listen? Mr. and Mrs.

McHail's son is . . . very unwell. His parents have come here all the way from America to try and persuade him to return home with them before . . . um, ah . . ."

Mr. McHail leant across the table and patted Luciano's arm. "'Scuse me for butting in here, but I think your good lady here needs to hear it from the horse's mouth. Mrs. uh, Mrs. Sega—"

"Please, call me Baci." Signora Strega-Borgia smiled encouragingly.

"Pleased to meet you, ma'am. I'm Lex and this here's my wife, Jolene. So, Back-shee, it's like this. Our son's in big trouble. Heck, ma'am, I can't remember a time when that boy *wasn't* in some kind of trouble or another. Right from when he was a little kid, he seemed to have a wild hair up his . . ." Lex coughed, shot a look of apology at his wife, and continued, "Seemed to us Alex was just wired up differently, and though we tried our darnedest, there was nothing his mom and I could do to change that. First, it was small stuff: getting kicked out of school, running away from home; but pretty soon it got much worse: getting into fights, stealing cars—and before we knew what was happening, the police were pitching up on our doorstep so often we could set our clocks by them. Well, see, Jolene and I, we're not the kind of folks to give up on a job halfway through, and we weren't about to give up on Alex without a fight. No way, ma'am. We ain't quitters, me and Jolene. Since the day that boy first got into bother with the law, we've tried to do our best by him. Psychiatrists, therapists, analysts, behaviorists, psychologists—

you name it, we've paid for every 'ist' you can think of and some that haven't even been invented yet."

Struggling to stay afloat in this tide of information, Baci distractedly filled the teapot with milk and poured hot water into the sugar bowl.

"The long and the short of it is, after we tried everything, all that those fancy doctors could tell us was that our son needed to find an outlet for his aggression. Since he wanted to go around hurting people, blowing things up, and setting fire to stuff, they suggested he join the armed forces—"

"That worked for a while," Jolene interjected. "He joined up, did his training as a munitions expert—"

"And then we don't know *what* went wrong," Lex interrupted. "It was as if the Special Forces training made him worse, not better. Like he'd somehow gotten hooked on violence, till even being a soldier wasn't enough for him. . . ." Lex paused, rubbed a hand across his eyes, and continued wearily, "Last time we saw him, he'd been dishonorably discharged and was holed up with a bunch of long-haired criminals in a trailer park in Illinois. . . . We tracked him down, persuaded him to come home with us, then a week later he just vanished off the face of the earth, leaving Jolene and me heartbroken—"

Concerned that this unfortunate stranger was about to break down and cry, Baci intervened, "Mr. McHail, I'm not quite sure how we can help you find your son. . . ." She sneaked a glance at the mantelpiece clock. Where on earth *was* Zander? It was nearly half-past ten, for heaven's sake.

"Oh no, ma'am. Back-shee, I mean. You don't have to help

us find him. We found him." Lex leant back in his seat, causing it to creak in protest. "We found him, all right. He's been here, somewhere."

"*Here?* At StregaSchloss?" Baci squeaked, aghast. "You mean there's a violent crim— Sorry, sorry, sorry, you mean your poor unwell son is somewhere lurking around our house? Our garden?"

"Afraid so, ma'am. But you weren't to know. Besides, he's gone, now—" Lex suddenly looked old, his face drawn and pale with the strain of talking about such things.

"That last time was the final straw," Jolene interrupted, her mouth spitting out the words like bitter fruit. "Last time, he emptied Lex's checking account, helped himself to my most valuable jewelry, and headed out of town in my car. Lex and me, we spent a fortune tracing him from South America, to Angola, and then over to some godforsaken hole in Russia . . . We lost him for a while, till he surfaced in Yurp, where he spent nine months bumming his way around, never staying in one place longer than a couple of weeks . . ." She paused, as if to gather strength for what she was about to say next.

"You know, it's not the money, or the jewelry, or the fact he trashed my Cadillac. It's none of those things that really hurts. No. What really burns me up is that he told your husband here that *his* mom and dad were dead. He just wrote us out of his life, like we never existed."

"Oh. My. God." Baci sat down gingerly, as if she feared she'd shatter with too sudden a movement. "Your son is *Zander?*"

"Yup," Lex stated baldly. "Ale*xander* McHail was our boy."

"Was?" Baci whispered.

"Thing is, Back-shee," Lex continued, "when a child puts his parents through all that pain and then ends up saying you don't even exist, pretends you're dead and buried . . . well, far as we're concerned, he might as well be dead, too. It's . . . it's a *tragedy*. Like, uh, the *feeling*—you understand, you're a mother yourself, you know I loved that boy but . . . the feeling's gone . . . and we just can't . . . go on kidding ourselves any longer. Jolene and me, we're going to head back on home and go get ourselves an attorney to cut that young man out of our lives for good."

In the silence, they could all hear Mrs. McLachlan and Damp, chatting as they came downstairs from the nursery.

"Watch out, dear. That's an awfully big step there. Careful now . . ."

The McHails stood up slowly, hiding their distress under a veneer of politeness.

"Thank you for your time, folks. Sorry you had to be involved in this . . . stuff." All Lex's bluster had gone, his self-confidence deflated like a leaky balloon.

As they turned to leave, Jolene murmured, "And don't you worry about him turning up here again. He's gone for good. We traced him to Glasgow Airport. He dumped his bike in the overnight parking lot. He ain't coming back no more."

The Strega-Borgias followed the grieving Americans to the front door, where Damp was sitting on the step while Mrs. McLachlan helped her into a pair of shoes.

"Oh my. Your daughter's just like a little fairy angel . . . ,"

Jolene said, squeezing into the passenger seat of a rental car and turning aside to wipe her eyes with a tissue.

Visibly uncomfortable, Lex opened the driver's door and climbed in, opening the windows to let in some air. Baci and Luciano stood silently on the steps, unsure what to say or do. Slipping out of Mrs. McLachlan's arms with only one shoe on, Damp squeezed between her parents and waved good-bye to the strangers.

"Oh! Isn't she just *darling*?" Jolene gasped. "Look—with her little wand and all . . ."

Mrs. McLachlan stiffened. Wand? Damp's other shoe fell from her hands and she stood up to see what was going on.

"Thanks again, folks." Lex was pulling away now, one hand on the wheel, the other waving out of the window to Damp. "What can I say? Life goes on? Another day, another dollar . . ."

"'Nother day," Damp repeated firmly as Mrs. McLachlan plucked Leonardo da Vinci's purloined paintbrush from the little girl's chubby fist.

Damp's *Rain, rain, go 'way* spell dissolved as the heavens opened. Forty-eight hours of magically pent-up rain turned the rose-quartz drive a deeper shade of pink, poured into Tock's empty moat, and drove the Strega-Borgias indoors.

Ring of Stone

Not even torrential rain could dampen Ffup's prenuptial enthusiasm, much to the annoyance of her fellow beasts. Lost in a lacy world of wedding plans, the dragon was unaware of anything other than her own drama, dragging every topic of conversation, no matter how unrelated, back to the Wedding of the Decade.

"With *you* as a role model, I doubt my daughters will have the sense to stay out of the rain," Tarantella observed gloomily, peering out of the kitchen window at the puddles forming on the ground.

"I just hope it doesn't rain on Mummy's Big Day," Ffup cooed to Nestor, who was clamped to his mother's breast in a state of blissed-out infant oblivion.

"Thank you for your

empathy," Tarantella snapped. "Actually, I was hoping you might offer me a lift down to the loch so that I can check that they're all safe. . . ."

"Won't they just make the sweetest little flower girls?" Ffup murmured, her eyes glowing. "I can just see them all in a line, each one holding a daisy, or even a forget-me-not."

"I'm working on it," Knot muttered. "But you keep reminding me."

"And heavens, I must write myself a reminder to order up some invitations. You can't imagine the amount of paperwork involved in getting a wedding under way. . . ."

"No. You're right. We can't even begin to imagine how we're going to restrain ourselves from gagging you if you don't stop obsessing about it." Sab's voice had risen to an aggrieved roar, but it didn't put so much as a dent in Ffup's armor of self-satisfaction.

"Train . . . ," she muttered, plucking Nestor off her breast and reaching for a pen. "The train . . . What d'you think, guys? Forty meters of white organza? Or should I just push the boat out and go for raw silk?"

"The only boat you'll be pushing out will be your funeral barge if you don't shut *up!*" Tock clamped his jaws around a leg of the kitchen table and gnawed it for comfort. This was unbearable, he decided. Ever since she'd been given that awful, vulgar ring . . .

"Tock, *dear,*" said a voice. "How many times do I have to tell you? If you feel the need to chew something, there's a pile of logs in the woodshed needing to be turned into kindling—"

"He was provoked," Sab interrupted, rising to the croco-dile's defense. "Trust me, you'd be chewing table legs too, if you had to put up with *her.*"

Mrs. McLachlan didn't reply. She was staring at Ffup's engagement ring in stunned disbelief.

Maybe it was a girl thing, Sab thought, yawning pointedly. Himself, he couldn't care less about such fripperies, but there they were, the only females in the room, apart from that lippy tarantula, both of them going off into raptures about a com-pressed lump of prehistoric carbon. . . .

"What an extraordinary gem," Mrs. McLachlan managed. "Such an unusual setting . . ."

"Isn't it?" Ffup squeaked. "He made it himself, the clever old thing. But look what it's *done* to my talon. . . ." She held out a paw for the nanny's scrutiny, pulling off the ring and indicating the place where her scales had turned an unappeal-ing shade of gray beneath the iron band.

"Dear, dear." Mrs. McLachlan turned Ffup's paw over and *tsk*ed sympathetically while her thoughts raced off in an alto-gether less pleasant direction.

She didn't have much time left, she realized. Somehow she had to get that *thing* out of the house, away from the family, and hide it somewhere safe. . . . Safe? Her mind reeled. Where on earth could she hide the stone? The answer filled her lungs with ice. Nowhere on earth was safe. Nowhere in this life. Forcing herself to breathe, she looked up into Ffup's innocent golden eyes.

"Ffup, dear, I think I have some cream upstairs in my first-aid kit. I'll just go and fetch it, shall I? Tell you what, I'll see if I can find you a Band-Aid as well. . . ."

"For my talon? Does that mean I can't wear my ring?" The dragon began to hyperventilate. "Ever again? Like, I'm going to break out in pustules every time I put it on?"

"Calm yourself, dear." Mrs. McLachlan picked up the Chronostone and tried to smile. "It's not a big problem. All I have to do is put a Band-Aid *inside* the ring, and that way the metal won't be in direct contact with your scales. Let's give your poor talon twenty-four hours to settle down, and then we can try again, hmmmm?"

Ffup peered at her talon dubiously, wondering if it would ever return to a normal color, and if so, when. Mrs. McLachlan reached over and patted her paw gently.

"It'll be fine, dear. I'll make sure this doesn't happen again." And forcing herself not to run, she headed upstairs with the ring clutched in one hand.

Stone of Power

No one was sure where the photographer had come from, or indeed which paper he'd claimed to work for. In fact, he'd been remarkably uncommunicative, chewing on the end of a slim cigar, which he kept relighting with a surprisingly realistic lizard lighter. Titus had wisely left him standing on the doorstep, not wishing to be responsible for filling the house with cigar smoke, and also because, as he later confessed to Pandora, the guy gave him the creeps.

"It was seriously weird, you know. Like he had some kind of force field around him. Or *we* did. He put one foot over the threshold, then jumped backward like he'd had an electric shock."

"The StregaSchloss force field," Pandora sighed. "Somehow, I don't think so."

"Well, he stayed out there for *ages*"—Titus yawned—"waiting while we all got ready. What a complete *pain* that was. All that fuss, just for a stupid engagement photo? The Strega-Borgias and their bridal beast? Boring, boring, boring."

"Boring *and* pointless," Pandora corrected. "No groom in the photo and no engagement ring. Let's hope things improve by the time Ffup gets around to organizing wedding photos. . . ."

"They could start by getting a different photographer," Titus muttered. "One who didn't smoke . . ."

". . . *and* remembered to take a bath occasionally," Pandora added. "Talk about force fields . . . he didn't *need* one—he smelled like he'd crawled out of a swamp."

She looked over to where Titus had opened his wardrobe and was scribbling something on a bit of paper stuck inside the door. Curious, she stood up and walked across the room to see what he was doing. "Titus? What are you up to now?"

Titus finished writing and turned around to smile at her. "I just remembered what Dad said when we'd been standing there on the doorstep for at least an hour and he suddenly caught a whiff of . . . that bloke."

Pandora peered at Titus's list of phrases frequently used by parents, and burst out laughing. The last entry read, " 'Phwoarrr, Titus, was that *you*?' (3, none of them me, actually)."

Not being strictly family meant that Marie Bain, Latch, and Mrs. McLachlan had been excluded from the group photograph. This was something of a blessing, since Marie Bain would have attempted to upstage the bride-to-be, Latch would have passed out with terror upon recognizing the photographer, and Mrs. McLachlan would have been unable to appear on the doorstep since, at the time, she was utterly preoccupied with holding the demon photographer at bay by means of magic. The nanny had been forced to extend her circle of enchantment somewhat to include not only Damp and Pandora, but also to encompass the entire household and the fabric of StregaSchloss in an unbreakable web of protection. She managed to hold this enchanted mesh intact until the demon's car had driven away, at which point her strength gave out and the web collapsed. Mrs. McLachlan was certain the demon would return when darkness fell, and this time she'd be too weak to prevent him taking the Chronostone. However, she vowed, *that* simply wasn't going to happen. Next time he came, she'd be ready. With the stone as bait, she was going to make sure the demon had no choice but to follow her into the realm of Death.

She took the stone from her pocket and looked at it, wishing with all her heart that it didn't exist. The fragile checks and balances that maintained the wobbly equilibrium between the powers of Light and Darkness could be swept away with this shining stone. The Chronostone represented true power in its most elemental, raw form. In itself, the stone was not magical at all; but when applied *with* magic . . . when it was used as the energy source to empower a magical spell . . . Mrs. McLachlan shivered. The stone conferred unlimited power on its owner. Unlimited and absolute. The kind of power necessary to stop the earth from turning. The kind of power that could raise the dead and turn back Time itself. An absolute power that corrupted absolutely everything it came into contact with. And if it fell into the hands of a thing from the Darkness, a creature of the Pit . . .

In Mrs. McLachlan's hands, the Chronostone glowed softly, shedding a warm light on her pale skin. Of course, she thought, I *could* use it to protect those I love. With it I could weave my protective mesh around Damp and use it—this unexpectedly beautiful gift—to make my spells invincible. Nothing could stand in my way, I wouldn't have to leave, I could stay here for ev—

She looked down, shocked. Blood welled out of a hole in the palm of her hand where an iron spike from the Sleeper's ring had penetrated her flesh. Flinging the Chronostone away from her, Mrs. McLachlan began to weep, aghast at how close she'd come to failing, devastated by her frailty and utterly horrified at what now lay ahead.

"Please, no . . . ," she whispered. "Do I have to do this? My heart's breaking at the very thought of hurting them. . . ."

Silence beat down upon her, pounding in her ears, crushing her to the floor. She curled into a ball, dimly aware that this was pathetic behavior on her part, but also aware that she had no choice but to allow the tides of feeling to wash over and through her.

Some time later, she stood in the bathroom, splashing cold

water around her eyes and trying to patch a smile back on her face.

"Right then, Flora," she said to her reflection. "Ready or not, here I come."

The reflection's bottom lip quivered for an instant, and its eyes were remarkably shiny, but the entire face now radiated absolute unstoppable determination.

The mirror did not lie.

Into the Dark

Strega-Nonna lay asleep in her freezer, exhausted by the events inside the icehouse. The old lady's body was wrapped in tinfoil like a Hollywood version of a pre-millennial astronaut, and her head was pillowed on a catering-sized bag of frozen peas. Around her lay the bodies of hundreds of miniaturized clones, a deep-frozen reminder of the perils of ill-considered scientific experiment and, in their suspended state, offering Strega-Nonna little in the way of companionship. In the old lady's lonely dreams, she returned to her sun-drenched childhood of hundreds of years ago. She was playing with her best friend on the sandy fringes of a dark wood, with the smell of lavender blown across the dunes on a warm breeze. . . .

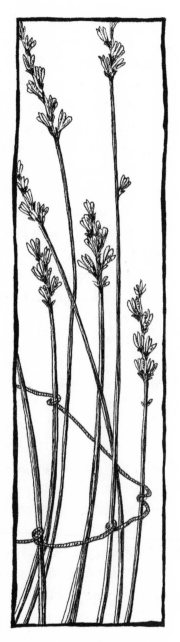

They'd dug a blackened marble out of the sand—a wondrous find—and once they'd cleaned the glass, they began to squabble over who should have it first. "Amelia," her friend was saying, her voice urgent, her grip surprisingly strong for such a scrawny waif. "Amelia. This is important. Listen to me."

She ignores this, because the marble is rolling away across the sand. A cloud swallows the sun and the smell of lavender intensifies. She looks up and sees her friend is now standing in the forest, her tiny body dappled with shadows.

"Amelia," the girl says, walking backward into the dark, "keep hold of the thread. . . ."

Amelia looks down at her hands. She is holding a silver thread between her fingers. It spans the ever-growing distance between her and her friend, her best friend, who is paying it out like a fishing line, a silver length at a time, spilling from her hands like spider silk.

"Amelia"—her voice is faint, far away now—"don't let go. It's up to you. I have to go back for a while."

Alarmed at how swiftly her friend is being absorbed by the forest, she tries to follow, but her feet keep slipping in the sand. "Flora . . . wait for me," she begs. "Don't go in there on your own. It's too dark."

Flora smiles at that and rubs her fists in her eyes. "Don't be silly, Amelia. Someone has to go and someone has to remain. You have to wait here and pull me back when it's time."

She is almost invisible in the darkness, just a shadow amongst the gathering mass of blackness.

"NO!" Strega-Nonna howled, her voice echoing back at her.

"No ... no ... no ..." She stumbles over a buried root and falls, tumbling over and over ...

... and crashes to a halt, banging her head against something surprisingly cold and smooth. The inside of the lid of the freezer. In Strega-Nonna's mind she can still hear Flora, laughing now, calling over her shoulder as she disappears into the dark forest.

"Och, you always were a stubborn wee baggage. Now, if you've finally stopped having hysterics, perhaps you might be good enough to hold this for me?"

In the darkness of the freezer, Strega-Nonna doesn't need eyes to see the thread she now clutches between her fingers. In the silence, there is the faintest smell of lavender, and from that she draws what comfort she can.

Damp clung to Mrs. McLachlan, her small pajama-clad body quivering with the effort.

"Not go," she said, patting her beloved nanny's face and placing a hot little hand over Mrs. McLachlan's mouth. "Not say ba-bye."

"How about cheerio?" Mrs. McLachlan kissed Damp's palm and tucked the bedcovers around the child once more.

"*Not* cheer-oh. Damp too sad to cheer-oh."

Mrs. McLachlan bit her lip. This was even harder than she'd imagined. Not to put too fine a point on it, this was one of the worst moments of her life.

"Damp coming too," the little girl decided, struggling to sit up in bed. "Take Damp with you," then, remembering the miraculous powers of the magic word, she added, "please."

"My wee darling..." Mrs. McLachlan's voice wobbled. "Please don't do this. I must go. I don't want to, but I must. And you must stay here and be a good girl for Mummy and Daddy and look after your big brother and sister and the new baby...."

"Not want new baby," Damp muttered, adding somewhat surreally, "scratchy cardigans."

A tiny smile crept across Mrs. McLachlan's mouth, a smile that was promptly eclipsed by Damp's next utterance.

"Hubble bubble?"

"Yes, pet. Hubble bubble it is. Nanny has to go sort out the hubble bubble."

Damp looked up, her eyes wide and solemn. The child and the woman sat for a moment in silence, their gaze held steady on each other in wordless communion. Damp's eyes filled with tears, but still she didn't say a word, not even when the tears spilled over and ran down her cheeks into her pillow. Mrs. McLachlan stood up at last, unable to bear any more. Bending down to kiss the little girl's forehead, she almost expected to find two small arms flung around her neck in an attempt to cling fast, to delay the moment of parting. No arms came, and she straightened up, smoothed the covers over the still child, and turned to go.

"Night-night, my dear wee love," she whispered. "Sweet dreams." She had reached the nursery door when she heard a tiny whisper.

"Ba-bye," and then the sound of a child crying softly, without any hope of comfort.

In Deep

Tarantella's daughters dangled beneath the seats of the rowboat, instinctively avoiding the wet stuff currently falling out of the sky. Only twenty-four hours old, the spiderlings hadn't grasped basic concepts like "rain" or "seagulls" or even "loch." However, they all agreed that they'd really learned everything there was to know about love. They'd watched Ffup and the Sleeper's practical demonstration, then spent the next day attempting to learn by imitation. In little study groups of five spiderlings at a time, they proposed marriage to each other, accepted gracefully, waved their legs in what they assumed was an appropriate fashion, and then practiced mouth-to-mouth contact, as shown by Ffup and her Sleeper.

By the time they heard the thunderous approach of footsteps running down the jetty, there were only seven spiderlings left. Seven rather bloated spiderlings who gazed around in some confusion, wondering where they'd gone so disastrously wrong. Belching forlornly, they huddled underneath the wooden seat, wincing as two human legs thudded into the boat in front of them. The boat pitched violently, then settled into a regular rocking movement accompanied by the splash of oars meeting water. The familiar sound of waves lapping the jetty faded away, and now all the spiderlings could hear was loud breathing and the rhythmic creak of oars in oarlocks as the boat pulled away from the shore.

Isagoth trained his binoculars on the silhouette of StregaSchloss rising out of the mist-wrapped meadow. Lights shone into the darkness, giving the house the appearance of an ocean liner far out at sea. The demon waited, willing the family to turn out the lights and go to bed, thus giving him the opportunity to patrol the house until he found a weak link in its magical armor.

Isagoth had been astonished to find any protection in place. The first time he came to StregaSchloss, he'd strolled straight in through the front door and overwhelmed the servant without breaking a sweat. This time, he'd been rebuffed with such force, he'd been convinced he was having a heart attack.

Isagoth didn't like that feeling at all. He didn't like the hammering in his chest, or the cold sweat that followed, and he most definitely didn't care for the unaccustomed feeling of being out of control. These are *mortals* I'm dealing with, he reminded himself, tracking a patch of shadow outside the kitchen door. Mere mortals, suitable for hunting, but ultimately disposable, doomed . . . He hurled the binoculars into the darkness and launched into pursuit. The moving shadow had broken cover and was running flat out across the meadow toward the loch. Fear must have given it wings, because Isagoth simply couldn't keep up. Years of driving a desk in Hades had taken their toll on the demon's physique—to say nothing of the cigar habit that was currently clogging his lungs with black tar. Moments later he was forced to a halt, wheezing pathetically as he tried to drag a mixture of oxygen and gnats into his worthless lungs.

Ahead of him, the figure sprinted along the jetty, bent to untie the mooring rope, and leapt into a rowboat. With a feeling of deep unease, Isagoth realized that this was no nighttime fishing expedition. Hardly able to breathe, he forced himself to run, despite the gasps of protest coming from his chest. Brambles clawed at his face, his ankle twisted as his foot plunged into a rabbit hole, and his lungs labored like two clots of wet sponge. He stumbled across the pebbled foreshore and stopped to see what manner of creature waited out there in the water.

In the middle of the loch, his quarry had shipped the oars and was watching him through the rain. Even in such poor visibility, Isagoth could see what it held in its hand. He stepped into the shallows, shivering as the cold water flooded his shoes.

"A bit chilly, isn't it?" the figure observed, the pitch of its voice marking it out as female. "But never mind, you won't be feeling the cold for too much longer . . . ," she continued, watching with little evidence of fear as he waded toward her.

"I'm sure you thought this was a freshwater loch, didn't you, dear?" she murmured. "But it's not. It's a sea-loch, full of salty sea water. . . ."

Salt? *In* the water? Isagoth trod water, craning his neck to look back longingly at the shore.

"Your kind aren't too keen on *salt,* are you?" she said calmly, turning the Chronostone over and over in her hands, and adding, "So why not just go home, hmmm? Save yourself the bother. . . ."

Little wavelets slapped at the demon's face, but on he swam, stroke by stroke, measuring the distance between him and his goal.

"Don't be ridiculousss," he hissed. "D'you really think a puny bit of salt's going to make the slightest difference? Is that the best you can do?" His words turned to choking sounds as his face disappeared beneath a wave. When he emerged again, much closer now, his mood had turned ugly. Vomiting up a mouthful of loch water, he continued, his words freighted with menace.

"Just give . . . me . . . the stone," he wheezed. "You know I'm not going to stop now. Save yourself, mortal. Give . . . me . . . what's mine. . . ." He swam closer, his eyes locked on hers as he drew near to the boat.

Mrs. McLachlan waited, forcing herself to be still until the demon's hand clasped itself around an oarlock, and then she stood up, towering above him.

"You poor lost soul," she whispered, then, steeling herself, she seized Isagoth's hand and threw herself into the loch.

The little boat pitched wildly, thumps and scraping sounds vibrating through its keel and causing Tarantella's daughters to moan in terror. Gouts of sulfurous gases bubbled to the surface of the dark water, and had the spiderlings been brave enough to look, they might have seen the woman and the demon still struggling several meters below.

When all was quiet and still once more, the seven spiders crept out from their hiding place and looked around. Their wooden world floated in an aching vastness of sky and water, water in which objects bobbed to the surface and knocked against the boat's sides. One by one, the spiderlings watched them come. A clear glass marble, then a drowned salamander, and finally a small bedraggled paintbrush; but even these were soon swept away on the incoming tide.

Latch Alone

Latch stood in his small attic bathroom, drawing an old-fashioned razor across his throat in careful sweeps, revealing his skin beneath a layer of shaving cream. Splashing water over his face, he looked up at the steamed-up mirror over the sink and his breath caught in his throat. She'd kept her promise, then. One word written in steam:

Throughout the ghastly time that followed, Latch moved through StregaSchloss like an immensely helpful ghost. Dealing with hysterical dragons, distraught employers, and devastated children,

he soothed, calmed, and passed the Kleenex with masterly self-control. When the police launch towed Titus's rowboat back to shore, it had been Latch who waited on the jetty, his face half hidden under a moth-eaten black umbrella. He stood in the rain and watched the boat being loaded onto the trailer that would take it to Glasgow for forensic examination, remaining silent when he saw seven tarantulas scuttle for shelter as the trailer began its slow journey across the pebbly foreshore.

When the untended roses in Baci's garden blossomed, bloomed, and fell, it was Latch who picked a small bunch of blood-red buds and placed them in a vase on the kitchen table. As summer slowly turned to autumn, Latch chopped kindling, picked fruit for jam, and kept his own counsel. By her own request, Pandora's birthday came and went, unmarked by chocolate meringue cake or candles, and no one had the heart to insist that it be otherwise. When a significant layer of dust had gathered on top of Pandora's unopened birthday presents, Latch tactfully removed them to the seldom-used map room and left them to wait for some happier time.

The Strega-Borgias stayed indoors, ignoring the seductive charms of the sunlit world beyond their windows, preferring to surround themselves with the kindness of shadows and the unchanging permanence of their home. Thoughts of Mrs. McLachlan occupied their every waking moment, but her name wasn't spoken out loud. Her bedroom remained as it was the night she'd disappeared, its closed door a mute reminder of all they had lost. The nanny's sensible shoes still stood in a row in front of her wardrobe, and her handbag sat untouched on a chair beside her bed. Sometimes the sound of muffled crying could be heard coming from behind the closed door, but when Pandora emerged from the nanny's room, no one said a word.

The trees turned golden and the evenings began to grow cold. Waking shivering in bed one night, Latch found his pillow damp with what he initially assumed were his own tears. He sat up in bed and reached for the little lamp on his bedside table, knowing from experience that all hope of sleep had gone. Blinking in the light, he turned to flip his pillow over, dry side up, and his eyes widened. Beside where he had slept unknowing, some unseen hand had placed a strand of seaweed. A long strand, almost the length of his arm, carefully arranged in the shape of a heart. When he reached out blindly to touch it, to reassure himself that it was real, hardly able to see it through his tears, he found that it was still wet.

The Witnesses for Hope

Pan?"

"Go away, Titus."

Titus slumped outside Mrs. McLachlan's bedroom door. This was going to be even harder than he'd thought. He turned the handle and gently pushed the door open.

At first he couldn't even see her in the gloom. Someone had closed Mrs. McLachlan's curtains and the room was full of shadows. Then he heard a gasp and saw a movement over on the bed.

"Oh Pan . . . ," he breathed, his words clotted with pity.

Pandora didn't reply. She pulled the covers over her head and burrowed deeper into the fading scent of lavender. Titus forced himself across the floor to her side, where he stood feeling utterly hopeless, uncertain how to proceed.

"Pan? There's something you need to see," he began, reaching out a hand to touch his sister's quivering shoulders. His hand paused in midair and hovered inches above her; then, overcome with embarrassment, he knelt down beside the bed and tugged gently at the covers.

"Go *away*."

"No, I won't go away, Pandora." He tugged harder, pulling the covers off a face almost unrecognizable in its grief. Pandora flinched, curling into an even tighter ball, her swollen eyes squeezed shut in denial. Titus tried not to look as he continued to unwrap his sister.

"Pandora . . . *listen*. I know you feel awful, we both do. Just because I'm not crying my eyes out doesn't mean I don't care. I *do* care. I miss her too, you know."

Renewed hiccupy sobs came from beneath the covers but Titus pressed on, willing his voice not to wobble and blinking his eyes against the tears he knew weren't far away. "Everybody misses her. Especially poor Damp. Think about her. . . . She's only little, she can hardly even speak . . . or understand. How d'you think *she* feels?" Swallowing with difficulty, Titus continued, "Anyway, I need you to come and see what I've found. It's . . . important. I don't know if I'm imagining it or not. . . . Oh, for God's sake, Pandora, would you *listen* to me? Stop shutting me out. You haven't said a word to me since . . . since . . ." Violently pushing himself upright, Titus lunged across the bedroom and dragged the curtains open.

"THERE!" he yelled. "Happy? Now we can both see ourselves. Pathetic, aren't we? I can almost hear her saying, 'Now, dears, that's quite enough of *that*. Blow your noses, wash your faces, and we'll go and have a nice cup . . . a nice cup . . .' "

Pandora blinked at the daylight flooding in through the open curtains. Titus glared at her, his face wet and furious, making no effort to conceal the tears rolling down his cheeks. She half fell out of bed, dragging the covers behind her like a discarded cocoon, limping over to where Titus stood haloed in sunlight. Knowing that if she hesitated for one moment, she'd lose not only Mrs. McLachlan but Titus as well, she fell forward, hoping he'd not turn away. She hadn't realized how tall he'd grown until she felt his chin pressed hard against the top of her head. And Titus, in turn, held his small sister tight, his arms around her shoulders, his awkward hands patting, patting, and patting her back.

"Tell me this isn't just a cunning plan to force me into opening my birthday presents?"

Titus sighed. Pandora was standing at the desk in the map room, regarding the dusty pile of unopened gifts as if one of them might contain an unexploded bomb.

"Leave them for now," Titus said, grabbing Pandora's arm and turning her to face the fireplace. "Look. The map. Tell me I'm imagining things. . . ."

Obediently, Pandora looked up at the hand-drawn map in its gilt frame. This map in particular was immensely valuable—partly because of its age but also because of the exquisite nature of its draftsmanship. It had been drawn by a long-dead ancestor whose obsession with accuracy had driven him to build a hot-air balloon to assist in his surveys of Lochnagargoyle and its surrounding lands. In a time long before airplanes and satellites, the hot-air balloon was the closest man could get to achieving the aerial view necessary for accurate mapping. It was the viewpoint of gods and angels, soaring high above ancient Caledonian forests and looking down at the turning earth below, allowing an almost sacred glimpse of mountain peaks and shining lochs that must have so impressed the balloonist that he then dedicated the rest of his life to producing the most beautiful map in the world.

Time had not faded the map's colors; in the darkness of the map room built below StregaSchloss's central courtyard, natural daylight never shone. Hanging over the empty fireplace, this map was one of many such charts lining the walls, but it alone gave an accurate representation of the way the land lay hundreds of years ago. Pandora's breath misted the glass of the frame, and she reached up to wipe it clean.

"WHAT?" she squeaked, recoiling in alarm and peering at her hand.

"I can't tell you how glad I am you said that," Titus muttered. "When I felt it, I thought for a minute I was going mad, but if you felt it too . . ." He trailed off, turned around, and grabbed a magnifying glass off the desk, passing it to Pandora without saying anything more.

"It was . . . burning hot," Pandora moaned. "My fingers are on fire. What's going on?"

"I wish I knew," Titus whispered, watching as his sister held the magnifying glass to the map and peered within.

Moments passed in silence as Titus waited for Pandora to work it out.

"Hang on . . . where *is* this?" Pandora drew back and tried to get her bearings. "There's StregaSchloss, and then the meadow . . . and the loch . . . but since when has there ever been an island out in the Kyle?"

Titus nodded. She'd reacted exactly like he had. He was about to tell her to keep going, to look more closely, but she was already there, her eyes widening at the discovery he knew she'd made.

"Titus?" She spun round, her face awash with tears, her mouth barely able to frame the next words. "You saw it too? The little campfire and the—"

"The wet clothes, laid out flat, drying in the sun. Yes. I saw them as well." Titus felt waves of relief wash over him, and he watched her turn back to examine the map again. Checking for what he knew was there.

"Her clothes," Pandora whispered. "The ones she always wore . . ." She corrected herself, "The ones she always *wears* . . . that means she's not . . ."

"She's *not* dead, Pandora. I don't know where she is, but somehow I'm sure she's safe." And, hugely comforted by this knowledge, he thought, I'm sure she wanted us to know that.

On the island, the little driftwood fire glowed, frozen in time by the mapmaker's hand. Painted in reds and pinks, the flames were the color of hope, burning away doubt and banishing grief back into the shadows. Neatly folded and laid over a rock, Mrs. McLachlan's tweed skirt, cream-colored blouse, and assorted undergarments were a guarantee of her presence somewhere nearby.

It was as clear a message as Titus and Pandora could wish for, and for the time being it would have to do.

Gliossary

ANENOME, AN ENEMY, AN ENEMAAARGH: The correct medical term is an "enema," as in "I'm going to give you an enema, so just lie down, roll over onto your side, and relax. . . ."

This somewhat medieval procedure involves a pair of disposable gloves; a small rubber bag filled with warm, soapy water; a long, flexible rubber hose; as little eye contact as is humanly possible; and a mad dash to the toilet by way of an ending. For more details, look in a medical dictionary under "anal irrigation," but please, not immediately after dinner.

ANTI-SOCIAL HOURS: In the West of Scotland, these are usually times of day when it is possible to enter a public house (tavern) and purchase alcohol. Having to work during such sociable (social) hours is considered to be a cruel and unusual punishment (hence, "anti-social"). In this case, the use of the phrase "anti-social hours" refers to the fact that the taxi bearing the Strega-Borgias back to StregaSchloss has been hired at a time when most taxi drivers are tucked up in bed, sleeping off the effects of excessive hours of extreme sociability verging on drunken hug-fests.

CHEESE AND PICKLE TOASTIE: "Phwoarrr," as Titus might have said. This is one of the staple foods in Scottish households where teenage boys are in residence. It consists of two or more slices of bread (preferably nasty synthetic white bread-fluff) toasted on one side only. Toasted sides are buttered and sandwiched facing each other across slabs of sharp cheddar cheese and dollops of brown and sticky pickle, also known as relish. For those of you who have never tasted pickle, Titus would like to extend his deepest condolences, but his mouth is too full of C&PT to speak right now. I'll continue on his behalf. Take the half-toasted sandwich with its cheesy, pickly filling and either toast it again (the outside, if you've done this correctly, should be untoasted bread) or fry it on both sides in olive oil in a frying pan. The idea is to make the cheese melt into orange goo, which will meld with the brown goo of the pickle and, if you're very lucky, run through your fingers, down your arms, and across your kitchen floor, whereupon your parents will take your precious copy of this book and feed it to the garbage disposal.

COIRE: Not for the faint-hearted, this refers to an almost circular cleft or hollow in the side of a hill. Climbing a coire can vary in what mountaineers call "the degree of technical difficulty," as if falling to one's death down a rock face were a mere technicality. Scaling the walls of a coire can involve a good walk (turn the walker into a breathlessly pink and sweaty blob of cardiovascular virtue) or a stiff scramble (vertical ascent complete with Sherpas, ropes, and oxygen. Also can be spelled "choire," "corrie," "coomb," "coombe," and "come." Pronounced "caw-ray."

DOSH: As in "wads of dosh." "Dosh" is Scottish slang for money and rhymes with "gosh." This is no coincidence, since it's a rare thing to find any dosh whatsoever in one's pockets, especially when one is a teenager, a taxi driver, or, regrettably, a Luciano. "Gosh, I have no dosh whatsoever. Do you take American Express?"

FLY-TIP: "On the fly" means "secretly," and "tip" means "dump," therefore, "fly-tip" means "to dump something secretly." This "something" is usually an item that you desperately need to get rid of but would rather not be observed doing so. To our nation's shame, fly-tipping under cover of darkness is a well-known West coast of Scotland pastime. The results can be viewed at some of our most isolated beauty spots, where rusting caravans, old upholstered chairs with springs bursting out of the seats, and ominously wet and overloaded plastic bags are among the treasures to be discovered.

GREETIN': Not a "hail fellow, well met" but more of a "bwah-hhhh." Greetin' is the sound Scottish babies make when they cry (greet).

HACKED OFF: Slightly peeved, verging on the deeply displeased, and in this case, heading in the general direction of violently aggrieved.

HING OAN, SON: Roughly translates as "Hold on, my son."

IT'S BRINGING ME OUT IN SPOTS: I am acquiring an unsightly rash of pimples on my otherwise perfect complexion. Possibly due to the overapplication of one of the many moisturizers strewn across my dressing table, or perhaps caused by the hormonal swings occasioned by being pregnant, or, who knows, it might have been entirely due to something I ate.

JIS' LIKE A CRYIN' WEAN: Exactly in the manner of a weeping child. "Wean" is a contraction of "wee 'un" and is pronounced way'n.

KEECH YOUR BREEKS: Offload a large quantity of feces in one's underwear—due to either being in a state of extreme terror or having something awfully wrong with one's digestion (q.v. NAE IDEA WHIT'S GONE WRANG WI' MA BOWELS).

KEN: As in "I dinnae wat to throw up, ken?" This doesn't mean, "I don't wish to vomit, Kenneth," but instead means, "I don't wish to vomit, you know?" "To ken something" is to understand it. Now that you ken what I'm on about, let's press on, shall we?

LAY-BY: Scottish motorists' name for a rest area off of a main highway. Lay-bys are used for a variety of purposes: for parking to facilitate map reading, for parking to allow the toddlers in one's vehicle to make a brief alfresco bathroom stop, for parking to allow the driver to have a restorative nap, for parking to indulge in face-to-face contact as demonstrated by Ffup and the Sleeper, and finally, for parking to pour gasoline over one's vehicle and set it alight.

NAE IDEA WHIT'S GONE WRANG WI' MA BOWELS: I'm aghast at what has just erupted from my bottom and would like to

276

take this opportunity to pretend that I had nothing to do with it.

NORTON: British manufacturer of seriously powerful motorcycles. Many years ago, this author was trapped beneath a Norton, due to being asked to hold it upright while its owner dashed inside to take a telephone call. Twenty seconds after being handed this metal monster, I found myself toppling sideways with all of its oily, metallic heaviness crashing down on top of me. Thank you for your concern—yes, the scars are healing nicely.

NUMPTY: An idiot, as opposed to a Humpty, which, as you well know, was an egg.

PILLION: The dangerous backseat on a motorcycle. Clinging behind the maniacal motorcyclist who is deluded enough to believe that he's in control of ten tons of oily metal speeding along at 100 mph is the poor pillion rider, the passive passenger on the rear. Just say no. Or, as they say in the West of Scotland, "Oan yer bike, Jimmy. Ah'm no goin' on yon thing wi' youse."

PLASTIQUE: One of the many pet names for plastic explosives, although why one would wish to give a pet name to something with such a capacity to maim and destroy is quite beyond the scope of this gliossary.

PLONKER: Second cousin of the fabled numpty, a plonker is similarly challenged intelligence-wise.

PORKIES: Lies, damned lies. This oddity has been imported from London's Cockney rhyming slang and is arrived at thus: pork pies = lies. I haven't a scooby how the linguistic labyrinth of Cockney rhyming slang ever made it into the language of the West of Scotland, but it isn't the only occurrence. (q.v. "I haven't a scooby," meaning "I have no idea." This comes from the TV series *Scooby-Doo*, and is arrived at thus: Scooby-Doo = clue.)

PUFFED: Out of breath. "Puffless" would be more accurate but requires more breath to pronounce. "Phew. Gasp. I'm too puffed to say 'puffless.'"

RHYTHMIC PRESSURE AROUND WITH MY SEVENTH CHAKRA: An obscure way to describe rubbing the top of one's head.

SLITTERED: Dribbled in a messy fashion, usually out of one's mouth, down one's chin, onto one's T-shirt, and then onto one's lap (q.v. CHEESE AND PICKLE TOASTIE).

STONKING BASS RIFF: A deep and danceable bass rhythm that gets even the wrinkliest of geriatrics up on their tottery feet, stomping and swaying to the beat in a fashion guaranteed to embarrass anyone under sixteen.

SUPPER'S IN THE SUCCUBUS: Usually a Hadean precursor to "And I'm filing for divorce tomorrow, you heartless devil."

TARTAN TAT TOURIST SHOPS: On behalf of these horrors, I do apologize. These are emporiums where the innocent tourist is encouraged to spend vast sums of money (q.v. (wads of) DOSH) on a variety of hideous tartan merchandise (tat), most of which has been manufactured not in Scotland but in the Philippines. Just say no. Or, as they say in the West of Scotland, "Oan yer bike, Jimmy. Ah'm no wantin' any o' that rubbish, ken?"

THROW A SYNCHRONIZED WOBBLY: Simultaneous group eruption of a hissy fit.

TUGS: Not little boats, but little tangles usually found in children's hair or animals' shaggy coats.

WET AFFAIRS: The department of Hades that deals with anything involving decapitation, defenestration, evisceration, immolation, amputation, and assorted tortures too excruciating to mention.

About the Author

Debi Gliori admits that she can't tone down her "gross and disgusting" nature, and her many fans love her for it. She also confesses a certain similarity between the passionate, colorful Strega-Borgias and her own family. She is the author of *Pure Dead Magic*, *Pure Dead Wicked*, and *Pure Dead Brilliant* and has written and illustrated numerous picture books.

Ms. Gliori lives in Scotland and has at least five children and one golden retriever.